*Hiraeth – 'is a Welsh concept of longing for home. "***Hiraeth***" is a word which cannot be completely translated, meaning more than solely "missing something" or "missing home". It implies missing a time, an era, or a person, including homesickness for what may not exist any longer.' Wikipedia*

# Finding Love at the Christmas Market

Jo Thomas

CORGI BOOKS

TRANSWORLD PUBLISHERS
www.penguin.co.uk
Penguin Random House, One Embassy Gardens,
8 Viaduct Gardens, London SW11 7BW

Transworld is part of the Penguin Random House group of companies whose addresses can be found at global.penguinrandomhouse.com

First published in Great Britain in 2020 by Corgi
an imprint of Transworld Publishers



This book is a work of fiction and, except in the case of historical fact, any resemblance to actual persons, living or dead, is purely coincidental.



A CIP catalogue record for this book
is available from the British Library.

ISBN
9780552176859

Typeset in 11/14pt ITC Giovanni by Jouve (UK), Milton Keynes.
Printed and bound in Great Britain by Clays Ltd, Elcograf S.p.A.

Penguin Random House is committed to a sustainable future for our business, our readers and our planet. This book is made from Forest Stewardship Council® certified paper.

To my gorgeous daughter, and my very own baker, Ffi. So proud of you and to be your mum. x

# ONE

'Am I wearing Aunt Lucy's watch again?'

'Does anybody want a Fox's Glacier Mint?'

'It would have been much quicker if we'd flown!'

'Alice, we haven't even left the estate yet!'

'I'm just saying, me and my husband always flew.'

Everyone is talking across each other, and loudly. The minibus lurches as I take my foot off the clutch too quickly. It stalls. The passengers fall silent with the engine. 'I'm not even sure I can drive this!' I say, gripping the unfamiliar steering wheel and checking my foot position on the pedals. I look up and out of the windscreen at the early-morning drizzle outside the Lavender Hill retirement flats. If there ever was a lavender hill around here, it's long gone. Every bit of green space is now a building site. Blue plastic sheeting, covering pallets and skips full of building waste, flaps in the breeze.

'Remind me.' I turn to look at Pearl, sitting just behind me. 'Why are we doing this again?'

'Because it's what Elsie wanted. She loved Christmas. Her flat was full of lights. She left instructions to scatter her ashes "somewhere Christmassy in my home country". I can't think of anywhere more Christmassy than a German Christmas market. We're putting her to rest among the lights and joy of Christmas at its best. That's why we're all here. And you get to go on a fabulous date! Anyway, the power and water are out at the flats. We'd all have had to move out for the next week. The builders hit a pipe or a cable or something.' She waves a dismissive hand. 'I'd never have got everyone to agree to come otherwise.' She motions to the minibus full of Elsie's mourners.

'She really had no one,' I state.

'Never married. No siblings.'

We shake our heads.

'Now, come on,' Pearl says. 'Let's get this bus moving, or we'll miss the Eurotunnel. And you'll miss your date. The online date of a lifetime at the German Christmas markets. What could be more romantic?'

I take hold of the ignition key and hesitate. My stomach squeezes into a tight ball. 'The date of a lifetime?' I raise a sceptical eyebrow.

'I'm sure of it!' says Pearl. 'He's a lovely man.'

'That's because you found him online and messaged him for me. You and the Silver Surfers Computer Club you used to go to.'

'Before the new owners stopped all activities here at the flats. Said they were too expensive to run, just like the café.' Pearl rolls her eyes, then gives a wide smile.

I look at the building in front of us. I can just make out the fizzy-drinks machine in the foyer, the space where there was once a café for visitors. The new owners had also cancelled film nights and Sunday-afternoon teas as well as the computer club, which Pearl had loved. Instead Meadowsweet Meals had moved in, a weekly frozen-food service, delivering single-portion ready meals to the inhabitants. The hours had suited me when I'd started, but now there are more customers and I find it hard to do my deliveries in the allocated time and always end up working late.

'So, I'm going on a date that you've set up for me,' I say slowly, 'and you're coming too.' I laugh. It sounds ridiculous.

'Well, we get to fulfil Elsie's wishes.' She holds the urn tightly to her. 'Come on, this is for Elsie.'

I check the gearstick and turn on the engine. It starts up eagerly.

'And for you to meet your prince.' Pearl beams.

'Hang on there!' I turn back to her, feeling panic and excitement all at the same time.

She winks.

'It's just a date!' I exclaim. 'It's not like I haven't done a few already.'

'But this one is in a German market,' says Pearl. 'It'll be fun. We should all have a little fun before it's too late. Like poor Elsie. One day you're there, watching *Pointless* with unidentifiable fish in watery parsley sauce, the next you're gone.'

'I know.' I'm sad that Elsie can't be with us today.

'It's still a shock. No matter how old we get, we're never quite ready for it,' says Pearl, putting a hand on my shoulder.

'Well, I didn't expect to find her like that when I delivered her fish pie and toad-in-the-hole with onion gravy.' More mash than fish and more gravy than toad, I think. I wish, again, that I could be a part of future Meadowsweet Meals, making the food more enticing and enjoyable. I push the minibus into first and slowly release the clutch, rolling forward towards the main road.

If Pearl hadn't responded to the message from Heinrich, I'm not sure I would have done. But she did and we're going to Germany. I'm terrified. I take a deep breath. I just need to stick to my usual plan. If he doesn't tick the boxes, he isn't the right one. I think of my notebook safely in my handbag. Sam bought it for me last Christmas. I used to love Christmas when Sam was small. Even when his dad and I were drifting apart, it was always a special time with Sam. Before that, my mum and nan had always made Christmas great. Somehow, it doesn't feel very special any more.

I look in my rear-view mirror as I pull up at the end of the drive. Despite the Christmas songs on the radio, no one looks as if they have much Christmas cheer.

Apart from Ron, who's already asleep with a Santa hat slipping over one eye.

'You've been messaging Heinrich in Germany for weeks now. It's time you met up,' Pearl says excitedly. 'If Elsie hadn't insisted on us doing something Christmassy with her ashes, who knows when you'd have got round to meeting up with him?'

I'm a bag of nerves all over again. 'But it was you who replied to his message in the first place.'

'Of course!' Pearl smiles. 'He sounded just your type.'

'Pearl!'

'Well, after some of the disasters you've had online, especially *that* one,' she says, and I go cold at the mention of it, 'someone had to keep an eye on you and help you out.'

Cars pass us on both sides of the main road and I'm stuck, wondering whether to pull out or not. I wait for the right moment.

'I . . .' I want to differ but can't. I've had some right disasters since I started online dating, and Pearl now seems to want to torment me by listing them.

'. . . and then there was the one who sent you a picture of his thingy while you were ironing and you threw your phone across the room.'

'Okay, okay.' I hold up a hand. 'Enough!'

'This is the right way forward. Get your checklist and make sure he ticks every box. You've already made a good start on it. And you were always saying about the lad you met on that school exchange, years ago. I thought Heinrich sounded just like him . . . the one that got away.'

She's right. I'm not going to get it wrong this time. He has to be fairly close to being the right one, if I'm driving a minibus to Germany to meet him. And if he is, I'm not letting him get away.

'I love your weekly updates on your online dating news. So I thought I'd give you a hand. I want to be there to see you meet up. I want a bit of fun! And what better way than to see two young people fall in love?'

'I'm not sure love has anything to do with it, Pearl. It's seeing if we're a match.' I look down at the pedals again and let out a 'Phffff! . . . I'm not sure I can do this.'

'Nonsense!' says Pearl. 'You've been driving that little Meadowsweet van for years. Not that there's anything sweet about their ready meals.' In the mirror I can see her downturned mouth. I've never been able to stop feeling guilty about delivering their ready meals to my customers, knowing the picture on the box bears no resemblance to the contents.

'If it wasn't for you slipping us one of your lovely cakes, Connie dear, and looking forward to your visits, I'd have cancelled my subscription ages ago and lived off toast and marmalade.'

'You can't live off toast and marmalade, Pearl,' I say, waggling the long gearstick to check it's in neutral, just to be on the safe side.

'Well, it might be better than being killed off by the muck Meadowsweet send us. Not sure which would be the preferable way to go.'

'Oh,' I suddenly remember, 'I saw the postwoman when I arrived this morning. I told her we'd be away for a few days. She wished you all a lovely time and a happy Christmas.' I reach into my big handbag and hand Pearl the pile of Christmas cards and bills. 'There's one for you and a few others. Can you pass them round?' She takes them from me, as I watch in the mirror, looks at her own letter and slips it into her coat pocket, then hands around the others.

'Norman?' calls Pearl, like she's doing the school register.

Norman straightens his hat, taking the letter with a smile. 'That'll be from my sister, wanting me to go for Christmas again. But it's miles away and I always feel a bit awkward. I think they only invite me out of politeness.' He looks at Pearl, but her eyes are elsewhere.

'Mine'll be from my niece, hoping I don't go for Christmas again and telling me about her plans for a Caribbean Christmas,' says Maeve.

'And I'll have got one from my daughter, with her list for the grandchildren, all the expensive presents,' says Alice. 'She'll be inviting me for Boxing Day cold cuts. Nothing says "unwanted" more than being invited for the leftovers.'

'Why she can't just email like everyone else is beyond

me. You'd think that just because we're in sheltered housing we're senile,' says Pearl.

'And stupid, judging by what she'd like me to spend on her children,' Alice adds, opening the card and letter enclosed.

Phffff! The atmosphere in the bus becomes as miserable as the wet, dark weather outside.

'Right,' I say, feeling like the Grinch, stealing the Christmas spirit. 'Let's get moving.' Let's get away from all the things that are bringing these people down. Christmas is supposed to be happy, not like this, with people feeling unloved, put-upon and lonely.

I shove the minibus into gear, release the clutch, slowly this time, and we roll forwards smoothly without the kangarooing of my last attempt. There's a cheer from my passengers and I can feel their spirits lifting as we pull away from everyday life.

I double-check both ways for a break in the traffic and drive out onto the main road. My passengers let out a little cheer so I put on the radio and George Michael's voice fills the vehicle. With a bit of effort, I manage to get the windscreen wipers and heater working.

'Germany, here we come!' Pearl says, the smile plastered back on her face.

'Will there be a toilet stop soon?' asks Alice.

'What time will we arrive?' Maeve wants to know.

'I think I've brought the wrong glasses!' Norman says.

'As long as they don't make me eat sauerkraut! And I've never been a lover of big sausages either. Give me wind,' Maeve says.

'I'm sure this is Aunt Lucy's watch. It's not keeping time at all,' says Norman.

'Who'd like a Fox's Glacier Mint?' asks Ron, finishing his Bounty bar.

'It would have been much quicker if we'd flown. Me and my late husband always flew,' says Alice. 'He insisted on it.'

John hasn't said anything so far. He's looking out of the window.

Di and her husband Graham have their heads in their Kindles, as they always do. He loves romance, she goes for thrillers. Graham holds his stick in one hand – he's used it since the stroke – and his Kindle in the other.

What on earth have I let myself in for? But Pearl is right. I'm going to meet Heinrich. I must be mad, but she insisted I needed to get back in the saddle after my last disaster. I can't help but smile as the minibus rolls away from the estate and towards the motorway. The windscreen wipers creak to and fro. I check the rear-view mirror, and see a swinging piece of tinsel – a nod to the festive season. Half of me wonders if Elsie and Pearl planned this, just to get me back out on a date. I wouldn't put it past Pearl. But I'm doing it. I'm going on a date. Thanks to Elsie and Pearl.

'Come on, Elsie, let's find that Christmas market.

Let's take you home,' I say, remembering the urn in Pearl's lap.

And the bus falls into a sleepy silence as the residents of Lavender Hill retirement flats gaze out of the window, alone with their thoughts.

After a couple of hours of silence, apart from Ron and Maeve's snoring, my passengers start to break from their thoughts.

'What time will we get there, Connie love?'

'Would have been quicker if we'd flown,' Alice repeats.

I turn up the radio and watch the miles pass steadily by to the same Christmas tunes. I'm going on a date! We're taking Elsie on her final journey, and I'm going on a date. And who knows? This could be my perfect match!

'What time's the next loo break?'

'Soon, soon,' I say.

'Are you sure you know the way, love? I could always take the wheel,' says Norman.

'We have satnav!' I say. 'What can go wrong?'

# TWO

'Make a U-turn! Make a U-turn!' the satnav repeats, like a stuck CD, shredding my nerves.

'If we hadn't stopped for that last loo break, we wouldn't be lost,' says Maeve.

'If we'd flown—'

'Shut up, Alice!' everyone says in unison.

The atmosphere is as frosty as the nip in the air when we left. But we'll miss our crossing if we can't find our way back to the motorway soon. My heart's thumping.

'If there hadn't been that diversion . . .'

'Just follow the map. Who's got a map?' says Norman.

I focus on the satnav, but it keeps taking me the same way, not understanding the diversion. After all this time messaging each other, I may not get to meet Heinrich at all. My chance at meeting my ideal partner ruined because of a toilet stop and a diversion for a burst water main. I can't let it happen.

'Right!' I say loudly, over the cacophony, swinging the minibus around and going in totally the opposite direction to the way the satnav is telling me. At least we're off the roundabout we seem to have been circumnavigating for ever.

'Completely the wrong way! Let me drive! We'll never get there in time!' Ron says.

'If we'd flown . . .'

I block out all the noise and unhelpful advice coming from the back of the bus.

'Go on, Connie,' says Pearl, quietly, behind me, as I ignore the satnav and offers of the map and head in what I hope is the right direction, away from the little town where we stopped and its diversion. 'You can do it.' Pearl's voice again, among the noise. The only thing I can do is follow my gut instinct. It doesn't look like the right direction, but it feels right and suddenly we're back on track, heading towards the motorway.

As we pull up at the Eurotunnel port, there's a cheer from the back of the bus.

'Knew you'd do it, Connie love,' Pearl says, as dawn begins to break and we drive onto the train that will take us under the Channel.

I breathe a sigh of relief. Let's hope the rest of the trip runs more smoothly.

*

'So, come on, then, tell us about this man you're going to meet,' says Alice, as we sit on the minibus and glide forward under the sea.

'So everyone knows about my online dating life?' I look at Pearl and frown. So much for me trying to keep this to myself. 'They were only supposed to know we were going to scatter Elsie's ashes,' I whisper.

'I couldn't help but mention it.' Pearl shrugs. 'It seemed like a bit of excitement at a sad time. Elsie would have loved to see you on your Christmas market date. You two just needed a little push in the right direction.'

'I'd call that a bloody great shove,' says Maeve.

'And what better excuse for us all to be going to Germany? Taking Elsie back home,' says Norman.

'And we all get to see you meet your man,' says Ron, opening a bag of Hula Hoops and crunching loudly.

'He must be pretty special if you're going all this way to meet him,' Alice says.

'Well, he . . .' I think about the conversations I've shared with Heinrich. We haven't Skyped yet. We would have done, but then, well, with Elsie passing and Pearl organizing this trip and my meeting with Heinrich, it's all happened so quickly. In any case, he's been working late on a big project, which I can't wait to hear more about.

'What makes this one worth the visit?' Norman asks.

'Well, we like the same things,' I say, thinking through

my checklist. 'Films, music, baking. He's in the business. And we agree on what we want from a partner. And he likes the UK. Spent time here as a young pastry chef during college and is keen to come back.'

'And how will you know if he's the one?' Alice asks.

'I'll have ticked all the boxes on my checklist,' I say simply. I've kept a note of every one of my dates since I started on the internet. And ticked off the boxes, or not.

'And what if he is, dear? Will you move to Germany?' asks Alice. 'It's a marvellous place.'

'We'll miss your cakes,' pipes up Ron.

I laugh. 'No, like I say, he's keen to visit the UK. We'd travel between the two. I couldn't just pack up my life and move to another country. But we're just going on a date. I'm not, like, marrying him.'

'That's right,' says Pearl. 'Just go and have some fun. Enjoy yourself. You deserve it.'

'Besides, like I say, I'd have to see if he ticks the boxes,' I say. It's how I live my life these days. Work, dates, worries: make a list. It keeps things . . . organized. Makes the days move in the right direction. Lists have seen me through the hard times. When my ex, Tom, left, lists helped, and so did recipes, which are like lists, aren't they? Lists of ingredients. What I needed to buy. What I already had. Which ingredient went with what. Since Sam went to university, I could have sat down and stared at the void in my life but he wouldn't want that. The recipes and the shopping lists kept me living life as

I should, day to day. So now I do lists when I meet potential partners online. I got it wrong last time, thinking I was doing fine and could cope without lists. And how wrong I was. If I'd only stuck to the list.

'Apparently, it all works like clockwork there,' Norman is saying.

I glance in the rear-view mirror at John, not saying a word, no doubt thinking about his beloved Violet. His loneliness is written all over his face. I know he's not the only one feeling like that. Christmas is going to be very strange for me this year.

'Mum, I've been invited snowboarding for Christmas!'

My heart said, 'Noooooo!' when he rang a couple of weeks ago. But my head said, 'Of course you must go!' And I found myself making a list of all the reasons why he should, rather than staying at home with me.

'It'll be amazing!' I smiled a watery smile. Because it will be. And who doesn't want their child to do amazing things?

'What will you do if I'm not there?'

'Oh, I have plenty to be getting on with. Loads going on at Lavender Hill,' I lied, although nothing happens at Lavender Hill these days.

'Really? I thought nothing ever happens there. Just a load of people stuck in their little flats.'

He was right.

'No, it'll be great. A real party this year.' I told him I'd be fine and I will. I'll have a box of Maltesers, a big one, and the *Gavin and Stacey Christmas Special*. It's just one day to get through. It's the lead-up to it that can get so tiring. Everyone asking you what your plans are and if you've finished your shopping.

'What would be on your checklist, Pearl, if you were having a Christmas date?' asks Graham, looking up from his Kindle.

'Oh, phffff! I'm too old to go on dates, dear. I've had my time. But I've got a great memory.' She points to her head and smiles wickedly.

'I'd like someone who listens to me,' says Alice, and we all turn to her. 'My husband never did.'

'I'd like to be with someone who wants the purple Quality Streets,' says Ron.

'I'd like someone who knows their own mind, funny and go-getting,' says Norman. He could almost be describing Pearl.

'There'd be no one like my Violet,' says John. 'I'd just like to be with her. She loved Christmas,' he adds, and a brief silence falls over us.

'Can't stand Christmas,' says Maeve. 'All this talk of going to parties, and family get-togethers. Not like that for us all.'

'Me neither,' says Ron. 'One long, lonely month.'

'If I wasn't in this wheelchair it might be different,' says Maeve.

'If I didn't have dietary requirements, I'd go to my brother's,' says Ron. 'But it's never been the same since Mam died.'

'My husband's family don't invite me,' says Alice. 'They always thought he married beneath him.'

'Why did Elsie love Christmas so much?' asks Norman. 'Sounds like we're all going to be sat alone, watching the countdown to the twenty-fifth, the TV adverts, radio tunes and social media overload, with a sense of impending doom.'

'She said Christmas made people happy,' Pearl said, her eyes fixed on the urn. 'She grew up in Germany and said the Christmas markets were just fabulous. They brought everyone together. I think it was the thing she missed most about growing up there. She said it was magical.'

'Well, it isn't magic to me,' says Maeve. 'Just a load of people telling you to enjoy yourself. And if you're stuck in a chair like I am, it's no fun.'

'We're doing this for Elsie. Her parents ran a hotel when she was growing up. She moved to Britain when she was nineteen to learn English, met a man and never went home. Now, we're taking her back to her childhood in Germany, to a Christmas market. It's what she wanted,' says Pearl, firmly.

There's a silence. Then Alice breaks it by saying what I reckon the others are all thinking. 'It seems the only time we all see each other is when we come out of our flats for another funeral,' she says.

'Got mine all planned!' Norman looks quite proud.

'Norman, we should be living life for the now, not planning for when we're not here,' Pearl scolds. 'That's another reason we're doing this. Elsie would have wanted us to have some fun. She left her small amount of savings to us to have a Christmas treat on her. A break will do us good, getting away from all that build-up. And trying to get us all to Tenerife would be an insurance nightmare.' She laughs. 'I found this guest-house on the internet and it was a cracking price, could take us all and is near where Connie has her date. Well, in the neighbouring town. We're not going because it's Christmas, in fact, quite the opposite, we're getting away from all that stuff at home. We're going because of Connie.' They all cheer again and join in with the Christmas songs on the radio, the tinsel swinging, as we reach the end of the tunnel. I reset the satnav with the address I have for Alte Stadt, Germany. 'You've got to make your own happiness in life, Connie love, not wait around for Fate to come knocking,' Pearl says. 'We need to get out of the flats, not wait around for Dr Death to call!'

'Okay, Ron, your turn to drive.' We're about to leave the train, but he's fast asleep, head on his chest, hat flopping forward, snoring.

Looks like I'll be in the driver's seat for a bit longer. Germany, here I come! I'm taking control of my life and making my own happiness, just like Pearl told me to. I may just find my perfect partner.

# THREE

'Blimey, carry on like this and I'll be rediscovering parts of my body I thought were dead years ago!' says Maeve, as I push her in the wheelchair, our cases on her lap, down a narrow cobbled street from where I've parked the minibus.

'Sorry, Maeve. I couldn't bring the bus down here.'

We reach the end of the narrow street and look out on the market square in front of us. It's like a Christmas card, just as I imagined. A quiet town, with tall half-timbered buildings all around, dark wood beams, tiny windows and very pointy red roofs. There are little chalet-type huts all the way round the square and even a carousel with painted horses and carriages. It's beautiful and so peaceful. It actually brings tears to my eyes. Maybe it's tiredness, but suddenly I'm gripped with fear. Part of me wants to turn around and head home. What if Heinrich is nothing like he is on Messenger? What if . . . what if he isn't like I've imagined him to be? What if this is one big mistake, like last time? Or, if he's as lovely as he sounds, what if I'm nothing like he imagined me? What if I'm a big disappointment? I'll be left with nothing. Maybe I was better off not knowing, enjoying our long-distance relationship . . . well, friendship. I expect you have to have met, maybe had some sort of physical contact, for it to be called a relationship. If only I'd told myself that last time! But I was enjoying Heinrich's and my friendship. Our nightly conversations with a glass of wine, discovering each other's interests and finding out new things about our lives and the businesses we work in.

'Don't worry, dear.' Pearl is at my side. 'I'm sure he'll be just like you imagined.' It's as if she's read my mind.

'But . . .'

'What if it's like last time?' She raises a pencilled eyebrow.

What if it *is* like last time? I've always thought myself to be a sensible, fairly intelligent person. But clearly not.

'We're all here with you,' she says. 'That's what friends are for. And you have your tick list. Stick to it, like you said, and you'll know for sure this time. Now, let's go in, shall we?'

The big wooden door, with a huge green wreath

and ribbons on it, is suddenly flung back and a short, large-chested woman with two plaits piled on top of her head smiles and holds out her hands. '*Willkommen!*' she announces. 'Welcome to the Old Town and our Christmas market.' She looks out towards the square, her smile slipping just a tiny bit. 'It's a little quiet at the moment, but don't worry, it will get busier!' she says, looking more hopeful than sure. 'On Sunday, this place will be the best Christmas market around. We even have an ice rink coming!' Then she laughs and her whole body wobbles. 'Although that's meant to be a secret. But as you don't know anyone, who can you tell?' She holds a finger to her lips.

'Thought we were running away from all the Christmas hype,' says Graham, with a wry smile and a slight slur.

'We are here because Con—'

I nudge Norman in the ribs to shut him up, which makes him cough, and then I feel bad.

'We're here for Elsie,' Pearl announces, drowning out all other voices. 'She was a resident in our flats.'

'Oh, lovely.' The woman looks around for Elsie.

'Here,' says Pearl, holding the urn and lifting it slightly.

'She loved Christmas,' says Norman. 'Christmas markets. She grew up in Germany. Moved to Britain. But she never forgot the Christmas markets.'

'So we're bringing her back,' says Pearl.

'It's a bit bonkers, really,' says Norman.

'Christmas just depresses us,' says Maeve.

'If it hadn't been for Elsie popping off, and the water being turned off . . .' I nudge Norman again. 'I'm just saying,' he explains, 'that we're not really fans of Christmas.'

The woman stares at the urn for just a moment. Then she smiles again, warmly. 'Of course. Well, come in. You are welcome whether you are here for the market or not.'

'We're after chocolate and beer!' says Ron.

'I'm here for the lederhosen!' Pearl laughs in a strange high-pitched way.

We all turn to her, not sure what to say.

'I like the way it squeaks,' she says.

'Well, we have pulled out all the stops this year.' Our hostess points to the market. 'We have Christmas . . . all wrapped up!' Suddenly she laughs like Pearl, loudly, at her own joke, and we all join in. This town, I think, like our hostess, is utterly charming.

'Maybe not the ice rink for us, though,' says Maeve, holding her hands tightly in her lap and pursing her lips.

'But it all looks lovely,' I say. 'Charming.'

'We hope this will be our year!' Our hostess sighs, letting her arm fall to her side and her shawl fall open. 'There was a time when this town was everything you could dream Christmas would be. Nowadays, ever since . . . Well, who knows? It could all change on Sunday.' She waves a hand in the air.

'Sunday?' I ask, wondering if this has anything to do with Heinrich and the project he's been working on.

'Yes, a big event. It's a very important day here in the Old Town, didn't you know? Come in, let me show you your rooms, fix you a glass of glühwein and I can explain it all. Now, some of you may need to share.'

'Share? I could have stayed at home and had my own room,' says Maeve.

'Without any water or heating, though, Maeve,' Di reminds her, as she guides Graham gently through the door. The pair look exhausted and I know she's still got to help him get ready for bed and be there for him throughout the night. It's never a rest for her.

'I don't mind sharing,' I offer, just desperate for some sleep.

'Nor me,' says Pearl, quickly. 'I'd enjoy the company.'

'That's settled, then.' Our hostess clasps her hands on her belly. 'I'm Anja.'

'Pearl,' I say quietly, 'are you sure about sharing? I mean, if it's not what you wanted, we could always go back.'

'Nonsense, dear! It's not what we expected, but it could be fun. And you have your date tomorrow. You're just getting cold feet.'

But if sharing a room is not what we expected, the

chances are my date won't be either. I know that from experience. We'll have come all this way for nothing and I'll be back to square one. A new list to start ticking off.

'And we're here for Elsie too, remember?' says Pearl, making me feel better that we're not just here for my date.

'I can't remember if I recorded *Coronation Street*,' says Alice.

'Hope it's a comfy bed. I do like a comfy bed.' Norman smiles.

'Not too many stairs,' Di puts in.

'I fancy a good pint. Nothing too fizzy!' Ron says, puffing by the second step.

'We're here now,' Pearl says, to everyone. 'Let's make the most of it.' Everyone looks shattered. 'Let's just stay until Connie has her date. If we're not having fun, and the heating and water's back on in the flats, we can scatter Elsie's ashes and then always leave if we want to.'

They agree and make their way upstairs behind Anja, who gives Pearl a grateful look.

I follow Pearl upstairs to our twin room, looking out over the square. As she uses the shared bathroom, I sit down on my bed. I pull out my list and the first box I need to tick.

'Is he real?' My pen hovers over the box.

My phone pings with a message. I pull it out of my shoulder bag, wondering if it's Sam. But, no, it's

Heinrich, checking I've arrived on schedule and if we can still meet for our date tomorrow. Pearl is emerging from the bathroom. 'It's him,' I say. 'Checking on our date tomorrow morning.'

Pearl smiles. But she looks tired too.

'So, you definitely have a date tomorrow,' she says, with a firm nod. 'Whether he's what you expected or not, it looks like he plans to be there.'

A bunch of excited butterflies have just been released in my stomach. 'Yes! Looks like it's really happening. I have a date tomorrow,' I repeat, letting out a long breath. This may work out. Now I just need to find out if he is who he says he is.

I message Sam: *I'm here! In Germany! The market is beautiful and the guesthouse really friendly. And Heinrich has checked that I'm here and ready for our date tomorrow.*

He messages straight back: *That's brilliant, Mum! Remember to take your notebook. Do it by the book. It's the only way. Let me know how it goes and that you're safe. And, if you want, I can ring you, just in case you need a get-out.*

I smile. *It's okay. I have Pearl with me. But thank you.*

*Have fun!*

*Thank you. Xxx*

*Love you Mum. Xxxx*

And this time I find myself holding my phone to my lips. 'Love you too, Sam,' I say to myself, with blurry eyes. I sniff away the itchiness in my nose, put down my phone and do exactly what my son has told me to do. Play it by the book. I pick up my notebook and read the first question: 'Is he real?'

If he's planning on meeting me tomorrow morning, I think it's safe to say that, whatever he looks or is like, he's real. Tentatively, I tick the first box, then hold the list tightly to me.

I can't get this wrong again.

# FOUR

It's the following morning. After last night's glühwein and the fattest, juiciest sausages I have ever eaten, I'd fallen into a deep sleep, on soft pillows and wrapped in a thick duvet. I felt like I was sleeping on a cloud. Now I stare at myself in the mirror. I've changed twice already and am about to change again. I can't work out what to wear.

'Morning, dear,' says Pearl, as I watch her from the mirror, propping herself up stiffly on her pillows.

'Sorry, Pearl, did I wake you? You go back to sleep. It's very early.'

'Not at all. At my age, the last thing you want is more sleep. Plenty of time for that when I'm pushing up the daisies.' She coughs. 'Is that what you're wearing?'

'You? Pushing up daisies?' I laugh. Pearl must be the youngest at the retirement flats. If not the youngest, then certainly the fittest and most energetic. If it wasn't for her and her organizing, I wouldn't be here now, wondering what on earth to wear and what on earth to expect of my date.

'Are you okay?' I ask, as she doesn't respond with her usual laughter.

'Fine, dear. I always take time to be thankful for another day, since that bit of bother I had a couple of years ago.'

'I presume you mean when you were ill.'

'Yes, that. But we're here and that's what matters,' she says briskly, and then her signature wicked smile is back in place. 'Now, you've still got a while before you meet him. Fancy going for breakfast or just a coffee?' She pulls her thin frame out of bed.

'Actually,' I swallow nervously, 'I thought I'd go and suss out the place where I'm supposed to be meeting him. Give myself time, in case I get lost.' I look out of the window. There's just lights in mist from the buildings opposite and streetlamps. Nothing else to see at the moment: it's too dark.

'Good idea! Do you want me to come with you?' She plumps up her hair with both hands. 'Just to be on the safe side.'

I smile and take a deep breath. 'No, but thank you. I'll text you to say I'm safe and sound, like we arranged. But I need to do this on my own. And I hope it reassures me I'm not the total idiot I've been feeling I am. I just need to find my confidence again, I suppose.'

'Just because he contacted you in the first place doesn't mean he's a fake,' Pearl says.

'No, but the fact that you answered him on my behalf is debatable.' I laugh and so does she.

'I couldn't help it when I saw it sitting there unanswered in your inbox.'

'I told you, hacking into people's accounts is not good. You learned bad skills at the Silver Surfers club! It wouldn't surprise me if you had a tracker system on me right now.'

She winks at me, playfully.

'But, seriously, thank you. If you hadn't given me a nudge, I wouldn't have done this.' I take a deep breath. 'I just hope . . . I just hope he's who he says he is. That I can . . .'

'Trust him?'

Tears spring to my made-up eyes, infuriating me, and I wave my hands in front of them, hoping it will dry them.

'It'll be fine. I'm sure. He wouldn't be checking on what time you were meeting if he wasn't,' Pearl reassures me.

I take a deep breath and lift my chin.

'One last go. You promised Sam.' Pearl looks at me.

'Yes, one last go at internet dating. If this one doesn't work out, I'm giving it up for good.' I point a finger firmly but in jest.

'I can't bear the thought of you giving up on it so soon.'

'But you can't say I haven't tried. I have. And look where it got me. After this, I'm happy staying at home with reruns of *Friends*!'

She frowns. 'You're always doing so much for everybody else. Baking for us, spending time with us when you make your deliveries, even if it does make you late, and running errands when you can. It's time you thought of yourself for once.'

'I promised Sam I'd get out there and start dating once he'd left home. And I did it. And mostly it's been awful.'

'But I've loved hearing about all your dates. We just want you to meet someone who deserves you.'

'Perhaps, but this is it now, Pearl,' I say, more firmly and seriously. I waggle my notebook at her, filled with dates, times, the set questions I have for each one, a round-up and verdict. 'You can't say I didn't give it a go. It does seem the way to find your match is online these days . . . but there's a lot of frogs out there, with very good filters on their photos. But for you I'll give it this one last go.'

'Okay, love. Have fun.'

'Do I look okay?' I run my hands over my high-necked knitted dress, which I've had for years, warm, cosy and figure-hugging, with a soft cream scarf around my neck that I got in last year's sales as a treat to myself. 'Not too tarty? Or frumpy? Or—'

'You look gorgeous. He's a lucky man. I hope he's the one you've been looking for.'

'Me too, Pearl.'

'Just one thing, dear. What happens if he is the one?'

'What do you mean?'

'Well, if it is the perfect match. It's all very well coming out here on holiday and going out on dates. But what if it's serious? You can't be popping over to Germany every other weekend and him to the UK. You'll have to work it out. And quickly.'

My excitement fizzles out, like droplets of water on birthday candles, fizzing and hissing. 'Pearl! You were the one who said to just have some fun! "You don't have to marry him," you said!' I stare at her.

'Just thinking aloud.' She shrugs impishly.

'Let's see if he's who he says he is to start with.' I pull down my hat firmly and put all other worries out of my mind. First things first. I'm not going to let myself get burned again. I'm doing exactly what Sam told me to do: playing it by the book.

'Well, you have just five days to find out.' Pearl grins. 'Now go and do it!' She beams and coughs, waving me off.

Just five days to decide if I've met the man I want to share the rest of my life with. It's not possible, is it? In five days, could he tick every box? I laugh as I walk through the drizzle, much like the drizzle we left at home, taking in the little town and its Christmas market. The stallholders are gathering around their chalets, preparing for the day and night ahead. The bar is being restocked and the cleaners are out in force, emptying bins, sweeping the streets and clearing away any evidence of the day and night before.

On the skyline, high above the square, I can see the outline of a castle. Below it, the town falls away like a beautiful ballgown, glittering as lights begin to turn on in the houses and down the cobbled streets to the square I'm standing in. I walk through it, looking for somewhere to get a coffee to help settle my jangling nerves. Or maybe just to warm me up. It's cold. I shiver. But maybe I'll wait for coffee until afterwards. I don't want to be looking for a loo on my date. I follow Google Maps down a dark alleyway and wonder if I've done the right thing in coming out so early – it's barely light.

I pull my coat round me. It has to be near here somewhere. We're due to meet at eight, before Heinrich goes to work. It's a busy week for him, and I'm assuming that's because it's nearly Christmas. He has an early-morning meeting here. 'First thing,' he said. 'We'll have a breakfast date and take it from there,' were his words. Very sensible. Then, if we don't like each other, we can just move on with the rest of our lives. But everything about his work ticked boxes. He even runs a bakery. I turn down a narrow cobbled street and stop, catch my breath and stare. It's love at first sight.

I stand outside the little shop, an orange glow pouring from the small panes of glass at the bay window. It's just like the Werther's Original and the Lindor

Christmas adverts all in one. This is where Heinrich arranged for us to meet. It's perfect! Magical, almost. That's a big tick. I pull out my notebook and open the page, drops of rain creating wet circles on it. I quickly write down the name of the place, how it makes me feel, and give 'Meeting Place' a big tick. I wonder if this is his bakery. I put away my notebook and take a photograph of the shop. I step forward for a closer look. There's no one around, but the smell of baking fills my nostrils and wraps around me, like a soft cashmere blanket, making my mouth water.

All of a sudden, I hear voices and I'm gripped with nerves, the usual worries whizzing round my head. What if he's nothing like I'm expecting? This place is just perfect. What if he's just as perfect? What if I'm about to meet my Mr Right? I'm not sure I'm ready. I need a moment to compose myself. This dating malarkey has a lot to answer for. I was a together, confident person, in control of my own life before I started hanging around in doorways, waiting to meet strange men. I don't want to be there first, maybe seeming over-eager. Or like I want to get the meet over and done with. I have to get this right.

I dart into the shadows of a narrow street opposite, slipping on the wet cobbles and sliding against the wall. I can still see the little shop from the shadows and a figure moving around inside. I think it's one, maybe more, but I'm not sure with the drizzle distorting the orange glow from the windowpanes. I try to photograph the shop again to post to my online baking group, but my hands are shaking with cold and nerves. This is it: this could be the moment I get to see him, the man I've been messaging for a couple of months. My cheeks burn at the memory of the last man I put my trust in. 'It's like falling off a horse,' Pearl had insisted. 'You've got to get right back in the saddle.' With that, she had opened up her iPad, then my profile page on the dating website, handed it to me and went to make coffee in her kitchenette.

I watch the door of the bakery, my heart pounding. It's like waiting to enjoy a freshly baked cake as it cools, hoping you've got it right, and that it'll be as glorious as it looks in the recipe book. You're aching for it to be delicious and bracing yourself for disappointment.

I shiver as raindrops run down the back of my neck. What am I doing here, hiding in the shadows, trying to get a glimpse of my date?

I hear voices again, not from the shop this time but in the square. I listen. They're familiar. I snap my head round. It's getting lighter and I can see, gathered under a big metal streetlamp, Pearl, Norman, Ron, Di and Graham, who is leaning heavily on his stick, his bobble hat sliding over one eye, Alice dressed to the nines, pushing Maeve, her handbag on her lap, and John at the back.

'What on earth . . . ?' I say under my breath.

'I'm sure this is the place,' says Norman.

'Maybe she won't want us here,' Di points out sensibly.

'What time did you say she was meeting him? I don't think this is my watch. Could be Aunt Lucy's,' Norman says.

'I just want to check she's in the right place,' says Pearl, and shushes them all loudly.

I hear voices from inside the shop again, raised voices, getting louder. My heart is beating faster. My head snaps back to the bakery doorway.

'She said it was a bakery. It's lovely!' says Pearl.

'Just because it looks pretty on the outside . . .' says Maeve, from her wheelchair.

'Well, let's just make sure she's here, safe and sound.' The group starts moving towards the bakery.

I stand in silence, frozen to the spot in horror. It's as if Mum and Dad have turned up on my date, except I'm a grown woman and it's a group of pensioners I deliver meals to, about to stick their faces up to the window. What on earth is he going to think when he comes out to meet me . . . and my friends? He'll run a mile! I've come all this way – and this could ruin everything.

'Pearl! I hiss. They don't hear me. I try again, louder this time. 'Pearl!'

This time, to my relief, she turns.

'What are you doing here?' I frown.

'More's the point, dear, what are *you* doing *here*?' She gestures at the alleyway where I'm hiding.

I feel my cheeks flame.

'I thought you were on your date. We thought we'd just wander by, discreetly, check you were okay.'

'Check him out, you mean. And that I haven't made a fool of myself again. That he actually exists.'

'We can all make mistakes, Connie love. Life wouldn't be the adventure it is if we didn't.'

I feel such a fool when I think about how taken in I was.

There's more voices from inside the bakery.

'I'm just waiting,' I say. 'I don't want to be the first to get here, and I'd like a moment to see if he's what I'm expecting. It's just what I do. First impressions.' I hold up the notebook Sam gave me for Christmas two years ago when he went to university and explained to me about making a list for my dates. 'That, and choice of venue.'

'Well, that gets a big tick,' says Pearl.

'Ah, there you are, Connie,' says Ron, who has taken over pushing Maeve in the wheelchair.

'Look, it's lovely of you all to come and check on me, but, really, I'm fine. I'll tell you all about it later. Why don't you go and find somewhere to have coffee? Text me. I'll meet you,' I say hurriedly, keeping an eye on the shadow in the doorway now.

'We were hoping to get something round here,' says Ron, lifting his nose into the air like a sniffer dog trained to search.

Suddenly, the shadow in the doorway gets bigger and I see the outline of a figure. Bigger, broader than I was expecting. My heart leaps into my mouth.

'Quick!' I say to the group. 'Over here!' I beckon

them into the shadows of the street where I'm standing in the wet December morning light. They do as I say, hobbling over the cobbles towards me and tucking in against the wall, their heads popping out over mine or, in Maeve's case, beside me from her wheelchair. We stand and listen. All I can hear is my companions breathing or, in Ron's case, wheezing, their breath creating plumes of condensation in the early-morning air. And then a man comes out of the shop, holding not one gingerbread heart as arranged, but a whole handful. I catch my breath.

# FIVE

'Catfished! That's what you've been,' says Norman.

'What?' The others turn to him.

'Sssh!' I try to quieten them, my heart thumping, head pumping and a hot sweat breaking out around my brow.

'Catfished!' he repeats, in a very loud whisper, presumably thinking that makes it okay. The man holding the gingerbread hearts by their strings, my date, it seems, looks around and frowns. 'Nothing like the photo Pearl showed us.'

They've even seen a photo of him! I roll my eyes.

'Sssh!' I say again, waving a gloved hand in Norman's direction but not taking my eyes off the man with the gingerbread hearts, his unruly dark hair. He's not tall and blond, or smart and fit. He raises an eyebrow, clearly amused, in the direction of the alleyway we're standing in. My fists tighten.

This is not what I was expecting, not at all. He promised he'd be carrying a gingerbread heart, but that's about the only thing that's right with this image.

The beautiful building in the narrow cobbled street is not what I was expecting either. A black cat runs across the street with little raindrops, like diamonds, scattered across its back. It hurries across our pathway, stopping only briefly to stare at me, then run on.

'See? It's a good-luck sign,' says Pearl, trying to be positive. 'It crossed your path from left to right.'

I'm still speechless. This man looks nothing like the guy in the pictures I've been sent. I'm trying to match the voice on the phone to this face, not the one I'd imagined. I pull out my phone to check that I'm in the right place at the right time, meeting Heinrich carrying a gingerbread heart. My notebook comes with it, tumbling from my bag and falling onto the wet cobbles. The gold writing on the front catches in the orange glow from the shop: 'hopes and dreams'. I have a feeling my hopes and dreams have plummeted down the drain with the rainwater that's trickling between the grooves of the cobbles, like liquid mercury. I pick it up and shake off the wet. I feel like someone's pulled the plug on a lovely warm bath filled with bubbles that I was about to enjoy, and instead I'm cold and wet, shivering, with only a damp towel to cover myself.

I pull up the picture Heinrich sent me on my phone and hold it up. Pearl and the others crane their necks to see, then look at the man outside the bakery, who is shaking his head as he starts to hang the gingerbread hearts under the awning over the window. Is he wondering why I'm not there on time?

I look at the clock in the tower on the square. It's almost eight. My mouth is dry and my chest tight. We agreed that timekeeping was important to us and if I don't go over now I'm going to be late.

'Definitely catfished!' says Norman again.

'What is "catfished"?' Pearl asks, handing back my phone, which they'd passed between themselves, looking at the picture and tutting.

'When you send a picture that looks nothing like you or pretend to be someone you're not. Like him . . . nothing like his picture.'

'How do you know all this?' Pearl asks.

'Done enough online dating myself to know all about catfishing, ghosting, orbiting,' says Norman.

'I never knew you'd been online dating,' Pearl says in surprise.

'Well, why would you? We don't really see each other, any of us, do we? We're all living in the same building but barely know our neighbours. If it wasn't for Connie, we might not know what's going on at all. She's the glue that's keeps us together. Without her visits . . .'

'And her online dating updates,' says Alice.

'. . . we'd barely know each other's names.'

A silence falls over the group.

'He's right. You've been catfished. It wouldn't be the first time,' Maeve joins in.

I don't really hear what else they're saying. It's all a bit of a blur. How could I have got it wrong again? I'm not stupid. I'm not desperate. I've followed all my own guidelines. The questions are bouncing around in my head as I'm trying to back away into the shadows even further. I don't want to be here. That man is not who I came to meet. Norman's right: I've been catfished. And Maeve is right too, not for the first time. I've come all this way and I've been taken for an idiot. Again! Angry tears spring to my eyes. My cheeks burn with embarrassment and humiliation. The man I came to meet, the one in my picture, is tall, blond and lean. This man has wild, dark hair, with a bandana round his head, for heaven's sake. He's shorter than I was expecting and with broad shoulders. Nothing like the Heinrich I've spent nights fantasizing about. I'm furious for agreeing to come, for making a fool of myself again. I was much happier when I could just think about him. Our nightly chats online were lovely. It was safe! I couldn't get hurt. Now I'm really hurt, and feeling foolish.

I keep stepping backwards.

'Where are you going?' hisses Pearl.

'Not staying here, that's for sure,' I say. 'Norman's right. He's nothing like his picture.'

'But he might be nice.'

'But he's . . . untrustworthy,' I say. 'He's not who he said he was. All this way to have it happen again. The Heinrich I was messaging does not look like that. I'm being taken for an idiot – again! I'm not staying.' The words catch in my throat. I back away and straight into something that sends me tumbling, arms flailing, losing my balance.

Suddenly, there's a right commotion along what was a silent road and alley, before my friends and I arrived.

'Steady there, Connie!' shouts one.

'Watch out for the bin!' shouts another.

'I've got her! . . . Oh, no, I haven't!'

'Argh!'

There's a clatter as the bin I've fallen over hits the ground, with me quickly after it.

'Do we need an ambulance?' shouts Alice.

'Who's our first-aider?' Ron yells.

'I'm fine! I'm fine!' I say, grovelling in scrunched-up paper bags, clearly from the bakery opposite, as I try to stand. Evidently the road sweepers haven't made it up this alley yet. If only everyone would just move back, I might be able to get to my feet. So many arms and walking sticks are being held out to me that I haven't the space to stand.

Then a hand breaks through and holds itself out to me. A hand covered with white flour.

'Are you okay?' says a deep, gravelly voice, with a strong German accent.

It's him! My tongue twists in knots. Where do I start? Of all the audacity!

'I'm fine,' I jolt myself into replying. My embarrassment rises a couple more notches, if that were possible, making me sound much sharper than I'd intended. A space clears around me, the hand takes hold of mine and pulls me to my feet. All eyes are on me, and the man. I dust myself down, hoping to hide my embarrassment and work out exactly what to say to him, in his chef's whites and his bandana, my cat-fishing date standing in front of me with amusement on his face.

I swallow hard, and straighten. I'm roughly the same height as him. Pearl hands me my bag. I struggle for words but she decides to help me out.

'This is Connie.' She holds out a hand and grins. 'From the UK. She's come to see you.'

'Pearl!' I scold. I really don't want to be here. He's not who I thought he was and I don't want to carry on with this pretence now. My dating disasters have just hit an all-time low – well, after the man who scammed my life savings from me. I'm never putting myself through this again.

'Has she? From the UK?' says the chef. A smile tugs at the corner of his mouth. 'Well, I'm flattered. Are you sure you're okay? That looked like quite a fall you took there.'

'I'm fine,' I repeat. 'I . . . just had a bit of a shock, that's all!' I say pointedly.

'Well, I hope you're okay now.' He turns to walk back to his shop.

'It's just that you don't look anything like your photograph,' says Maeve, direct and to the point as always. I cringe, but if anyone is going to tell him what I think of him, it's going to be me.

'Oh, well, maybe it was an old photograph. I haven't had my picture taken in a long time,' he says, suddenly thoughtful. 'Not since I came back . . .' He tails off.

'It's not just an old photograph, it doesn't look anything like you.' I suddenly find my voice. 'I've come all this way to meet you and well, phffff, frankly, I'm . . .' What am I? Disappointed? Cross? Feeling foolish?

'Look, I'm not sure what you were expecting.' He frowns, as if I'm some sort of deranged stalker, infuriating me even more. We've talked. We agreed to meet here. At this time. Him holding a gingerbread heart.

'Well, certainly not . . . not . . .' I circle my hand in his direction. How do I say he's a scruffy-haired, shorter, darker, far wider man than he told me he was? Nothing like my usual type. Nothing like a perfect match.

'She's just upset because the photograph you sent her wasn't anything like you. But she's here, for your date.' Pearl gives me a nudge forward.

He looks at me, fresh from the gutter where I've been rolling around with the rubbish. And I can't help but feel I'm being sized up. The cheek of it! I didn't send a totally false photograph. Well, okay, it might have been a few years old, but at least I still look like me. Clearly, though, he doesn't think so.

'I'm sorry.' His eyes narrow and he looks at the group of pensioners standing around me. There is silence, apart from the bell beginning to chime eight o'clock in the clock tower in the square. 'I have no idea what you're talking about. I'm not looking for a date and if I was . . .'

'Huh!' Norman takes a sharp intake of breath. 'Ghosted!' he announces. 'Means they just ignore you and hope you'll go away.'

I want the ground to open up and swallow me there and then. I'm furious. My cheeks are on fire, raging red hot.

'If I was looking for a date it certainly wouldn't be . . .'

I knew I shouldn't have let Pearl persuade me into doing this again. Internet dating seems to work for everyone but me. I should have given up after the last time. I swore I would! I don't think my perfect date is out there. He doesn't exist. Like before . . . I try to blink away the tears in my eyes.

Just then, as the bell in the clock tower chimes for the eighth time, a tall, blond man, carrying a small gingerbread heart, dips his head and steps out of the low bakery door opposite, bang on time. He looks up and down the street, then at me and . . . smiles.

# SIX

'Heinrich!' I recognize him straight away from his photograph. Tall, blond, neatly dressed, and holding one gingerbread heart. Tick, tick, tick! Exactly what I was expecting.

I could kiss him, actually kiss him, there and then. The corners of my mouth twitch, then draw back into a wide smile to meet his.

I turn back to Pearl and the shorter, dark-haired man, who glowers in Heinrich's direction. I'm still smiling. I pull my hat straight and dust myself down.

The bin men have arrived, sweeping the street and emptying bins behind me, and I don't think I've ever seen cleaner streets. In fact, all of a sudden everything about this place seems perfect. I turn back to the man in front of me, who might have been about to tell me he wouldn't fancy me if I was the last woman on earth. He raises a questioning eyebrow.

'Excuse me,' I say, and straighten my hat again. 'And, um, I'm sorry,' I cough, 'for the misunderstanding.' I'm not sorry I indicated that I was as disappointed by his looks as he seems to have been by mine. 'I have a date to go on,' I say, lifting my chin.

'With Heinrich?' He nods towards the other man.

'Yes, with Heinrich.' I nod firmly back. Tall, smart, attractive Heinrich.

'And you're meeting here . . . ?' He shakes his head. 'That makes sense.' His smile drops. 'Treating the place as if he owns it,' he growls.

What's that supposed to mean? 'Well, he does, doesn't he? And you'd probably do well to remember that,' I say, far more haughtily than I mean to, still embarrassed by having mistaken one of Heinrich's employees for Heinrich. The man does that eyebrow-raising thing again.

I want to challenge him but, actually, I don't want to waste any more of my precious time here in the Old Town. I want to enjoy every bit of it. I turn back to look at Heinrich, whose smile slips when he sees me talking to this man.

'Excuse me, I have to go,' I say, taking a deep breath and turning to Heinrich, full of nerves all over again. I take a step towards him. His smile slowly returns and my nerves settle as I walk towards him.

'Go on, Connie!' I hear Norman say behind me, as I walk across the damp, shiny cobbles.

'Have a good time!' I hear Pearl call.

'I will,' I tell her, and turn back to Heinrich.

'Um . . . Connie?'

It's the deep, gravelly voice again. My nerves stand to attention, on high alert. I turn slowly back to the man in chef's whites and the bandana.

'Yes?' This time it's me who raises an eyebrow. I just want to speak to Heinrich, the man I've travelled all this way to meet. He's making me think that all the internet dating's been worth it, if he's as lovely as he looks.

The annoying chef points, his lopsided smile tugging at the corner of his mouth.

'You have . . . some . . .' His forefinger circles.

I'm irritated by this man delaying me now. I look back at Heinrich, whose smile slips again. I turn back to the man, wanting to get away quickly. 'What is it?'

'Some rubbish, caught.' He steps forward and peels a greasy paper bag from last night's street food, left behind by the street cleaners, from the back of my thigh and holds it up. 'Sorted!' He grins, infuriating me all the more. I blush with humiliation. If I never see this man again it will be far too soon.

I turn back to Heinrich, take a huge breath and blow out slowly, determined not to let the chef ruin this for me, I straighten my hat for the third time and smile back at him. Little butterflies of hope do a happy dance in my stomach. I remember I have just four nights to decide if he's the one. It certainly looks as if it'll be worth staying to find out.

# SEVEN

'Hi!' says Heinrich. I gaze up at him, taking in all the details of his face, as if I'm reading the blurb on the back of a book, having liked the cover. Small, neat features. Neat blond hair that sometimes falls forward when he brushes it back. He's wearing a black fleecy neck snood, an expensive ski jacket and warm gloves to match. I can't really believe I'm standing here. I've dreamed of this moment for weeks, hoping it would be . . . well, just like this. He smells of a complex aftershave, not sweet, or too citrussy. Spicy almost. I can't quite work out whether I like it or not. It tickles the inside of my nose. But I can tell it's expensive and he's not been shy with it. That's a good sign. A sign of cleanliness, and . . . generosity. I make a mental note to put it on my pros list and tick both boxes.

'Hi!' I say nervously, no idea whether I should kiss

him or not and, if so, once or on both cheeks. Or just shake hands?

He bends towards me. I slowly go on tiptoe and as he hands me the gingerbread heart he's holding, I go to kiss his cheek as he embraces me in a strong hug so I end up with a broken heart and kiss his chin.

'Sorry!'

'Sorry!'

We both laugh nervously, glancing at the cobbles, then at each other again.

'Nerves,' we say together, and laugh again. I hear a ripple of agreement and remember my little audience. I glance over to the group huddled together, like a family photo, with Maeve at the front in her wheelchair. And there beside the group, as if he's part of it, is the man in the chef's whites, his arms folded, taking as much interest as the rest of my party. I bristle at them all. I make eye gestures to Pearl for them to go away, but she doesn't move, just stands there smiling. She probably can't see my subtle messages because she's too vain to wear her glasses. I try a nod, to get them to leave, but no one is moving. Not even the chef in whites, who seems to be as entertained as if he's watching a Christmas movie. My dating life is not a spectator sport, I want to tell them. I'm suddenly paralysed with embarrassment, like I'm a young woman again. I'd forgotten that part of being young. I remember the carefree joy, but I'd forgotten the lack of confidence.

He clears his throat and I lift my head, remembering I'm not that sixteen-year-old girl any more. I'm forty-one and have life's scars to prove it.

'I see you know William.' He nods to the group of pensioners.

'Who?' I'm suddenly confused. The little bubble we were standing in just seconds ago has burst, and it's cold without it. I shiver.

'William. He owns this place.' He nods towards the shop, still lit with an orange glow from under the awning, which is festooned with tiny white lights and hanging gingerbread hearts.

'He . . .' I look back at the chef, his arms folded across his chest, alongside the beaming pensioners, like they're at the finals of *Strictly Come Dancing*, willing their favourite to win.

'Oh, no.' I shake my head. 'We just met when I was waiting for you.'

'Waiting for me? But we said eight on the dot, didn't we?' He looks concerned and checks his expensive blue-faced watch.

'Yes, yes, we did. I just got here early.'

'Early?' He seems surprised, then smiles. 'That's good.' And for a moment I wonder if he's making a mental list in his head, too.

'So . . . you don't own this place?' I ask, realizing my mistake and feeling a little disappointed.

'No, my shop is in the New Town. It's on the outskirts of the Old Town here. Although we are officially part of this town, it grew and began to spread outside the city walls, over the bridge. We have much more space there.' He glances around at the narrow streets and high half-timbered buildings. 'We are really separate towns altogether. There has been a feud for many years. We believe the New Town is the real hub of the community, and here, they try to maintain that they are the heart of it. We know it isn't true. Progress makes things better. We have a much better functioning town . . . and market for that matter.'

I look back at the small bakery and the sign above the door. I'm not sure anything could be more perfect than this. 'I can't wait to see it,' I say. 'If it's half as good as this . . .'

'It's much better. More efficient. Besides, he asks way too much for his gingerbread. No wonder he and the rest of the Old Town are going out of business.' I'm a little taken aback by his bluntness. Or am I? Maybe his honesty and truthfulness are exactly what I've been looking for. Refreshingly honest. Wasn't trustworthiness one of the most important qualities on my list? Aren't they the same things? Honesty and truthfulness? I make a mental note to mark it on my pros list, double-tick those boxes, and smile.

'Still, it looks like he has found some customers. Tourists are always suckers for this kind of sentimentality.' Again, I'm taken aback. 'They come for the look of this place, but the locals want what we have to offer.'

I look at Pearl and the gang, and Pearl waves.

'You know them?' he asks.

'Um, well, sort of . . . Yes.' I don't want to tell him they're with me. That I've come on my date with a group of pensioners, one of whom thinks she's Cilla Black reincarnated while the others are acting as my personal bodyguards.

'Just some people I – met while I was waiting. Not that I was waiting long. Just . . .' Phffff. I link my arm through his, desperate to move us on. 'Let's go somewhere for coffee, shall we?' I say decisively, determined to make every moment count.

'Sure. We'll head back to my hometown on the other side of the bridge. I've finished here.'

'Finished?' I stop and look at him.

'I had a meeting with William. I needed to speak with him. Not that he was in the mood for listening. It seemed a good place to meet. It was good for you?'

'Lovely.' I think of my box for meeting-place choices. It was perfect. Still is perfect, I think, even if it was more out of convenience for him.

'We have plenty of places to eat and drink in our town. Not like here. I cannot wait to show you our market. It's going to be our best yet.' He throws a look at William, then directs me down the lane.

'You can't even bring cars into this town.' He shakes his head. 'It's so infuriating. Follow me. I'll take you to mine.' He leads me to his car at the end of the lane, under what I think is a fairly universal sign for no parking, and opens the door for me. Tick. I know it shouldn't matter, but it makes me smile that he's thoughtful.

'Oh, wait! You have something on your shoe.' He grabs my foot, pulls off a piece of paper.

I climb into the car, leaving a dusting of sugar on the carpet. I blush. 'Sorry.'

'Don't worry. It happens at Christmas market time. There is food and drink everywhere. It's a big job for the towns to keep the streets clean. Really, it's not a problem.' But I can see he's not keen on getting it in his car.

He dusts off his hands, then gets into the driver's seat and I give a brief look back at the group standing by the bakery. They're waving me off cheerfully, and beside them an amused-looking chef is returning to hang more gingerbread hearts on hooks outside the pretty little bakery.

We drive towards the bridge and to the town on the other side. All the way across it, we're snatching glances at each other, like a game of Grandmother's Footsteps, trying not to be caught out and smiling each time we are.

# EIGHT

The market is in full swing already. In fact, it may still be going from last night. There is a big square, with big-name shops and well-known food chains, modern flats and offices all around it.

'This is my town,' says Heinrich, parking his car in front of a large, modern, glass-fronted shop on the main square. 'And this is my business, mine and my family's.' He points to the shop, and what looks to be a big industrial kitchen behind.

He smiles. His teeth are very white. And he's here, he's real and looks just like his picture. And he really does have his own bakery business. It's not the pretty Dickensian-style place we've come from but that is definitely his family name above the door. It's all true. I feel like I'm over the first and biggest hurdle. He's here and he's real and he's very attractive. I smile back, allowing myself to relax just a little. So far, things are looking good, really good.

'Come on, let's get some breakfast.' He unclips his seatbelt in the smart, leather-lined car. 'There's plenty to choose from in the market.'

We step out and I can hear the market already. He locks the car with a *beep-beep* and checks his watch. 'I need to be back in the office in one hour. Is that okay for you?' he asks earnestly.

Once again, I'm a bit surprised by his directness, but I quite like it. I know exactly where I stand. Some of my other online dates didn't bother to let me know what they were thinking, or tried to make me believe something totally untrue.

'Great,' I say, watching the blue and pink lights coming from the far end of the market, lighting up a big glass building, where the street cleaners are working hard.

'Great,' he repeats. 'Let's go.' He slings his arm around my shoulders and at first I'm a bit taken aback but, actually, I quite like it and let him leave it there. 'Then we can decide if we want to see each other again,' he says. Again, straight to the point. But what if he doesn't want to see me again? I'm suddenly not relaxed at all.

We walk through the market, which the stallholders are setting up. It's quite early. Anja told me that the market where we are doesn't really start until eleven. Here, the fairground waltzer is still covered, as are the other rides, which look as if they exist to scare the life out of you, loud music blaring and lights flashing to add to the thrill. Some businesses are opening the wooden shutters at the front of the little huts, much more modern and brightly coloured than the rustic ones in the Old Town. Perhaps they're hoping to catch early-morning shoppers, smartly dressed young people with rucksacks, suitcases and laptops, carrying refillable coffee cups on their way to work. The air is full of the smell of coffee and, if I'm not mistaken, warm doughnuts.

I'm suddenly feeling quite hungry as we walk closer to the stall selling spirals of dough covered with sugar. The bearded vendor pops his head out of the kiosk and offers me a piece to try. I hold up my hand to refuse, even though I want to try everything. I must be myself, I think, not what I'm imagining Heinrich is expecting me to be. But Heinrich stops at the stall. 'Would you like one?' he says.

'They do smell delicious,' I say, feeling as if it's a test. If I say I'd like one, will he think I have no self-restraint? If I say no, will he think I'm too buttoned-up? He orders anyway, taking the decision out of my hands. I have to sort myself out. Be myself. I can't try to second-guess this. Anyway, I'm here to see if I like him just as much as he is seeing if he likes me. It's a two-way street. And right now, he's handing me the delicious, sugary spiral doughnut and a hot coffee.

'I remember you saying how much you like sugared doughnuts,' he says, 'when we spoke. I thought this might be exactly what you'd like for breakfast. No need for restraint. You're on holiday! One won't hurt.' He points towards a covered seating area.

I'd once mentioned liking doughnuts and how I have to resist them when they're on offer at the end of the day in the supermarkets. 'You remembered,' I say quietly, looking at the treat in my hands. 'Thank you,' I say, touched. He gestures to the seating area and I follow him. All around the outside are wooden pods like huge wine barrels, benches and tables, and small blackboards showing the times when the booths are reserved. He leads me to stand at one of the tables to drink our coffee and eat our doughnuts.

I gaze around, taking in the market. Heinrich, though, is keen to make the best use of our breakfast date. He describes the town's layout, pointing to the big modern theatre, the cinema and bowling alley, and I look at the big shops and their Christmas window displays.

'So, how do you like it?' he asks, and for a moment I'm not sure if he means the town or the doughnut, which is very tasty, if a bit too sugary.

'It's lovely,' I say, to both. 'Thank you.'

'And your journey here was okay?'

'Yes, fine. Actually . . . I came with some friends,' I say, trying gently to introduce the fact that the elderly tourists surrounding me earlier had been with me all the time.

'Ah, good. I'd like to meet them. How does this compare to your hometown?'

'It's . . . not that different. But this is totally unlike the other market,' I say. They're like two different towns, not one that's expanded.

'Oh, yes, we are very different from the Old Town. Our market has much more going on.'

'So, you had a meeting with William this morning? Are you friends?' I ask, and put the last piece of my doughnut into my mouth.

He laughs and shakes his head. 'No, I wouldn't call us friends.' He checks his watch.

'But, if you aren't friends, why did we meet at the bakery in the other town?' I ask, dabbing my mouth with a napkin in an effort to wipe the sugar off my lips. 'Oh, sorry, ignore me. None of my business. One of my faults. Always interested in other people's lives. Some might even call it nosy!' I laugh, a little too high-pitched, and continue trying to deal with the sugar.

He chuckles, and hands me another napkin.

'Thank you.' I'm trying not to say anything else that might put him off me.

'It's fine. We're here to get to know each other,' he says, taking out a little bottle of antibacterial cleanser, spraying his hands, then offering it to me. 'I have been trying to do some business with William. But he is . . . reluctant to face the facts.' He shrugs.

'His shop is beautiful,' I say. 'Not that yours isn't! It's beautiful too!' Shut up, Connie.

'Yes, but . . . there really isn't room for two markets

like this side by side. I'm offering to help him out. We take over the market, I buy the shop and stock it with my cakes. He's had a bad run over the past few years. Their market hasn't won the annual competition in ten years now. Ours is getting bigger and bigger, year on year. It would make sense. I could take over his shop and we merge the businesses and the markets. But he is stubborn and refuses. But it will all change on Sunday. Hopefully he will see sense.'

'What happens on Sunday?'

'It's a big day for our towns. The baking competition.'

'Like *The Great British Bake Off*?' I remember Anja telling us about it.

He laughs, a proper laugh. It's nice. A hyena-style laugh can be very off-putting. I should add it to the list.

'This is so much more than *Bake Off*,' he says seriously. 'There's a lot at stake. Especially this year.' He glances at his watch again. 'Come on, let's take a walk around and then we can decide if we want a second date.'

We put our rubbish into one of the many bins provided and return our mugs to the kiosk. I pull on my gloves and follow Heinrich as he strides out from the table area into the busy shopping street. He's so tall I barely come up to his armpit.

'You should try this,' he says, as we pass a bar setting up. 'Eggnog with cream. A traditional drink. Would you like some now? I know you have a sweet tooth.'

'Um, isn't it a little early for hard drinking?' I laugh.

And I'm reminded of a breakfast date when my partner ordered pints of lager. Off-putting to say the least. Especially when I ended up paying for it all because his card was declined. He still asked for a second date.

'Not at Christmas,' he tells me, and orders one anyway. 'Here, try!'

'Are you not having one?'

'I have to keep a clear head for today. We are working on our cake for Sunday.'

I take a sip of the sweet, creamy drink, almost like melted white chocolate should taste. It's lovely, but sickly. I sip it slowly as we walk around the town, Heinrich pointing out the activities that take place throughout the market in the run-up to Christmas, the silent disco, the stage for bands and DJs, the light show and ice bowling alley.

As our hour comes to an end, we walk back towards his shop and car. The bright white lights are on. There is a glass counter with rows of cakes and staff wearing white coats and hairnets.

'So, how did you enjoy our date?' he asks.

This time I'm ready for his directness. This is what I wanted, isn't it? No messing around. 'Very much,' I say firmly. Then I swallow and ask, 'And you?' After all, this is about how we both feel, and suddenly I feel nervous.

'Yes. I did. Perhaps I can show you my factory some time.' He points to the brightly lit shopfront.

'I'd like that.' I smile, relaxing a little. He wants to see me again and I want to see him. This is great! 'I . . . Well, I like making cakes,' I say. I can really start to be myself: the first test is over. My shoulders drop. Getting a second date was great. From now on, it's about finding out who we both are.

'Of course, I remember. It's what first brought you to my attention. We have a lot in common. That's why I was so happy when you wanted to meet,' he says. 'We tick a lot of each other's boxes.'

I'm wrongfooted, like I've been caught out, then smile. 'You have a list too?'

'Of course! Who goes internet dating without a list?'

We laugh.

'Something else we have in common! So, would you like a second date? Tonight? There is a band playing here. Locals will come and meet friends, drink glühwein and beer.'

'As long as it's not another warm eggnog,' I joke.

'You didn't like it?' He looks crestfallen.

'Oh, it was lovely. Just a bit too sweet for me . . .' I trail off. Gosh, dating and trying to say the right things are like walking over eggshells.

He glances at his watch yet again and I realize I'm holding him up.

'But, yes, I'd love a second date,' I say. 'I'd like it very much.' Oh, shut up, Connie. 'That would be very nice.'

'Okay.' He consults his watch. 'I have to go. I need to get my team organized for Sunday. Like I say, it's a big event here. Hopefully after that, William will see the sense in my proposal.'

'Sounds exciting,' I say.

'I hope so.' He smiles again and it's a very attractive smile, but I'm not sure if he's talking about the big event, his expansion proposal or even me. But I find myself smiling back, liking the sound of all three.

'And by then perhaps you and I will know if we will become a couple and make a plan of our own?'

'By the end of the week?' I say.

'Of course. We will know if we want to be a couple, don't you think? If all the right ingredients are there, so to speak? We know so much about each other already, and you have come all this way. No point in wasting time. We're not getting any younger. If everything is right, if we are a match, we should make a plan.'

I'm rooted to the spot. I hadn't expected that. But he's right. There's no point in wasting time if everything is right. I've blown too many years on the wrong dates, and false dreams.

Then he leans in and kisses me and I'm not sure if it's going to be on the lips or the cheek. I turn slightly and it lands, neatly and perfectly, on my cheek. I'm kicking myself, though. I would have liked to taste his kiss on my lips. But that would be too soon, of course. There will be plenty of time for kissing . . . and who knows? What if we really are meant to be together? I shiver with excitement.

'Yes, of course. By the end of the week.' I'm slightly dazed, as if I've just been catapulted from shadows into the limelight. But he's right: if you know, you know, don't you?

'By Sunday, our lives could have changed for ever.' He smiles that big white smile again.

# NINE

The light rain seems to have stopped and it feels colder as I walk back towards the Old Town, over the bridge, having turned down Heinrich's offer of a lift. I don't want to keep him away from his work and his competition piece. Anyway, I want to take in every bit of what's just happened. I feel like a teenager replaying her first kiss, and smiling, feeling the tingle where his lips touched my cheek. Replaying every bit of our conversation, trying to analyse if it meant more than the words we used. He remembered I loved doughnuts. Some of my dates have struggled to remember my name! And after so many online dating disasters, could I have got it right this time? And if I have, it's because of Sam and the list. If I haven't, I'm not going through this again. This is it. My last attempt.

As I walk out of town, I turn back to see the pink and blue strobe lights from the square still lighting the buildings and the sky behind me. As I head towards the bridge to the Old Town, I see the castle high above, looking down on the Old and New Towns. I stop on the bridge and gaze up at it, casting its long shadow over the Old Town, reaching out to the New Town at its foot. I lean against the bridge and stare down the watery boundary between the two, so different in identity yet both celebrating Christmas. It goes to show that Christmas is different things to different people.

Christmas has changed for me over the years. Now Sam will be away and it will be just me. Despite our differences, his father, Tom, and I always made Christmas nice for him. But as soon as Sam was off to university, Tom told me he was leaving. He'd stayed for Sam's sake, and now Sam was leaving home, he was too. Double whammy. That was when I'd started baking. For me, Christmas this year is about wishing for it to be over so life can get back to normal and I'm spared all the happy-family images on the television adverts.

Not everyone is celebrating being with family at this time of year. Take Pearl and the others. Not one of them is looking forward to a traditional family Christmas. There's Alice. She was married to a colonel in the British Army. She's widowed. She has a daughter, a son and grandchildren but they barely see her. Then there's Maeve, who has a sister and a niece. They always invite her for Boxing Day, never Christmas. She can't stay over because there's no downstairs loo and she's confined to the wheelchair. Norman's sister always invites him but he never goes. Pearl? Pearl was married three times, I think, but none of them lasted. She went to art college and ran her own gallery for a while, but sold up and lost most of the money in her divorces. John recently lost his wife and is bereft without her. And Di is exhausted from looking after Graham since he had his stroke.

I look out at the river, then back up at the castle. I pull out my notebook and flip over the dating disasters until I get to Heinrich's page.

Reliability, so far, tick. Timekeeping, yep. Financially independent/stable job, tick. He has his own shop. Own car, tick. Shoes. I think you can always judge a man by his shoes, that and the way they hold a knife and fork, but I've yet to see that. Laughter, that's the one I'm adding. Well, he's made me smile, but we haven't laughed properly together. But I did hear his laugh and it was nice. Appearance, a definite tick. I still need to find out about his family and how they get on, and how he feels about travelling to the UK for more dates. I suck the end of the pen. Just then, a Toy Town train passes me, giving a cheery toot, with the group of pensioners aboard, looking no happier than they did when we first arrived. Pearl and Norman wave. I push the book back into my bag and follow the little train to where it's stopped on the outskirts of the Old Town. It's more like a tractor pulling carriages, dressed up like a train with a big smiley face at the front. The tall, thin, familiar figure of Norman, dressed head to toe in beige, gets out and helps the others off, including Maeve in her wheelchair, and Di, leading Graham. More tourists get on board, younger people, families, tourists heading for the Christmas market over the bridge. There's a pattern here. It's getting busier. Only my crowd are getting off in the Old Town. Most are heading to the New Town, for the funfair and later, presumably, for the bands.

'Yoo-hoo, Connie, how was it?' Pearl is waving at me.

'It was good.' I realize I'm smiling.

'I want all the details,' she says, linking her arm in mine. 'How's the list going?'

'Great. How was your trip?' I look at the little train. 'Did you go to the New Town?' I narrow my eyes at her. 'Were you spying on me again?'

Pearl waves a hand. 'No, no.' She shakes her head but I'm not convinced.

'It was awful!' says Maeve. 'All that noise and all those people. And the day's barely started.'

'Ah,' I say. 'So you were in the market. I'm surprised I didn't see you.'

'Pearl said we had to keep out of sight,' said Ron, a bag of sweet treats hanging by his side.

I give Pearl a hard stare. She shrugs. 'Just keeping an eye and checking you're safe,' she says. 'Dating dangers and all that.'

'But it was good?' says Norman, putting a hand on my shoulder like a concerned parent, wanting to know, but not being intrusive.

'Thanks, Norman. Yes. It was good. And the market was huge.'

'And you're seeing him again?' Pearl raises her eyebrow and looks fit to burst with excitement.

'Yes, Pearl, I'm seeing him again.' I put her out of her misery and she squeezes me to her.

'Does that mean we're staying here longer?' says Maeve, looking bored and fed up.

'Well . . . we have to find somewhere to scatter Elsie's ashes, like we promised. But if you want to, and the others agree, we can go after that if you like, Maeve.' I can hear the words coming out but a voice in my head says, *Stay! Stay! I've only just started ticking my boxes and I want to tick more!* But I can't think only of myself. 'I'd hate you to be here longer than you want. I can always come back and visit Heinrich again.'

'Absolutely not,' Pearl insists. 'One, you can't afford it because you lost all your savings, and two, we're here for Elsie. We're here to have fun!'

'And we don't know that the water is back on at the flats yet, Maeve. They said with it being such a busy time of year, it could take a week. You'd have to go and stay at your sister's.'

Maeve shudders. 'Can't go there! No downstairs loo! There's no dignity in having to take a Portapotty and having to sing loudly if I need to use it to stop anyone walking in on me! Bloody chair! My bloody joints! Taken all the joy out of life.'

'Well, there you are. Come on, let's get back to the guesthouse,' says Pearl. 'Maybe a spot of lunch in a bit will cheer you up.'

'How was your first trip to the markets?' asks Anja, when we arrive. She invites us into the small dining room where the smell of soup wraps around us like a warm hug. There are cold meats and cheeses too. And a tray of gingerbread biscuits beside a large pot of coffee. And although my stomach is knotted with excitement from this morning's date and the prospect of tonight, it rumbles at the sight of lunch.

'Noisy,' says Maeve, clearly not pacified by the smell of the soup and freshly baked bread.

'Sorry,' I say, not sure whether Maeve is talking about the New Town or my stomach.

'Ah . . . you went on the train to the New Town,' Anja says, understanding.

They all nod.

'Did you find something there to eat and drink?'

They take turns to complain about the cost of food and how it wasn't quite what they wanted.

'I just wanted a hot chocolate,' says Alice, 'but there was so much cream and so many marshmallows, I'm not even sure I got to the hot chocolate.'

'You like hot chocolate?' says Anja, smiling. 'Have

some soup and a sandwich, then come with me,' she says. 'Let me take you for hot chocolate.'

When they're revived by potato soup and bread, and despite their reluctance to go back outside into the cold, Anja ushers everyone through the heavy wooden door, with its large green wreath, onto the cobbled side street, where the weather has turned bright and cold. She guides us into the market square, waving to stallholders as she passes. They clap their hands together, blowing into them, and wait expectantly for customers to welcome to their red-roofed wooden chalets, hoping to make some sales today.

'This is Elias.' Anja holds out a hand. 'He's been coming to the market for years,' she says. 'His father was here before that.'

He waves from behind his stall where he is selling wooden ornaments and nutcrackers in the shape of soldiers, large and small. Next to him a stall offers rows of scented candles, which could certainly brighten my little house back home. Glass baubles hang from the ceiling of another, and I can see moulds for Christmas cookies across the square. There are handmade leather bags, hats and gloves, golden amber or silver jewellery, and food stalls selling all sorts of festive treats: flavoured vodkas, honey and jams, homemade chocolate and spicy salamis. The owner of a stall with an open fire is cooking fish, while another is grilling bratwurst, big fat juicy sausages. The seller waves his long-handled tongs at Anja as we pass. The smell of cinnamon and spices, and a hint of vanilla, fills the air as we pass a bar setting up, advertising glühwein, red, white or rosé, and spiced apple juice.

I think about the eggnog I had with Heinrich. I liked the idea of it more than the taste. I make a note to tell Sam about it, when we're back. He's very keen to hear about my progress. I get a twinge of homesickness. Not for the house, or my job, but for Sam and being with him. I think about him with Amy, his girlfriend, and smile, happy to know he's found love. Is it Sam I'm missing or am I missing love in my life, being with someone who wants to be with me? Someone to cook for, share the household chores with and battle with over the remote control. I haven't shared everyday life with a partner in a long time. It's the little things I miss, having someone to talk to as I stir the Sunday-lunch gravy, hearing the news from the papers as he reads through his Facebook feed and sorting the recycling together as the truck comes round. Someone who remembers I like doughnuts, I think, and a smile tugs at the corners of my mouth.

We walk on. 'And that is Christian! Serves the best hot chocolate in the whole of Germany!' Anja's round face lights up.

'What's that space for?' I point to an empty area in front of the clock tower, by the big Christmas tree, which must be ten foot high. 'Were you let down by stallholders?'

'That's where the ice rink will go,' she says, in a lowered voice. 'It's supposed to be a big surprise.'

'Why the surprise?'

'Well, we like to keep our main attractions a secret until the big day. The Sunday before Christmas.'

'How will people know to come if it's a secret?'

'That is a problem but, you see, we don't want news of our plans getting out.'

'But why?' I'm confused.

'Come, let's get hot chocolate and I'll explain.' She guides us towards the covered area, by the hot chocolate. I can't help but draw in the smell. It reminds me of something I can't quite put my finger on, but I like it. Something missing in my life. Something that feels a lot like homesickness.

In the bakery shop, just off the market square, William's head throbbed. He held the bandana wrapped around it with one hand in the hope it would pass. With the other he pressed the phone to his ear, keeping an eye on the oven behind him and wishing he could get back to his work. He had just made a batch of royal icing that would now be hardening. He'd have to start again.

The tirade he'd been listening to at the other end of the line ended and the line went dead – he'd barely managed to get a word in. He sighed and hung up too. When had Christmas become so stressful? He just wanted to see his son, that was all. Why did it have to be a battle every time he spoke to Marta? Why did she hate him so much? His life had changed overnight when she'd left with their son. It was like his family had been stolen from him and with it any dreams for the future he might have had. Were they ever going to find a middle ground? He doubted it. The Christmas spirit had long since got lost in all of this.

He looked down at his dog, which was in the back room, away from the shop and the ovens, looking up at him loyally. It barked, making William smile. He thought about Heinrich's visit, about him sneezing before he'd even seen the dog and, once again, pointing out that he could report him to health and safety officials for having a dog on the premises. He needed to make sure that didn't happen. His dog was all he had right now, that and the shop, and the chance of putting things right for the town on Sunday. He bent down and rubbed his friend's head. Always there when he needed him.

He walked back into the shop and looked out the bay window towards the market square, the empty space that would hopefully put this market back on the map and draw the crowds back to the Old Town. He could see Anja, sitting with a group of people under the wooden-roofed terrace, by the open fire, passing around blankets from the backs of the wooden chairs. In the New Town everyone stood around high tables to socialize with friends. You could get more people into a bar area that way, but here, his father had insisted, people wanted to sit by a fire with a blanket and everyone had agreed.

As he watched Anja, he realized she was with the group of people from the UK he'd met earlier that morning, after Heinrich's visit to the shop. Once again, he'd come to make an offer to buy it. And this time, it wasn't half as insulting as the last. It had certainly given him food for thought. His only mistake was telling Marta about it when he'd rung to talk about Noah. She'd goaded him, saying he wasn't doing anything to make things right between them. She couldn't understand why he was hesitating, why he hadn't just accepted the offer. It had come from Heinrich's father, William knew, so why couldn't he just give in and walk away from the business that was barely making him a living these days? But something was stopping him: he just wanted one last chance to prove to his wife, his family, that he could win the town baking contest, to put things right where he'd let them down in the past and bring the cup home to the Old Town. Then, if he did have to sell to Heinrich, he could leave knowing he'd brought the cup home at last and that the market was thriving.

The ice rink was his last attempt: He'd borrowed against the shop to pay for it, and in the new year, he'd have to start repaying the loan. If it didn't work out, he'd be forced to accept Heinrich's offer and he really didn't want to think about that.

He carried on watching the group by the fire,

drinking hot chocolate. And then he looked closer. There was that woman again. The one who'd been here to meet Heinrich. She was with them. Why would she come all the way to Germany to go on a date with a man she'd clearly never met before? Love, dating, relationships . . . It was a mystery to him and not something he planned ever to get mixed up in again. Right now, he'd stick to baking and trying to get his show-stopping cake finished for Sunday. All he wanted was to show his son the best he could do and hope his boy understood why he'd found it so hard to walk away. Baking was all he knew. If he wasn't a cake-maker, who was he?

His dog barked again.

'Okay, okay, Fritz,' he said, knowing the dog wanted to go out for some air. He couldn't help but think that Fritz wanted him to get some air too. Maybe it would shift his banging headache. He'd start the royal icing again when he got back. It was going to be a late night if he was to finish his sculpture on time. But he had to. He had to win this year. He had a lot of people relying on him. He couldn't let them down again.

# TEN

'How long has the market been here?' Pearl asks, as I watch her hand round mugs of hot chocolate.

'Well, for as long as I can remember,' says Anja. 'It was a part of our growing up. Christmas began when the market stalls and lights went up, leading to the big tree being lit on Christmas Eve. After that we brought the smaller trees into the houses. But, of course, Christmas is very different from when I was a child.'

'Tell me about it,' says Alice, as Pearl gives her a mug.

'I used to love coming here with my grandparents. They ran the guesthouse then, and my parents after that.'

'Elsie's parents ran a guesthouse too,' says Pearl. 'Our friend,' she explains to Anja. 'The one whose ashes we've come to scatter. She was sent to London to learn English and work in a hotel there. She never went back. But she loved Christmas, and the traditions. She said Christmas always brought happiness and magic into people's lives.' We all take a moment to think about Elsie.

'The Christmas market has always brought families and friends together as well as customers and visitors to the town. But now . . . not quite so much.'

'Why's that?' asks Pearl, sitting down, pulling a blanket over her knees, wrapping her hands around her mug and breathing in the deep, rich aroma rising on the curling steam. I do the same. Its bitter yet sweet smell is the perfect combination, unlike that of the eggnog, which was sweet on sweet. Sometimes you need some bitter to balance the flavour.

I pull out my notebook and make a note of the chocolate's flavour to post to my Facebook baking friends. It's a friendly group. There's no upset or arguing like in other Facebook groups, just a bunch of people who like baking. We talk about flavours and recipes, and share experiences. It's been a godsend to me. It feels like I've found where I fit in, even though I've never actually met any of them. I love talking cake. Cake was my lifesaver when Tom announced he wasn't happy and had met someone else. I found myself watching reruns of *Bake Off*, then making cakes, loads of them. When I couldn't sleep I got up and baked. When I thought I was going mad and couldn't see the wood for the trees, I baked. When getting out of bed every day was a struggle, I baked. It wasn't the eating that was the thing, it was the making. While I was baking, I was focusing on the job in hand, the weighing, the timings, the decorating. I wasn't thinking about the pain inside.

But as the cakes piled up I realized I had to do something with them and started handing them out with the meals I delivered. It became a real ice-breaker with residents I hadn't really got talking to before. John barely spoke after his wife died, but he did enjoy my sponges and Welsh cakes with a cup of tea in the afternoons. Their teatime was when he missed her most, and since she'd died, he'd stopped it. My cakes made him feel life was getting a little bit of normal back into it, he told me. It became a focal point in his week: I made a delivery and he'd brew a pot of tea and eat the cake. He'd put two cups on a tray, and I'm not sure if one was for his wife or me but I stayed and drank the tea anyway.

In fact, I drink a huge amount of tea on my rounds. It seems the least you can do is stay for a cup of tea and a chat. My boss, Islwyn, owner of Meadowsweet, is always telling me off for taking too long on the rounds. But I can't not stay. I just wonder what'll happen when he sells the business: his recent heart attack has made him realize he needs to retire before he ends up in sheltered housing eating his own awful ready meals. I would have given anything to take it over but I can't, not now my money's all gone and there's no chance of getting it back. My hackles rise. It's not the money, it's the fact that someone stole from me, stole my dreams, my plans, my happiness . . . took me for a fool.

'We're struggling because people prefer the New Town now . . .' Anja considers it. 'I guess they love the bright lights and bands. They have big laser light shows, big band names, bigger every year. The fair is getting bigger, faster rides. They've done well ever since . . .' She changes the conversation. 'How's the hot chocolate?' she asks. Everyone nods, except Alice, who is lost in a world of her own, staring down at her china mug, her eyes filling with tears. I don't think she's happy to be here at all and I feel bad. Maybe we should just go home. I nudge Pearl and nod towards her. Pearl looks concerned.

'Tell me about the castle, Anja,' I say, trying to distract Alice.

'It overlooks the two towns. You can see.' She points up to it, just below the church on the hill above us. 'The owner, Wolfgang Richter, loved the Christmas markets. He lived for this time of year. It's because of him we have the cake competition, for all the problems it has created.'

'Really? I thought it sounded fun.'

'It was supposed to be. But it is way out of hand. Everything now rides on it. People's livelihoods. When the New Town began to spread outside the city walls and over the bridge, he loved the two markets but couldn't decide which he loved the most. So, when he died, he left a sum of money in his will. Every year the two markets compete to be better than the other and bring more customers to our towns. And on the Sunday before Christmas, this coming Sunday, the final one in Advent, there is a bakery competition. He loved all types of cake, you see. So, the town's top bakers produce their creations to celebrate Christmas and the markets. The best market, and the best Christmas cake, wins the pot of money towards next year's market.' She smiles tightly.

'And do you usually win?' asks Norman, soaking up the atmosphere around the fire, the white fairy lights strung all around beginning to shine in the cold afternoon as the day starts to darken.

Anja's smile drops. She looks at Christian, the hot-chocolate-seller, whose head shakes. 'Sadly, no. We have not won for a while.'

'Ten years,' Christian joins in. 'It is the Cologne curse.'

'The what?' I ask.

'We used to win every year,' Anja explains. 'Our village baker was the best around. Him and then his son.' She has a twinkle in her eye. 'He used to have a business partner, but they went their separate ways. The partner wanted to get bigger premises, grow the business, use modern techniques. They parted, arguing, having resolved nothing. The cake competition became a battle of honour between the two. Our baker, here in the Old Town, his creations were wonderful. Everyone came to see what he would bake next.

There would be whispers and ideas all around the town. Then each year it was revealed and the crowds would pour in.'

'So what happened?'

'Well, the son was asked to go to Cologne and work with a master baker there, doing celebration cakes for celebrities and the wealthy, and big sculptures for events. Extreme cakes! 'We won the year he left, but then the old baker's wife died.' His son came back, took over the shop and threw everything he had into making the annual cake. But somehow nothing worked. From then on, the New Town has won, their cake getting bigger and better every year.'

'Like their market,' says Christian, tipping hot chestnuts into cones and handing them around for us to try.

Anja shrugs. 'It is the Cologne curse. Since Joseph's wife died, and his son went to work away, it's as if the spirit of our market has disappeared.'

'So . . .' I say quietly, putting two and two together, 'your baker, Joseph, and his son . . .'

'William, who runs the bakery now.' She points towards the cobbled street where I met Heinrich. I feel a prickle run over my skin. He's the son who went away and came back. The one Heinrich has offered to buy out. 'And what will happen if you don't win again this year?' I ask.

'The market,' Anja sighs, 'will close. There just isn't enough money to keep putting it on. If we could have won one year, and got the money from the will, it would have been different. But nothing stays the same for ever. The New Town keeps winning so has more and more money to put into their market, and their competition pieces get bigger and bigger every year.'

We all sit with our thoughts for a while. Heinrich's creation is happening now behind closed doors, away from the bustling market. I look around at the gentle pace of the market we're sitting in and feel sad for Anja and the stallholders.

'Well,' I say, noticing that Alice is still looking glum, 'maybe we should be getting back into the warm.'

Alice looks at me. 'Not on your nelly! This is the best hot chocolate I've ever had! And I'm not leaving until I've had another!'

After a moment's stunned silence we all burst out laughing.

# ELEVEN

Alice draws another long breath and shuts her eyes, then opens them slowly. I see tears.

'Sorry, silly I know . . .' She sniffs and rubs her nose quickly.

'No, not at all,' I say, realizing the hot chocolate has unlocked some kind of memory for her. From her smile, it's a good one. Her face looks totally different. Gone are the pinched lips and tight jaw. In its place there's softness. It's a glimpse of the young woman she once was.

I breathe in the scent of the hot chocolate, letting the cinnamon, vanilla, dark chocolate and nutmeg work together. No swirly cream or marshmallows, just warm, spiced, rich chocolate. I sip slowly, letting the flavour sit on my tongue before swallowing. 'It's wonderful.'

The others agree.

'It's made locally and sold here on market days,' Anja tells us.

'It . . .' Alice tries to speak, but the words don't come.

'Go on, Alice,' Norman says.

She looks up to stop the tears forming. 'Phffff . . .' She exhales, pushing out her lips, her warm breath making curls of steam in the air. 'I'm sorry,' she says. 'It's just this hot chocolate reminds me of when I was newly married. We were stationed here, in Germany. It reminds me of when my husband still looked at me as if I really mattered, before the children came along and, well, we seemed to drift apart. When I became almost an annoyance in his life – at least, that's how it felt.' She swallows.

'Elsie used to say hot chocolate reminded her of her mother and grandmother. She always made this at Christmas time, sitting by the fire. She said hot chocolate was everything that was Christmas,' Pearl says.

'She always offered me a cup when I went there,' I add. 'She said it told her how much her mother loved her, even when she didn't always show it. Her mother was a very . . . practical woman. Not what you might call demonstrative.'

Anja nods and seems to understand.

'When she came to the UK to work in a hotel, she said it was the first time she'd been offered a day off. She didn't know what it was.'

'Same for me,' says Anja. 'But this cup . . . In this cup I knew I was loved.' Her eyes fill, as do Alice's. I take another sip.

'This was what Christmas was all about to me,' Alice says, her eyes bright.

'It was the woolly jumper my mum used to knit for us every year,' says Norman.

'Stirring the Christmas pudding,' says Di.

'I loved singing carols. I'd love to sing carols with a choir one last time,' says John. 'I met Violet at the church choir.'

'I loved the Nativity play. I always wanted to be Mary,' says Maeve, surprising us.

'What about you, Connie?' Anja asks.

'Me?'

'What did you love about Christmas?' Anja smiles.

'Christmas cake?' asks Pearl.

'Mince pies? Yours were brilliant this year,' says Ron.

I think about the Christmases when Sam was small, the pile of presents, opened in pyjamas by the fire, and before that, when I was young . . . A memory suddenly comes into sharp focus in my mind, maybe the thing that started my baking obsession, like a security blanket in scary times.

'Gingerbread,' I announce. 'My grandmother always made a gingerbread house with me. Some years it would turn into a whole little village.' Suddenly tears are in my eyes too, just as they are with Anja and Alice, as they remember Christmases gone by. Where did the magic go? Is it just that we grew up? When did we all start wishing it could be over? Clearly Elsie had known something we don't.

'I think we should write a list between us, of something we loved about Christmas and want to do again,' says Pearl. 'Our Christmas memory list.'

'Why would we want to do that?' says Maeve, back to her more obstructive self.

'It's Elsie's wake, remember? We're doing it for her. She'd have loved it. And if we want to remember Christmases past, and what made us smile, then that's what we should do. Something that made us feel special at Christmas or something we'd loved to do. A Christmas wish that money can't buy. And when we've completed the list, we'll scatter Elsie's ashes, so she goes with all our happy Christmas memories and thoughts. Agreed?' Pearl looks around the group.

'Agreed.' They nod and smile. Apart from Maeve, who humphs. Persuading her to join in may be hard. I'm not sure Maeve's Christmas spirit can ever be found again, no matter how fabulous the setting. But we'll give it a try, for Elsie's sake.

# TWELVE

'Gah!' Maeve clutches her bag to her stomach and her hot chocolate to her chest.

'Maeve?' Pearl and I spin round to her in surprise. Even the others look up from their drinks and their memories.

Maeve nods several times, her eyes wide. We all turn to see what she's staring at. From nowhere, a long-legged gangly dog is galumphing towards us at speed. We all hold onto our drinks, waiting for a collision. But, as quickly as he came, the beautiful, silky-smooth dog stops without crashing into us. He comes to Anja first to have his head stroked, then noses his way into the centre of the group and greets us all in turn, gently pushing his head into everyone's lap and, as he does so, a smile appears on their faces. Mine, too – he says hello in the gentlest way. If a dog can have good manners, he certainly does.

'Whassat?' Ron wakes from his power nap, or after-lunch doze. He has a knack of catching forty winks whenever and wherever. He lifts his chin from his wide chest, not having spilled a drop of the hot chocolate he's still clutching in both hands. 'Oh, hello, fella.' He caresses the dog's ears.

Finally the dog stops at Maeve. When she doesn't greet him, he nudges her arm and she raises her hands, holding her hot chocolate higher. When he persists, she lets go of her handbag, tentatively puts out a hand and pats his head. He doesn't move on. He just sits by her and she goes back to ignoring him.

'Oh, William.' Anja waves at someone.

I turn. Oh, no. My heart sinks and my cheeks burn. Not him! But he doesn't hear her, thankfully. He's on the phone, looking intense. He seems to be pacing around the empty space where the ice rink will be. He finishes his call and runs his hands through his thick dark curly hair. Then he spots Anja and raises a hand. At least he isn't coming over. I let out a sigh of relief.

'Isn't that the man from the bakery?' asks Pearl.

'The one I thought had catfished you,' Norman says.

'The one you thought was your date, but wasn't,' Alice joins in, peering at him.

'He had quite a look of shock about him.' Norman laughs.

'Yes, all right, Norman,' says Pearl, patting his knee to quieten him as she can see my embarrassment escalating.

Anja waves again and this time he spots the dog. He raises another hand, shoves his phone into his pocket and hurries over. Oh, no! I hunch into my big thick scarf and clutch my hot chocolate to my face.

'Hi, sorry,' he says, pointing to the dog. 'Fritz is deaf. No amount of calling gets him to come back.'

'Whassat?' asks Ron.

'He said he's deaf,' says Pearl, loudly.

'I'm not deaf. Just windy, that's all.' Ron looks up and around.

'You can say that again,' mutters Pearl, and I can't help but smile. Ron thinks no one can hear him when he passes wind, which he does frequently. 'Put your hearing aid in!' Pearl says loudly.

'Hearing aid? I don't need a hearing aid. I'm not deaf, you know.'

Fritz is still sitting by Maeve's wheelchair and I can see her taking snatched, wary glances at him.

'William! How are you? Will you join us?' Anja asks, holding out a hand to the fire and the group. 'These are guests of mine, from the UK.'

He holds up a hand in greeting. 'Yes.' He smiles at everyone, then looks at me. 'We met this morning. Here on a date, I gather.' Heat runs up my neck and I sink lower into my scarf.

'A date?' Anja twists round to me, her eyebrows shooting up.

'Not all of us,' Pearl explains.

'Just Connie,' Norman pipes up.

'You were meeting Heinrich.' His smile slowly falls. 'After his visit to me.'

'Heinrich? From the New Town bakery?' Realization slides across Anja's face.

I swallow. 'Yes. We've been talking for a while.' I feel the need to explain. 'We met online.'

'Online?' Anja nods. 'Everything seems to happen online these days,' she says sadly. 'No one gets out there and shops any more.' And I don't know if she's talking about dating or the Christmas market.

'And he came to see you again?' She turns to look at William, who confirms it with a slow nod.

'He came to the shop. This morning. To make me an offer I couldn't afford to refuse, apparently.'

I see the muscles in his jaw clench. For a moment no one says anything, looking between Anja and William, wondering what is being left unsaid between them.

'Well.' William breaks the silence. He looks around at the group and then at me, clapping his hands together to keep out the cold. 'I hope your trip was worthwhile and you found what you were looking for.'

'I hope so too, thank you,' I say crisply and politely. Pearl looks at me and I can't decide if she's intrigued at how I'm feeling about Heinrich or about why William seems to bring out the worst in me and makes me bristle.

'I wish you all a happy Christmas,' he says politely, and turns to leave.

'And is all okay with the . . . ?' Anja asks, stopping

him before he goes, nodding towards the place where the ice rink is due to go.

'It will be . . . As soon as the bank sends over the money, the men will bring it and set it up,' he replies, gazing down at the phone. 'Should be all ready for Sunday.'

'I used to love ice skating,' says Maeve, letting on that we know what's coming.

Anja shrugs and smiles apologetically at William, and says, 'Me too.'

He smiles back. 'Word will be out soon enough,' he says. 'It'll be too late for the New Town to copy it anyway. They will have made their plans, whatever they may be.'

'Perhaps you can all try when the ice rink arrives.' Anja beams, gesturing to where it will be.

'Not me!' I say.

'Scared of falling?' says William, and I have no idea why his words feel so loaded.

'Yes,' I reply. 'It hurts. Better not to take the chance.' And for a moment I hold his stare. I have no idea what made me reply with such bluntness either. There is just something about this man that seems to get under my skin.

'I loved it as a child,' says Anja.

'We were just talking about Christmas memories and what we wish we could do again. What about you, William? What did you love about Christmas? What would you wish for again?' asks Pearl.

'For my life to go back to how it was,' he says. He

glances around the market. 'To break the curse . . . And who knows? If we win on Sunday,' he looks straight at me, 'we'll bring the cup back to the Old Town, where it belongs. Tell your boyfriend. This time it's coming home.'

'Oh, he's not . . .' I stop myself. He's not my boyfriend, I was going to say.

'Yet,' says Pearl, raising an eyebrow.

But he could be! He could be just that, come Sunday. 'Boyfriend' seems such a young person's word. But suddenly I feel torn between wanting a win for Heinrich and celebrating with him on Sunday, and wanting the Old Town and its market to survive. Because if Heinrich wins, this market and its traders will be no more. William's and Anja's businesses will suffer. Maybe this market will be just another Christmas memory for people like them. I look around the group. Christmas memories are important, I realize, and I'm determined to help my friends revisit and relive theirs. It's the least I can do to repay them, especially Pearl, for pushing me into coming here. I'm glad they did, I think, with a warm glow. Because if they hadn't I wouldn't have met Heinrich and he deserves to win just as much as William does on Sunday. Maybe more so, who knows? He certainly seems to be putting in the effort.

'Let's make this a Christmas to remember for everyone,' I say, including Anja. 'To the Christmas memory list!' I say, and hold up my mug, determined to tick off a memory for each of them.

# THIRTEEN

I watch as William summons his dog by getting in his line of sight and waving an arm. Then, as if he's noticed his owner for the first time and is delighted to see him, the dog leaves Maeve's side – is that disappointment on her face? – and galumphs back to his owner.

For a moment, we all stare into the fire pit. The sky has darkened and it's much colder, making my nose tickle as the cold pinches it. I wonder if we should be getting back, but Alice is on her second hot chocolate, staring into it as if it's showing her an image from her happy time.

'Life is all about making memories, isn't it?' she says. 'Because that's really all you're left with.'

'You never want to look back at life and think what if . . .' says Pearl.

Then I remember my school trip to Germany when I was seventeen. I met someone. It was a week when I fell in love and thought I would never feel the same again. And, to be honest, I'm not sure I have. We vowed to find a way to be together. We wrote all the time. He even came over to stay with my family. But after he went back, his letters began to trail off, with longer and longer periods between them. I'd rush to the postbox to send a reply to one of his by return, then wait and wait for a response. Until, eventually, nothing came. I often wonder what would have happened if he had replied. If we'd gone ahead with those impetuous plans to be together. He was the one I thought was my soul-mate. The one who got away. Eventually my family moved house, and I'll never know if he wrote again or tried to find me. I've looked him up on Facebook, but he has a family and seems happy. I just wonder if he ever thinks of me. Then I met Tom, Sam's dad, and life was straightforward, not the rollercoaster ride it had been, waiting for letters that didn't come. With Tom, we liked each other, we were friends and got on. It was sensible and steady, and we enjoyed the same things. There were good times, and at first we were happy, but eventually he started wanting other things, and by the time Sam was ready to go to university, he'd moved on too. But I wouldn't change it for the world because I wouldn't have Sam, and he is definitely the best thing to happen to me. Sam wants me to meet someone now. He wants to see me happy and not alone.

I think about Heinrich. I have to go for it, if I think it's right. I can't be scared. Pearl's right. We're making memories, not regrets. I want to look back on my life and smile, like I do when I think of Sam's dad in the happy times we shared. And like I do when I remember that summer and believing, at seventeen, that anything was possible.

We fall back into our own thoughts as the fire spits and smokes and glows. I try to imagine Heinrich visiting me at home, me coming back here in the summer. I try to imagine him and me at this time next year.

'We should make that list,' says Pearl, interrupting our reveries. 'A proper list.'

'What sort of a list?' asks Norman.

'The one we were just talking about!' says Pearl, tutting.

'I'm lost without a list. Can't remember a thing,' says Maeve.

'As long as it's not a Christmas present list!' Alice pipes up. 'Truth is . . .' she says, clearly thawed by the hot chocolate '. . . I can't afford it. I can't afford all the presents my daughter wants me to buy for her kids. They've had it all! I've helped them out with houses and holidays so the money's gone. And what with the pension age for women changing, well, I . . .'

Alice has always given the impression of being well off. I had no idea of the truth. I don't know what to say. Instead I take her spare hand and just hold it.

'No, not a present list. That's where it's all gone wrong,' says Pearl, and I agree.

'Remember, we were talking about a list of Christmas

memories of things we loved or something we dream of doing again. Then when we've made all those memories real, we put a candy cane in a mug.' I hope they don't think it sounds ridiculous. I look at Pearl, who smiles widely. 'One for each memory we tick off.'

There's a moment's silence. John is the first to speak. 'I'd like to sing, like I was back in the choir on Christmas morning. Singing just because it was Christmas, as if Violet was by my side. Because . . . well, just because it made me feel really happy.' His voice cracks. 'I'd like to sing like that again. Just for fun. As if no one is listening.'

'I never knew you liked singing before now, John, or that that was how you and Violet met,' says Graham, slowly and slurred, because the stroke had pulled down one corner of his mouth, but everyone listens.

John shrugs sadly. 'I'd forgotten how much I enjoyed it, I suppose.'

'Singing it is then!' announces Pearl, her hand in the air. 'We shall find somewhere to sing carols. Connie, get out that notebook you carry everywhere and make a list. Our very own Christmas list . . . and not an Xbox or an iPhone in sight! Christmas memories! Who's next?'

'I'd like to watch a Christmas movie with other people and eat popcorn. I love Christmas films,' says Graham, who is always on his Kindle.

'And I'd like to dance,' says Di, smiling. 'Like we

used to. Christmas Eve in the local village hall where we met.' She gives Graham a watery smile and touches his cheek.

'I don't think I'm made for dancing now,' he says slowly and with effort, 'but we used to cut a rug!' He chortles.

'And snow. I miss snow at Christmas. In the winter of sixty-three the snow was so high it reached up to the tops of the hedges,' Alice says.

'Connie? What did you love doing at Christmas? What's your Christmas wish?'

I have no idea how to say I'd like a boyfriend for Christmas, to be part of a couple, to find the one I know is the right one for me. I'd like to fall in love, just once more, like I did when I was seventeen. 'I . . . I . . .' My grandmother and her gingerbread house pop into my head again. I remember how it made me feel. Loved. Everything about those times did; in that house, with my mother and grandmother, I felt loved. And I hope Sam felt that too. I hope that's what I passed on to him. No matter what happened between his dad and me, I always wanted him to still feel loved. Like he wants for me now.

'I'd like to make gingerbread,' I say finally, 'a gingerbread house.' And again I think of Heinrich. It could be the perfect date for us. We could really find out whether or not we're a match if we can work in the kitchen together, share our passion for baking.

'Write it down,' Pearl insists, and points to my

notebook. I make a note, then flick through the pages where my date details will go. I think about Sam sitting me down at the kitchen table and helping me decide on all the things I should look for in a man. Let's hope Heinrich is the last in my dating diary.

I think about him and how he reminds me of my seventeen-year-old love. He makes me feel young again. And safe. Like everything is mapped out. I get the feeling I'd always know where I stood with Heinrich.

'I've always wanted to skate,' says Maeve, looking out from her wheelchair to the space where the rink will go. I look at Pearl, who raises her eyebrows and nods to the book.

'Oh, I'm not sure . . .' I start.

Pearl gives me a firm look and I do as I'm told and write it down. I seem to have a habit of doing as I'm told when it comes to Pearl.

'I'd like to see a Nativity . . . a living one,' says Alice.

'And wear a Christmas jumper,' says Ron.

'I love a Christmas jumper,' says Norman.

'Decorate a Christmas tree. Simply. No tinsel!' says John, brightening up and getting into the swing of it. 'Violet hated tinsel.'

'Stroke a donkey!' says Norman.

'See a shooting star!' says Di.

'Get tipsy!' says Pearl. 'And find a man wearing lederhosen!' She giggles some more. Everyone looks at her and laughs. It's been a long time since I've heard laughter like that. And apparently it's the same with them: they suddenly stop, surprising themselves, giving little coughs.

'Find gifts that mean something and don't cost the earth,' says Alice, and we slip gently back to earth.

'Well, these memories don't cost anything . . . not really,' I say, trying to lift the mood. 'I think we should try to do as many of them as we can before we leave on Sunday. Don't you, Pearl? And when we have, we'll scatter Elsie's ashes. We'll find the best place to keep her Christmas spirit alive.'

Pearl looks at everything I've written down.

'We're making memories. No regrets, isn't that what you said?' I ask her.

'It is!' She nods. 'We'll do the list, even if we die trying!' There's a moment's silence, then everyone laughs again and agrees.

'Let's find out if there's any of that Christmas spirit we used to know and feel left in the world,' says Pearl.

And Anja claps her hands in delight. 'It's a time for making memories.' She looks around at the market, as if she's trying to imprint it in her mind. I want her to enjoy this time as much as us, to have the memories to hold on to if the worst happens and the market doesn't survive.

I agree and think about Heinrich. If ever there were the right ingredients to fall in love, I have a feeling this list has them all. If I can get him along for the ride, I'll find out if Heinrich really is kind and generous, and has a sense of humour. And if I am the woman who ticks all his boxes.

'Good luck with that,' says Maeve, and I'm not sure if she's talking about me and Heinrich or her ice skating.

# FOURTEEN

As we leave the square, moving away from the noise and the partygoers, Heinrich guides me through the crowds, with his arm around my shoulders. My ears are buzzing after the gig in the New Town square. It was like I was a teenager all over again and I can't help but smile. I have no idea who the band were, but they were loud and everyone seemed to be loving their sound. Heinrich had known I'd like them, he said, judging by my other musical taste, and he was right, they were great. Even if I did feel my age. There were lights all around the square, projections on the buildings of different-coloured falling snow, and the glühwein definitely hit the spot. Heinrich wasn't drinking and I only had a couple. He has to be up early to work on his cake and I'm dying to ask what it's like, but I know I can't with both towns sworn to secrecy.

He takes me towards the river. I peer up at the

white-and-rose-pink lit castle, and the white lights of the Old Town scattered across the hillside away from it and at its foot, like glittering snowflakes. I catch my breath. It's beautiful. Then Heinrich stops and turns to me. I look up at him and he looks down at me, then bends and places his lips firmly and confidently on mine, as if he had the whole procedure mapped out. I try to relax into the kiss, and when he finally pulls away, he's smiling.

'Good?' he says.

I smile back and up at him. 'Good.' We've got this sussed. It was good. And we're being open and honest with each other and that's great.

'And I'll see you tomorrow?' he says, more like a statement than a question.

'Yes, lovely. I have some things I need to do with my friends,' I start.

'The old people you drove here,' he says directly.

'Um, yes. My friends,' I reiterate.

'Do you have friends your own age?'

I'm thrown for a moment. Not really. But is that the wrong answer?

'Some,' I lie. There's my Facebook baking group.

'Okay, let's make a plan for tomorrow.'

'I'll message you,' I say, and I can tell he's a little on the back foot, not knowing exactly what the plan for tomorrow is. But I tell him I'll let him know as soon as I can.

I turn down Heinrich's offer to escort me back to

the guesthouse, preferring instead to walk across the bridge and give myself time to think about that kiss. It's cold now, really cold, but clear. Gone are the drizzle and gloom of the morning. I roll my lips, tasting his kiss on them. Gentle, soft and really quite nice, lovely even. He's a very neat kisser. I pull out my notebook. I could get used to that kiss. I want to remember everything about this trip. But I can barely write with my gloves off as my hands are so cold. I put away my notebook and walk back across the bridge, away from the bright lights and the disco beat that has started now the band has finished. I'd have quite liked to stay later, but with the competition only days away Heinrich needs an early night to keep a clear head, he tells me. I'm not sure if that's about me or the competition or both.

My feet ache and it's only ten, but I'll have to be careful not to wake Pearl when I get back to the guesthouse. It's been a long day and I can't wait to get into bed and allow myself to wonder what it would be like to go to bed with Heinrich. As lovely as the kiss, I expect. I think about some of the awful goodnight kisses I've had on first and last dates and shudder. This one was lovely. No clashing of noses or cheekbones, no scrape of stubble, or the taste of tandoori chicken as happened once. And it was real, which is more than my last date was. I like him and, by the sound of it, he likes me. I'm happy, determined to message Sam when I get in and tell him all about my successful date. I'm back in the saddle and I'm glad. I have a spring in my step as I head towards the market square, cutting through the little cobbled street, past the bakery where I first met Heinrich.

As I pass, the lights in the bay window are still on, creating that warm orange glow down the narrow street. There is something about the shop that just draws me to it. It's beautiful, almost magnetic. I feel a sense of loss, something from the past, something missing, but I don't know what it is, a feeling of belonging perhaps. I go to look in the window, and as I move closer, I suddenly see William appear from a back room, holding a cup of coffee and heading for a work bench. I reel back into the shadows. The last thing I want is for him to see me staring into his shop. He's the competition now, Heinrich's competition, and as I'm . . . What am I? Dating? Stepping out? 'Talking', as the younger generation seem to call it, these days, before officially 'coming out' as boyfriend and girlfriend. But I'm way too old to be talking about 'talking' and 'boyfriend and girlfriend'. 'Partner' is a better word.

From a distance, near enough to where I was this morning, I see William bend over his work bench. Around his head is the red and white bandana, tying back his unruly dark hair from his eyes. I feel as if I'm spying, but it is captivating to watch him work, so focused on the job in hand. I wonder what his competition piece is. And the rumours about the Cologne curse. I think about what he might have meant about life going back to how it was. I turn away, and suddenly I hear a shout from the end of the street. 'Come back!' It's an English voice I recognize, and now there's a commotion. Not again! They can't be following me still . . .

I walk quickly towards the square and see a donkey. If I'm not mistaken, the shepherd leading it around the market square is . . .

'Norman?'

'Ah, Connie love. Glad you're here. We're short of a Wise Man, if you fancy it.'

I stare at him incredulously. 'Norman, what are you doing?'

'The Christmas list!' He gazes at me as if everything is perfectly normal. I wonder if it's me or him who's the odd one here. 'This is Axel. He lives with Christian, the hot-chocolate-seller, just up the mountain.' He jerks a thumb in the direction of the castle. 'Anja said they were looking for people to help out with the living Nativity. Not enough cast members this year, apparently. So we offered to help. Everyone's here!' He points to a wooden stall under the clock tower, lit up and full of straw. There in the stable, among the straw, is . . . everyone. I throw back my head and laugh with joy at my friends, lit up in the stable against the night sky.

'So that's one ticked off the list, then!' I can't stop smiling, looking at them all.

'Two, actually. Remember the donkey!' Axel pulls on his rope and drags Norman off around the market to the laughter of the others in the living Nativity scene.

'Haven't laughed so much in years!' says Graham, holding his stick with both hands to steady himself.

'It's all right for you! I've still got rope burns from being dragged around that market.' Norman's grinning.

'Here, have a top-up.' Di pours him some more glühwein from the Thermos jug on the table as we sit on a bench under a wooden roof, bars around the outside keeping out the wind and cold, the fire pit burning in the middle, white fairy lights all around and gentle music playing in the background.

As we sit around sipping, suddenly I feel something wet in my hand on my lap. It's William's Fritz. Once again he goes around and greets each of us with a wagging tail and his head in our laps. Each of us greets him, smiling, even Maeve. My heart lurches as I hear the dog's name being called. Once again, embarrassment at my mistake this morning washes over me. William walks up to us, hands shoved into the pockets of his big worn coat, smiling.

'Sorry!' He puts up a hand. 'Good evening, all!' He nods to each of us and I lower my head to my terracotta mug. I can feel him smile – he knows how uncomfortable I feel and finds it amusing.

'I hear the Nativity scene was a great success this evening. Thank you,' he says. 'Let me get you some more glühwein.'

Some of the group say that would be lovely, others try to turn him down but end up saying, 'Oh, go on, then.'

I say, 'Not for me, thank you,' intending to head straight for bed, but I'm not sure he heard me.

He goes to the bar, orders a jug of glühwein and a beer for himself. Clearly not as dedicated as Heinrich, who headed off for an early night to get up early to work on his creation for Sunday.

Fritz greets the other few drinkers in the bar – stallholders having a nightcap before closing up – who know him well, pat him fondly and greet him like he's a regular, which he probably is. William brings over the jug and just the smell is intoxicating. The scent of cinnamon mixed with woodsmoke from the fire is like a warm blanket being wrapped around me and, surprisingly, no one is feeling the cold. William thanks everyone again, and I shrink into my big scarf to avoid catching his eye. Then he heads back to stand at the bar with the stallholders. Out of the corner of my eye I see him taking a long draught from his beer, closing his eyes, then putting down the bottle and opening them. I can't help watching him. He has things on his mind, clearly. Suddenly he looks at me and I turn away quickly, like I've been caught red-handed. I feel the blush around my neck and in my cheeks that always appears when he's around.

Then, as quickly as he came, he waves to Fritz, bids everyone at the bar goodnight and leaves, the dog happy to follow.

'To the Christmas list,' says Pearl, and raises her glass. 'And the first two ticked off.'

Looks like we're going to try to fulfil each and every one and my heart flutters as I remember the gingerbread date I have planned with Heinrich. I wonder where it might lead.

Back at the guesthouse we weave our way to bed, Maeve to the downstairs room and the rest of us upstairs, Di guiding Graham. Pearl gets into bed and quizzes me on my evening. When I've answered all her questions and described the band, the square and every last detail, we say goodnight and she settles into her pillows. I switch off the light and hope she sleeps well. She did a lot of tossing and turning last night. Right now, I'm wide awake. Sam has messaged asking how my day has been and I message him back telling him about Heinrich, the market and the living Nativity, ripples of laughter bubbling up in me every time I think of Norman, Axel the donkey, and Maeve as the Virgin Mary, her big blue dress like a tent, covering the wheels of her chair! It may have been a tablecloth. I think about Fritz, greeting us all in turn, making sure he didn't miss anyone, not even Maeve – particularly not Maeve – and making a fuss of Pearl.

My stomach rumbles and I wish I could make tea

and toast, like I used to when Sam came home from a night out. I couldn't sleep until he got back. It's different now. Now I don't know what he's up to, or who he's with.

I check on Pearl, who looks to be sleeping lightly. And then I look at the photographs Sam has sent through: arriving on the slopes with his attractive, dark-haired girlfriend Amy, with goggles on her head, smiling as much as he is in all the images. That's what I miss: someone to share things with, to watch a sunset and say, 'Wow, look at that!' To cook a roast dinner on a Sunday and open a bottle of wine. I miss the sharing. To be honest, I'm not sure I ever had it. When I met Tom, Sam's dad, I thought I'd found love. But after Sam was born, the sharing seemed to fizzle out, and I think that's what I missed most. He'd eat at separate times, go to bed at different times, and had taken a job working away so that he just came home at weekends. The sharing disappeared and I'd love to have it again. I was lonely in our marriage for a long time before Tom left. Sharing is how I want to show love and feel loved, I suppose. Sharing the cakes I baked with the pensioners saved me, really.

I think back to those nights at Christmas, making the gingerbread houses with my grandmother, sharing that time with her, making memories together. Then I remember the gingerbread heart in my handbag, the one Heinrich gave me. My stomach rumbles so loudly, I worry it might wake Pearl. I reach in, pull out the heart and peel off the wrapping, as excited as a child on Christmas Eve. Pearl seems to be sleeping soundly.

I snap off a piece. The smell is gorgeous as I put it into my mouth and scroll through Sam's Facebook pictures, wondering what else I can tell him about Heinrich's and my first date, other than that he seems to be who he says he is, is clean and smart, and I had a lovely time. Suddenly I sit up. What on earth?

# FIFTEEN

I feel like . . . I don't know what I feel like. I'm sitting upright in bed, chewing gingerbread. It's not just my mouth that feels alive. Every bit of me feels alive, warm, fuzzy, like I've been hugged. My mouth is warm with spice. I break off another piece and chew it, slower this time, registering all of the flavours and letting it take me wherever it wants to. I feel as if I'm at home, as a child, with my grandparents and all the excitement of Christmas Eve, knowing I'll never be able to sleep. I remember feeling so excited, happy and loved. Just like Alice with the hot chocolate, I'm right back there. Nothing bad could happen. Life was wonderful. We didn't have a lot of money, but there was my grandmother's gingerbread, which I'd helped to make. The house smelt of it for days after she'd baked the gingerbread house, now in pride of place on the dresser. As we decorated it, I'd put one Smartie on the house and one in my mouth.

I remember the carefree laughter. It was the same laugh I remember hearing in Sam. A laugh I remember from when I met my boyfriend on that school exchange trip. Before I met Sam's dad and became pregnant and life took a different path from the one I was expecting. I don't remember laughing like that for a very long time, except tonight, at the living Nativity. I haven't laughed like that with any of my online dates. Especially not after the one who stole everything from me, my confidence and dignity with it. That was why Sam had bought me the notebook and insisted on 'the list'.

Why did I suddenly go off piste or, at least, off list, ignoring all the signs? Was I just flattered that someone could want me as much as they said they did? I take another bite of the gingerbread heart, which seems to rebalance my world. If it hadn't been for Pearl I would never have considered online dating again. Things could be going my way at last. I take another bite of the gingerbread and wonder if Heinrich and I will laugh together with carefree abandon.

I pick up my phone from among the dips and folds of the duvet and go to message my Facebook baking group. Then I open my Messenger tab. Sam is always telling me off for keeping too many tabs open, but it's easier if I want to dip in and out of a conversation, or have a conversation on the go with more than one person, like when Heinrich messaged this evening. I've become pretty dextrous at swapping between tabs as I chat to him, Sam and the group. He's messaged me now: *Goodnight. Looking forward to our next date tomorrow. Is there anything you would like to do?*

Make gingerbread, I think, and smell the remainder of the heart, snap a shot of it, then pop it into my mouth. I post the picture and a message to the baking group: *Most amazing gingerbread I have ever tasted, made right here in the Old Town. How on earth do they get that flavour? It takes me right back to being a child, happy Christmases and carefree teenage years all wrapped up in one. What's the secret?* With the gingerbread and the glühwein finally making me feel sleepy, I press send, shut my phone case and settle down to sleep. I was meant to come to Germany. It's all going to be okay. I can't wait to see what tomorrow brings.

# SIXTEEN

*Ping!*

William stopped and hesitated. His hand hovered over his laptop lid, which he was just closing for the night. Should he read the message or leave it for the morning? It might be Noah. He'd check quickly, and if it wasn't his son, he'd leave it for the morning. If he went to bed now he'd get a few hours' sleep before getting up to work again. But sleep never came very easily, these days. He slid his gold-rimmed glasses onto his nose in front of his tired, sore eyes, narrowed them and read: *What's the secret?* He was confused, if not a little intrigued. He reread the message on his Facebook page, then checked the sender's profile.

Even more intrigued, he reread the message, shaking his head and smiling. *Most amazing gingerbread ever.* Lebkuchen, not gingerbread. He tutted. 'Well, she's not wrong,' he said to Fritz, lying on his bed in the corner of the shop, asleep a long time ago. He laughed to himself, pulling off his glasses. As if he was going to tell her the secret to his lebkuchen. His father and grandfather had made it every winter. He wasn't going to give out the recipe to a stranger who happened across his Facebook page.

He looked at the profile picture again. Put his glasses back on. The picture wasn't a close-up but he vaguely recognized the woman. But where from? That would have to wait until tomorrow. He took off his glasses and closed down the computer, walked around the counter to the front window and pulled down the blinds. Then he looked out of the front door, over the shadows of the street outside, and locked it. He loved this time of night on the cobbled street, as the market was shutting. But it was also his loneliest time of day, when he missed going upstairs to the apartment, kissing his sleeping boy and joining his wife in their bed. She would have been asleep for a while, fed up of waiting for him to finish work and join her. And he'd be up again before the house woke in the morning. They'd become ships that passed in the night. Fritz had been there, always at his side, no matter what hours he worked. A baker's hours were never the same as other people's. It was a duty to have the shop stocked by the time people wanted their breakfast, and the gingerbread was freshly baked for the start of market. Now, of course, there was the baking competition. They had to win it this year. They just had to. Because if they didn't, there wouldn't be a next.

He looked into the shadows once more. Of course! That was where he knew her from. He chuckled, thinking about the Facebook message. She was the woman waiting for Heinrich this morning. His date. The woman who'd been drinking hot chocolate with the group who'd helped with the living Nativity, and glühwein later when he'd bought them drinks to thank them. Heinrich hadn't hung around to introduce her after their meeting that morning, but he recognized her now.

He rubbed his forehead, thinking about the meeting with Heinrich. Heinrich's father had been keen to buy the shop – he'd always wanted it, ever since his own father, Joseph, and Heinrich's had fallen out. Heinrich's father had wanted to mass produce the product they sold. William's had wanted to stick to traditional methods. But if William didn't win the competition on Sunday, he'd be practically bankrupt, having put all his money, topped up with a bank loan, into the ice rink. He'd have to sell up. He'd be left with no choice.

He didn't know what Heinrich's date was up to. What was she doing messaging him about his bakes? Was she buttering him up, trying to find out about this year's competition piece? Because there was no way he would tell her. No one, apart from himself and his father, Joseph, knew. And that was the way it was going to stay.

He turned off the lights and walked towards the stairs, passing his computer. He stopped. Opened it and reread the message.

He smiled mischievously and typed a reply, sent it and closed the computer once more, praying that sleep would come to him for the next few hours.

# SEVENTEEN

*With love!* I reread, trying to get my eyes to focus. What's going on? I was checking my phone for messages, having woken before Pearl. I'd had a reply to my baking post, thanking me for my comments and replying that all Becker und Sohn cakes were made 'with love'.

Oh, no. I groan, feeling a little fuzzy from the long day, the late night and the glühwein.

'What's up?' Pearl sits up stiffly, wincing.

'Oh . . . nothing.' I grimace. 'I just . . .' My mouth is dry. As if I haven't made a big enough fool of myself in front of this man already. I bristle. 'I just . . . mis-sent a Facebook message.' And to him! Of all people! Mortification floods over me as I fall back into my pillows and wish they'd swallow me.

'Easily done,' says Pearl, adjusting hers behind her.

I can just imagine the lopsided smile spreading

across his face, confirming in his mind that I am some kind of idiot.

I bite my lip, determined not to rise to the bait, or respond. But my fingers have other ideas, and before I know it, I'm doing exactly what the voice in my head is telling me not to do.

*Thank you,* my fingers type back. *Not a surefire recipe for a consistent bake, I imagine!* I press send, then go to close my phone. Determined that would be an end to it. Whatever happens, I won't respond again.

*Ping!*

I look at Pearl, who is brushing her hair, as she does every morning, then starting to pin it up. It can't be, I think. I open my phone case. And there it is, a new message – from him.

*Sometimes it isn't enough to have the right ingredients to get the perfect bake.* He ends with a smiley face.

Is he teasing me? I frown.

*The right ingredients in the right measures mean consistency, surely. A bake you can rely on and trust.*

Despite my best-laid plans, I press send.

Little dots appear on the screen, bobbing up and down. He's typing again! I hold my breath and wait.

The little dots stop bobbing. I let out a long breath. Then they start again.

What am I doing? Sitting here arguing about baking methods with a baker who happens to be Heinrich's competition! I go to close the case.

*Ping!*

'Someone's popular,' says Pearl, putting the last pin into place in her hair. She never goes out without full make-up and her hair done.

I blush and look down at the message. 'It's just Sam . . . and Heinrich,' I lie.

*It's all about alchemy,* William writes. *You can have and use all of the right ingredients, but if the alchemy isn't right, it'll be a disaster.*

Another message appears in my Messenger. It's Heinrich! My heart leaps into my mouth. I slam my phone cover shut.

What am I doing? Heinrich! I need to tell him what I'd like to do today. I take a deep breath, open my phone and type my reply. I'd like him to show me his bakery and how he makes gingerbread. It'll be a tick on the Christmas memories list and it'll show William. Because if you have the right ingredients, I have everything crossed, this will be the perfect bake!

# EIGHTEEN

'So . . . we get the ready-made mix from here,' he points to the large store over the noise of the machinery that's already at work, 'and it gets emptied into the vat over there.' He points to a woman who's wearing exactly the same as I am. 'This is . . .' He struggles for a moment.

'Klara,' she introduces herself.

'Klara,' he says, having been prompted.

She's about my age, I think, but we all look the same right now. I'm wearing a white coat, white boots and a hat with a hairnet, just like the workers in the factory. 'Each batch is measured out exactly. So we have the exact same bake every time.' He smiles, but he doesn't move. He looks down and I follow his eyes and see he's holding out his hand to me. I look at the soft, long fingers in clear plastic gloves and realize he's waiting for me to take his hand.

'Oh, yes,' I say, as I smile and do so. It feels nice. It feels good. As good as it can through wrinkled plastic gloves. But I do feel connected. I feel like we're nearly there. Nearly in a relationship. My stomach gives a hopeful leap. We're sharing something. He guides me around the factory, talking over the noise of the gleaming machines. He points to the offices, up a metal staircase, a wall of glass so that he can monitor the factory floor from every angle. There is a workshop too, he tells me, where this year's creation for Sunday's bake-off is being created as we speak. The woman I saw at the start of the tour is coming out of the workshop.

'Can I see it?' I ask, excited to hear about his design, plans and execution for the big show-stopping cake. He smiles widely. I'm coming to like that smile very much, and I'd like to kiss it, to remind myself of how his lips felt on mine.

He shakes his head, still smiling. 'On Sunday,' he says, and I'm a little disappointed. I would love to see something like this in creation, love to be a part of it. 'So, what do you think of our operation here?' he asks, holding out his arm to his empire. The bright modern shop at the front, with big glass windows and uniform cakes in rows behind more glass, the bakery and the workshop behind.

'Impressive.' And it is. I'd love to talk to him more, find out why he's dating online when he's so attractive and clearly successful. And with his 'own teeth and hair'. This was one of Sam's suggestions for the tick list, but the reality has not always been a joke.

So, why is someone like Heinrich looking for love online and overseas? Although he must be wondering the same about me. Is he really as good as he appears? Is he actually single? I catch my breath. That's a box I haven't ticked yet: single. Is he looking for a conveniently placed mistress in the UK? My heart starts pounding as my brain goes into overdrive.

He guides me out to the reception area and pulls off his white hat, revealing his short, smart, freshly washed blond hair. 'So, I have to go to work now.' He points to the office. 'But we could meet later, for dinner?' Everything in its place. That's Heinrich.

'Dinner? That would be nice.' I'll have dinner with him and ask him all the questions I need answers to.

'I hope you enjoyed your tour. Oh, wait.' He speaks to the young man behind the counter, dressed in white overall and hat, and points to something behind the glass. The young man picks one up with tongs, puts it into a box and hands it to Heinrich. 'For you! The gingerbread!' He smiles, handing me the box.

I look down at it, hoping to breathe in the smell of warm gingerbread, but it doesn't come. I hold it closer to me and try again. Nothing. 'Lovely,' I say, but the scent doesn't reach my nostrils. Neither does the gingerbread-making here stir my memories. I look at Heinrich – attractive, business-owner Heinrich. What's missing? Why doesn't this gingerbread smell as it should? And what about Heinrich? What am I missing there? I think about Pearl and the Christmas memory list, the mug we planned to fill with candy canes for every memory revisited. I can't help but think I've let them down.

'My family want to meet you.' Heinrich interrupts my thoughts.

'Your family?' Suddenly I'm on the back foot. I hadn't expected that!

'Of course! They are keen to meet someone who is important to me. Yes, my parents and I are very close. They'd like to meet you.' He seems slightly surprised by my sudden panic.

'Your parents . . .' I swallow '. . . want to meet me?' I feel like I'm twenty years old again, meeting Tom's parents for the first time, once it looked like we were getting serious and we realized I was pregnant. Is this all going too fast? Have some fun, Pearl had said. You don't have to marry him! Well, he must be single if he's inviting me to meet his parents. Tick. Is this going too fast, or is it exactly what I've been looking for?

'Um . . . that would be great!' I'm gripped with nerves and a part of me feels I'm being judged, just like that time I met Tom's parents. This is a first: I've never been invited before to meet the parents in my online dating history. Is it a good thing? What if they don't like me, don't want a single mother from the UK for their son? My dating radar is going berserk. First you meet someone you like online, then you meet them in person, and then you've got to get approval from friends and family.

'How about you meet my friends before we visit your parents? They'd love to meet you,' I say, wanting him to meet Pearl and wondering what exactly I know about him. Is he really too good to be true? Pearl will get to the bottom of it, I'm sure. And it's true, she is dying to meet him. They all are! 'They've heard so much about you already.'

'Have they?' He smiles, pulling off his white coat and boots and holding out his hand to take mine.

'Yes,' I say. And it's true.

But it's time I found out more about the real Heinrich and if he could be what I've been looking for.

# NINETEEN

I take my usual route, which I'm beginning to know well, past the theatre and the cinema, away from the market square, past the big shops with bright lights and elaborate window displays, past the blocks of offices and flats, towards the river and back over the bridge towards the Old Town. I'm thinking of everything I know about Heinrich and the time I've spent with him, and there is nothing that hasn't been lovely. Nothing that has made my dating radar stand to attention. He seems to be everything he says he is. And, from where I'm standing, that seems very good. I'm excited, and terrified that something's going to pop up to ruin it. I pass the castle, pull out my phone and take a photo or two to load into our online album that Pearl is creating on Facebook of our Christmas memories. So far all I have to show for it is a smiling gingerbread Santa that I'm holding in a box. I need something to add to the collection of memories. I send a picture of the castle to Sam with love from Germany.

I look back up at the castle, lit in the darkening sky. Little flakes start to fall. At first I can't make out if it's snow or not. It's like tiny pieces of glitter. It is – it's snow! I'm beaming with joy and sticking out my tongue to catch it like I did on snowy days as a child. It couldn't be more picture perfect.

Suddenly my phone vibrates, making me jump. It's Sam. My heart leaps and turns somersaults.

'Sam!' I say, as I accept the call and his face appears on the screen. My Sam, smiling and happy, with goggles on top of his head, and a huge snowy mountain behind him.

'Hi, Mum?' he asks, checking I can hear him.

'I can hear you. How lovely to see you!' I'm looking down at his face as I lean against the stone bridge wall, and little flakes of snow speckle the screen. Then a thought flashes through my mind. 'Are you okay?'

'I'm fine, Mum! Having a great time. And so are you by the look of the photo you just sent me. Amazing!'

I look up at the castle again and light snow falls on my nose and cheeks. 'I am,' I say, with a smile and slowly growing confidence. 'I really am.'

'Great! How's Heinrich?'

'Got all his own hair and teeth!' I joke.

'Amy's with me.' He pulls her into the shot and she waves. I'm so happy he's found someone lovely to be with.

'So, Heinrich, what's he really like?' he asks, a little more seriously. Behind him the sun is shining and people are skiing and snowboarding downhill. Sam and Amy seem to be standing on the wooden terrace of a bar.

'He's . . .' I gather my thoughts and Sam waits. 'He's . . . lovely.'

'Really?' Sam's serious face spreads into a smile.

'Yes,' I say. 'He's tall and attractive. He's punctual and attentive. He took me out for doughnuts for breakfast.'

'You love doughnuts!' Sam beams.

'I know! And he remembered!'

'And you're keeping your notebook with you, ticking off the list?' he asks.

'Yes!' I show him, as if the roles of parent and son have been reversed.

'And he's who he says he is?'

I nod. 'It seems that way. He's got his own business – well, the family have. I've just been there and I'm meeting them tomorrow.'

'Meeting the family?' Sam says.

'Yes. But he's meeting Pearl first.'

'Good. Pearl will give him the once-over. Look, I'd better go, Mum.'

'Okay.'

'Have fun! Stay safe. It sounds like you could have met your man. Keep to the list. And don't do anything daft like getting married before I've met him.'

'I won't. I promise.'

'And enjoy the ride!'

'The what?'

'That would be too much information for a son and his mother to share. I mean enjoy the journey. Enjoy getting to know him better.'

'Oh, right, yes.'

'Bye, Mum.' He waves, and a lump catches in my throat.

'Take care. I love you,' I say.

'Love you too, Mum.' With that, Amy waves into the screen and they're gone. But the smile stays on my face and the phone in my hand. Finally, slowly, like I'm getting a whole new perspective on this, I lift it up and take some more photos of the castle and the river and more of the Old Town at the foot of the hill, like a sparkling diamond necklace, as I head towards it. I want to show Sam everything about my time here. He's right: if I stick to the list I'll know. And, right now, that list is looking pretty healthy. I need to enjoy the ride. I'm still smiling from the phone call and repeating Sam's words, 'Looks like you could have met your man.' Looks like I could have done. Somehow telling Sam about him makes it all feel just a little bit more real.

I walk back over the bridge towards the Old Town, checking my pictures as I go, when I'm practically bowled off my feet. I look down to see William's Fritz, happily snaking around my legs.

'Hello, lovely boy.' I bend down and greet him, feeling as happy to see him as he is to see me. I hear the whistle. The dog doesn't. I straighten, patting him, and spot William, leaning out of his front door, little flakes of glittery snow falling around him and the awning where the gingerbread is hanging. I catch my breath. It's a beautiful scene. That gingerbread was so good and so different from what I've just seen being made. William comes outside now, his arm waving in my direction, trying to attract the dog's attention. His dog stares up at me and, just for a moment, my heart flutters, like the snowflakes around me and those lit up outside the little shop in the orange glow from the windows and the big lantern in the street there. I want to capture the image but I won't. Just in case he thinks I'm photographing him.

He drops his arm, looks at me and the dog, and shakes his head. I give Fritz one last rub of the ears, then point towards his master. But he doesn't move. I try again, and again he doesn't move. A little giggle bubbles up in me. He's reminding me of a naughty toddler, friendly but firmly refusing to go in after playing. He's just looking at me, big pink tongue catching the little snowflakes, wagging his tail. I laugh. Then I take hold of his collar and gently turn his head towards the bakery. But he's not playing ball. Just sitting and looking up at me. I have a new friend.

I walk around him, pointing towards the shop, and this time he follows, in the direction of the bakery. His warm breath mists as it hits the cold air. But still he is looking up at me, not down the cobbled lane to William. I take a deep breath and walk a few steps towards the shop and the dog follows. I stop. The dog stops and sits. I point again. I don't want to have to get too close. Just being this close brings back all the embarrassment of having that conversation with him online. What was I thinking? I can't believe I could have mistaken my baking-group Facebook page for his shop's, open because I'd looked it up when I was first meeting Heinrich. And then carrying on talking to him! Like he really was a member of my baking group. He's not. He's in competition with Heinrich and I need to remember that. I'm with Heinrich and he's the opposition, however sad I'll be for the Old Town when Heinrich wins.

William waves and whistles again, making me jump, as we near the shop. To my relief, Fritz spots him and runs joyously back to him, to be patted and then returned to the warmth of the shop, wagging his tail, seemingly delighted he's brought home a new friend. I slow right down so I don't have to get too close, but I don't stop walking altogether. I don't want William to think I've made a complete fool of myself, even if that's how I feel. Maybe I want to bluff it out. I lift my chin a little, which always makes me feel a little braver.

'Um, thanks,' he says, retreating into the shop. 'He's—'

'Deaf,' I finish. 'Yes.' I'm not sure what else to say. It's like I'm standing in front of the man I met yesterday morning all over again, flushing, rattled, anxious, terrified I've made another mistake. I wrap my arms around myself, like a barrier, not letting anyone close. Since my last dating disaster, I've tended to keep everyone at arm's length. It feels safer that way. That's why the list is so important. I hadn't known I could misread a situation so badly and now the only way I can judge things is in black and white. For a moment, we stand awkwardly, not knowing how to end the non-conversation.

'Well, thanks again for bringing him back,' he repeats, and waves a hand.

'No problem,' I say, grateful he doesn't want to chat. Why would he? We're not friends. And definitely nothing more . . . As he said, if he was going on a date, I wouldn't be what he was looking for, and he definitely wouldn't tick any of the boxes on my list. I shove my hands into my pockets, put my head down and walk on past the shop, feeling awkward as I pass him, as if I should have talked to him, found some common ground to establish polite boundaries and not appear rude. But I don't. I keep walking and wonder at which point he goes back into the shop and shuts the door, or if he's still there, watching me go. It isn't until I get into the town square that I take a peep behind me. He's gone. I breathe normally again.

In the middle of the market, under the cover of the open-sided terrace, the fire pit burning brightly, I see

Pearl and the others. Ron seems to be dressed as an angel and is handing sweets from a tinsel-covered sack to the occasional passer-by. The others are looking at a piece of paper and there are chairs all around them.

'Hello? What's going on here?' I say, as I climb the couple of steps to the terrace.

'Oh, Connie love, there you are! How was the gingerbread-making? Can we tick it off the list?'

I hesitate. I wonder whether to lie, and just say yes, but something in me makes me shake my head. I hold out the gingerbread Santa in the box. They peer into it and say nothing.

'Let's just say Heinrich's set-up is a little more commercial,' I say.

Pearl raises an eyebrow.

'It's a factory, is it?' says Norman, straight to the point.

'Well, um, yes. But amazing!' I say. Because it is. Perfectly precise and high-performing. 'Very impressive. By the way, why is Ron dressed as an angel?' I ask Pearl.

'He's the Christmas angel. Goes around the market greeting children. Ticks another one off the list on the Christmas list. Ron was supposed to be the Archangel Gabriel in the school Nativity play, but got tonsillitis and had to stay at home. He's never forgotten the disappointment.'

'Oh, right,' I say, as if this is all perfectly normal. 'And John?'

Pearl shakes her head. 'Not sure. Goes off in the morning, walking, and comes back in the evening without a word.' She shrugs sadly. I put a hand on her shoulder.

'So, what's going on here?' I point.

'Outside cinema,' Pearl announces, holding out an arm. 'Anja has borrowed a projector and we're going to be playing *It's a Wonderful Life* tonight at six o'clock sharp! There'll be snacks.'

'Won't it be cold?' I ask, worrying about Maeve and Graham.

'Not in these!' And Pearl hands out hand-knitted Christmas jumpers. 'Got a deal on them at the stall here in the market. Everyone is buying jumpers with Christmas logos and pictures on, these days. These are the real deal! A knitted Christmas jumper.'

Norman takes the jumpers from Pearl with a smile and hands them around. 'Boosted Frieda's sales! She's the jumper lady.' She points. 'We bought you yours as a Christmas present.'

'Thank you, Pearl!' I kiss her soft cheek.

She smiles at me. 'You do so much for all of us,' she says softly.

'If it wasn't for you, some of us wouldn't see anyone for days on end,' says Alice. I feel choked thinking of Elsie. I wish I'd done more, popped in more often.

'Oh, and I'll take one for Heinrich too!' I shove my hand into my handbag for my purse, searching for my euros.

Pearl raises her eyebrows and tilts her head.

'Thought I'd invite him here this evening to meet you all. This will be perfect.' I look around at the white lights strung from the terrace to the bars, the steam rising from the glühwein, the smell of cinnamon and sizzling sausages on the food stalls around us and the cosy seating area around the fire pit.

'That would be lovely,' says Pearl. She squeezes my hand. At least if they meet and like Heinrich, they'll stop asking me 'if I've met someone yet', like I'm the only person online dating who hasn't met their perfect match. By the law of averages, it has to be my turn, surely.

I make my way back to the guesthouse. There, I open my phone to upload my pictures for the Christmas memory album and to post in my baking group – my actual group this time. *Ping!* I jump with excitement and indignation at the same time. There's another message.

# TWENTY

*How was your date?*

It's him. William.

*Sorry if I seemed rude earlier. I had some lebkuchen that needed to come out of the oven. Thank you for bringing my dog back. It was rude of me not to ask how your date went.*

I look at the message and think about ignoring it. I walk away from my phone, but I don't close it. I just keep a watchful eye on it, although I have no idea why. I begin to get changed, though not in front of the phone. My hackles are up. I'm going to ignore him. I'm not going to respond. I think about him standing in the doorway of the bakery, thanking me for returning his dog. I'm not going to respond. He's goading me, teasing me. I pull off a boot. He's trying to start an argument. But why? Just because I'm here with Heinrich? Is that it? Or because Heinrich and I have put the effort into finding what we want, each other, and he can't bear to see Heinrich happy? I pull off the other boot and throw it down next to the first. I go to respond, then turn away. I'm not going to reply, I tell myself, and brush my thick hair roughly, enjoying working through the tangles the wind had made. What if he's just being polite? What if I could help resolve this feud between him and Heinrich? Find a way that they both get what they want and put an end to the rivalry. But I'm not going to respond. I pull out my make-up bag and start to reapply my lipstick, putting on far more than I intended. I stare at myself in the mirror. But what if I'm the one being rude? I sit heavily on the bed, wiggle my toes in their two pairs of socks and look at the screen. I'm still not going to respond.

At his work bench, William looked at his computer screen. Maybe he shouldn't have sent the message. But there was no way of taking it back now. Actually, he had no idea why he had. Just felt he should have said something when she saw him outside the shop and brought his dog back. Fritz had taken a shine to her and her friends. Who was this woman with her posse of pensioners? And what was she doing here, meeting Heinrich on a date? How had they got together? But the last thing he wanted to think about right now was Heinrich. Or his new girlfriend, for that matter. He had work to do. He rubbed his eyes. He was tired. But that was the life of the cake-maker and baker, like his father before him. He looked up at the picture of him and his father on the wall, taken the last time they'd won the cup, just as the bell tinkled, and the door opened, bringing with it a chilly gust but a welcome sight.

'Hey, Paps!' William was always happy to see his father, although he wished he wasn't on a walking stick and clearly aching from the arthritis.

'You look tired,' his father said, in German. 'You should get out. Go and see that boy of yours.'

'I try, Paps, but it's not easy with the competition coming up and, frankly, Marta is making it difficult for me. She knows the hours I work.'

'Tsk. You need time off. The competition can wait. Go to the film this evening, in the square. Take your son.'

'It can't wait, Paps. We have to lift the curse. We have everything riding on it this year, what with the ice rink.' He waved at the square. 'This has to be the year we finally win the competition again.'

'I wish I could help. These damn hands.' Joseph looked down at them, in fingerless gloves, and banged the walking stick on the flagstone floor.

'Don't worry, Paps. I'm going to make you proud of the shop this year, and the town.'

His father looked at him. 'You just need to be proud of yourself. Make your son proud of you.'

'Right now, he sees me as the bad guy. The one who chose baking over him and his mother. I don't know how to change it. I didn't choose baking. It's . . . just what I do. It's the hours. Well, you know that. You've been doing it all your life.'

His father nodded. 'Maybe it's time this place had a revamp. We should bring it into the modern world. Heinrich and the family are doing big business.'

William liked the shop as it was, but maybe Joseph was right. Now, though, he wasn't going to give in to the idea.

'Let the cake speak for itself, Paps. It's going to be as modern as it gets. There is no way Heinrich can beat it this year. Not unless he has spies in every corner of this town.'

'I hope so, son. The town has a lot riding on it. They're relying on you,' he said, lifting himself stiffly from the stool he'd sat on to one side of the old wooden counter. He turned to leave. 'I'll bring you back coffee. I want to go and listen to the choir singing before the film-showing in the square. Always loved the choir.'

'Great. I must get on,' said William. He went to shut down the laptop and put it away. The last thing he needed was any more distractions. He had to work, he thought, just as his father had done. The brass bell tinkled again, and he watched his father step out into the cold, snow-sprinkled afternoon, bent against the breeze.

*Ping!* A message popped into his inbox, stopping him in his tracks as he went to shut the computer, and making him smile. It was a rare feeling these days, smiling.

*

*Fine, thank you,* I type briskly, because I'm really not intending to reply at all. But at least I'm not being rude and ignoring him. I've been polite. I mean, I've no reason to ignore him. He's the cake-maker in this town, part of the community. I don't want it to be awkward when I see him, especially if Heinrich and I were to . . . get together. I'd be here. Visiting.

I message Heinrich too. His time for picking up messages is between one and two p.m., so I should just get in on time. *Hi, Heinrich. They are showing* It's a Wonderful Life *in the square here tonight at six p.m. I would love it if you could join me and meet my friends.* I press send, and as I do, a message pops into my inbox, making my heart jump into my mouth, worrying it's William replying. But it's not. My heart settles. It's Heinrich. Our messages must have crossed. *My parents would like to know if you'd like to join us for dinner tonight at 7 p.m. until 9.30 p.m.*

Heinrich is clearly very hot on timekeeping. At least I know where I am with him and he doesn't let me down. I wait a second and another message comes through from him: he's just seen mine. *No problem. I'll arrange my parents for tomorrow,* he says, and I smile but am also terrified again. I was scared enough meeting him, but now meeting his parents! That makes us official! I remember Sam telling me to enjoy the journey. I need Heinrich to meet Pearl and the gang first, just to make sure I'm doing the right thing. If Pearl likes him, I'll know it's right. I place my hand on my notebook.

*Ping!*

My head snaps back to the screen.

*How was your gingerbread masterclass?*

Phffff!

I could just ignore him. But this is a man who knows gingerbread, or lebkuchen, as he'd corrected me.

*Did you find out all you wanted to know?*

My fingers hover over the keyboard. *Not in as much depth as I would have liked,* I reply. *But I did get to try Bethmännchen.*

*Ah. A pastry made from marzipan. And did you like it?*

*Yes! What else is in it?*

*It's done with almond, powdered sugar, rosewater and eggs. They are usually baked for Christmas Day. Lots of chocolate shops around Frankfurt sell them.*

*And what about stollen?* I think about my baking group and how I can report what goes into stollen. Before I know it, I'm drawn into a conversation and the minutes tick by.

*Ah, but I much prefer Christmas cake to stollen.*

*No, no! That's a very British thing!* He puts a smiley face after it, making me smile.

*Show me one!* he says.

I hesitate and then think, Why not? I'm building bridges here between Heinrich and William. This is my way of helping the two get along and maybe for the competition to come to an end, if that's what it will take to save the Old Town market and the businesses there.

I resettle myself on the bed and send over a picture of a Christmas cake I made this year. He's impressed and sends me one of his.

I'm speechless. *It's incredible,* I type, looking at last year's competition cake. *And it didn't win?*

The other end of the conversation goes silent. I look at the screen. Did the connection drop out? I check the Wi-Fi and my charger cable, which I've had to attach as the battery has worn down during this conversation.

*Hello?* I type, feeling as if I've been ghosted, with no idea as to why.

How rude! What was I thinking, chatting to this man as if we're friends? He's been rude from the moment I met him!

*Ping!*

*Sorry, got to go. I have a date!* he messages.

*Oh, fine, no problem. It was . . .* nice to chat, I was going to say. But he's offline, no longer active on Messenger, and I'm left standing in an empty chat room, reminded of how I felt when I was last faced with silence at the other end of the message line. God! What was I thinking? That was . . . Well, if I'm honest, it was great just talking about baking, fascinating even, but weird, as it was that grumpy sod from the bakery I was talking to. It just felt like the most natural conversation in the world. I'll try to talk to Heinrich more about baking when we meet. I look at the time on my phone clock.

'Oh, God! Heinrich!' My whole body leaps into panic mode. Nerve endings included.

I slam the phone shut, pull on my big thick Christmas jumper with reindeer round the chest, grab my scarf and hat and run out of the room. How could I have lost track of time like that? I really don't want to mess this up. I couldn't bear to get it badly wrong again. As I'm running down the dark wooden stairs, with swags of greenery wound all the way down to the lights and decorations in the hallway, I'm replaying the conversation about stollen with the picture of William's cake from last year in my head. I'm coming to really like this place. How could you not like a town with cake and baking at the heart of it?

Anja is at the bottom of the stairs. 'Someone looks happy. All okay? Going well?' She beams, her cheeks red and rosy.

'Yes, great, thank you!' I suddenly realize I'm still smiling from my cake conversation. I risk a quick glance at my watch and see it's gone five.

'Off to the film?' she asks.

'Yes. I'm meeting Heinrich,' I say, as I pull back the heavy wooden door and swing out of it.

'Heinrich's coming here? To the Old Town?' she asks, her smile dropping slightly.

'Yes. I'm running late.' I grimace and make her laugh.

'Now there is a man who likes things to run to schedule. Like his father before him,' I hear her say, as

I'm out of the door into the chilly evening with soft snowflakes in the air.

I hurry as carefully as I can, slipping and righting myself, down the small side road to the main square. I can see Heinrich waiting by the clock tower. Tall, dressed smartly but warmly and, despite the big clock overhead, looking at his watch. He looks at it a lot, I realize. But, as I've said, I love that he's reliable. Did I say that word to myself – 'love'? 'Love that he's reliable'?

I make my way to him through the small crowd as quickly as I can.

Heinrich doesn't look happy. In fact, he looks positively anxious.

'Heinrich,' I call and wave, my scarf flicking up in my face. I nearly slip over on the cobbles again. Must get better boots if I come back, I think. He turns to me and breaks into a smile. When I come back, I tell myself.

'I was worried you weren't coming. Going to stand me up!' He manages a laugh despite the tension on his face.

'No, sorry,' I say, out of breath and trying to catch it, but the cold air hits the back of my throat, making me cough as Heinrich attempts to kiss my cheek, then backs off.

'Sorry,' I repeat. 'I got caught up. Delayed.'

'It must have been important. Is everything okay?' He looks serious.

If I say it wasn't important, will he be offended? It wasn't important, just fun. But what was I thinking? Chatting to a man who isn't important to me about cake.

'Everything's fine now, thank you,' I say finally. 'Now, shall we meet my friends?' I'm trying to take some control of the situation. It was just a chat about cake. So why do I feel disloyal?

I link my arm through his. It was just a cake conversation, I repeat to myself. I notice Heinrich peering at my jumper with surprise.

'My Christmas jumper,' I say proudly. 'Here, I got you one too.' I hand it to him.

He takes it. 'Thank you,' he says, but doesn't get it out of the bag. As we walk towards the covered terrace in the middle of the square, Pearl and all the others are there, in their matching jumpers. They turn round and smile, and I laugh. Heinrich is clearly baffled.

'Yes, these are my friends,' I say, holding out an arm. Then another member of the group, wearing a matching jumper, turns towards us and my smile freezes, as if I have a guilty secret.

'Heinrich,' says William, his hands pushed into his pockets, under his Christmas jumper. 'Didn't you get the memo? Christmas jumpers to be worn for free entry?'

'Er, no, I didn't.' He looks taken off guard for just a split second. 'But it's okay. I'm happy to pay.'

'But you have a jumper.' I point to the one in the bag.

'It's okay. I can pay.' He looks up at William. 'I can afford it.'

I'm taken aback by the jibe, if that was what it was. Heinrich suddenly seems back in his comfort zone, as if he's just won the first game in a tennis match. He pulls out his wallet and produces a note.

'Smashing,' says Pearl, taking it and handing it to Anja, who's holding a tin. 'Every bit helps towards the Christmas Fair Fund.'

I look at William and my hackles rise. Why did he have to make Heinrich feel uncomfortable? No wonder he retaliated. He's here for me and to meet my friends. And William's not one of them! I have no idea what I was doing swapping messages with him earlier. I certainly won't do it again.

Heinrich looks around at the Christmas market and I can see he's judging it, comparing it to his. Then he offers to fetch us drinks.

'Thank you. Glühwein would be lovely,' I say, touched by his thoughtfulness, the moment of his retaliation against William put to the back of my mind.

'Waiting for your date?' I ask William pointedly, lifting my chin and glancing around.

'Yes,' he says, and his shoulders seem to stoop. 'But I think I may have been stood up.' Suddenly I feel very unkind. There was no need for me to say that. His phone pings. He pulls it from his pocket and looks at it. 'Yup, stood up!' he confirms, and shoves his phone back into his jacket. 'A cold, apparently. The weather wouldn't be right for it! Phffff!' He breathes out heavily.

'Right, come on. Popcorn, everyone.' Pearl is handing round cardboard boxes, and Anja is helping Heinrich with the mugs of steaming, scented glühwein.

'Take your seats, everyone.' We all huddle close to the fire pit, which is giving off a glorious heat.

'Not staying, William?' Heinrich asks.

William looks up at the screen, which is showing a picture of a happy family. 'Some of us have work to do,' he says, and turns away, his dog at his heels. 'Sugar paste to make.'

Anja watches him go. 'That woman!' She tuts, and looks towards an old man who's also watching William walk away, leaning on a stick, his hands swollen and twisted with arthritis. He glances at Anja, who puts a hand on his shoulder and tops up his glühwein from a big jug. 'It'll be okay. It'll work out,' she says to him, and I follow what she says in my limited German. But the body language tells me all I need to know. They're worried for William.

Heinrich moves up closer to me on our bench and pulls a blanket over our legs, puts his arm around me and smiles. 'I brought you this.' He hands me a little gift-wrapped box.

'Thank you!' I say, untying the ribbon and feeling touched. I open the box to find a candle inside. I lift it to my nose. It smells of cinnamon and spice. 'I love it, thank you!' And I kiss his cheek. I can see Pearl looking on approvingly.

'So you will think of being here, even when you're not,' he says, and holds my gaze.

Eventually I look down and sniff the candle again. 'It's lovely. Really thoughtful of you.'

'Oh, and these,' he says, pulling out a bag of Haribo Starmix. 'I know you said you like the fried eggs best.'

Is there no box this man doesn't tick? He's even remembered which Haribo Starmix are my favourites from our online chats. 'And you can have the red hearts with foamy backs.' I open the packet and put it between us as I snuggle back into the seat. If it wasn't for William's face just now, the sadness etched there, and on Anja's and the old man's, I would be feeling like this evening was perfect. Heinrich hands me the mug of glühwein and I feel warm from the inside out as I take a sip. I feel like . . . we're a couple. I really do. But I can't help sneaking a glance over my shoulder to see the stooped figure of William, hands in pockets, returning to his shop with his dog by his side. I wonder if this was no ordinary date for him as the film begins. Heinrich and I reach for the Haribos every now and again, our hands meeting, and we share gummy bears, fried eggs and cola bottles. Practically perfect, I think, with a happy little smile, and find myself hoping that William will get his perfect match sometime soon, too.

# TWENTY-ONE

My thumb hovers over the keyboard. I shouldn't. But I'm feeling guilty for asking him about his date, and cringing even more at Heinrich's comment that he could afford to pay. I don't know if he meant it to wound or not, but I think it did. Apart from that, the evening was lovely. We all enjoyed the film, ate popcorn and drank glühwein. Heinrich kissed me goodnight and my friends gently applauded as we agreed to meet again tomorrow, for dinner with his parents, which I'm not really looking forward to. This is turning from dating and fun into something a little more serious and I'm not sure how I feel about that.

*You okay?* I finally type and press send really quickly. I know I shouldn't, but can't help myself, hoping the guilt will subside. *How was the sugar paste?*

*Sticky!* he replies, making me smile, relieved that my

silly swipe hasn't caused lasting irritation. I watch the screen.

Then nothing.

My thumb hovers over the keys. I go to shut my phone case, then open it again, just to be sure. The little dots are dancing to show him typing. I wait. I'm like a teenager, not sure who should make the next move towards a first kiss. Although this is clearly not a kiss. It's just a quick conversation. My fingers seem to be shaking slightly. What if he's about to tell me to mind my own business, not his? I feel hot and have butterflies in my stomach. Too much popcorn, maybe. I focus on Heinrich's goodnight kiss. It was lovely, like well-made shoes, reassuringly comfortable, smelling beautiful, perfect in every way.

*How's your gingerbread research going?*

My thumb hovers, start, delete and restart. *Need to do more!* I finally reply.

There's another awkward silence and I wish I could take back the message, I frantically search for the remove button. But too late. It's been read.

*Ping!*

*I could show you how to make gingerbread if you like?*

I stare at the screen and bite my bottom lip. Again, I hover over the keyboard. The little dots are dancing up and down again. *Pearl and your other friends have been really good helping in the market. I'd like to give something back, get you that tick on the Christmas list.*

I bite my lip, harder this time. Ow! And then, as if he's reading my mind, *You wouldn't have to tell Heinrich, if it would help. Keep it our secret.*

I'm not sure I could keep it a secret. I'd have to tell Heinrich. I can't expect him to be trustworthy if I'm the one keeping secrets.

*No worries if it's a problem, just wanted to say thank you to Pearl and the others for doing their bit. Don't worry. It was just a mad idea. I can see it would be difficult for you. Hope you manage to see some real gingerbread, lebkuchen, being made.*

He's right! This isn't about him or Heinrich. This is about the Christmas list and my friends. And Elsie.

*No, wait. Hang on!* I suddenly type. *It would be lovely. Thank you. Pearl will be delighted we've got another thing ticked off the list!* I'll be able to take photographs and put them in the Christmas memories album. I'm sure Heinrich will understand why I'm doing it. Or maybe he won't. Or maybe I'll tell him I'm trying to help seal his deal. But only if I have to. I'll tell him at some point. Just not yet.

*Okay. It'll have to be early tomorrow, when I start baking for the day.*

*Yes, of course. What time?*

*Say 4?*

I stare at the screen. Has he made a mistake?

*Is that okay?* he types. *I need to clean everything and prepare the ingredients for the day. I usually do that at 5 and start baking at 7, ready to open at 9.*

I cough and clear my throat just as Pearl is coming into the room.

'Lovely night, and your Heinrich is so nice.'

*Just checking, did you say 4? Meaning a.m.?*

*Yes.* I can almost hear the laughter in his voice.

'Who's that you're typing to?'

'Just the cake club!' I inexplicably fib . . . again.

*Fine. See you then,* I type and close my phone case.

'So, what did you think of William, I mean Heinrich?' I correct myself quickly and blush.

Pearl misses just a beat and I hope she doesn't read any more into that than was intended.

'Heinrich,' I confirm. 'What did you think?'

'I think . . .' she says, unwinding the scarf from her neck and hanging it on the back of the door, '. . . you may finally have found the one.' She smiles.

'You said it was just a bit of fun,' I tease her.

'I think, when you find the one, you just have to be brave enough to take a chance on love,' she says, as we undress.

'What about you, Pearl? Wouldn't you like to find love again?' We climb into our beds.

'I'm a great believer that, if it's meant to be, love will find you,' she says. 'I've had my time. I felt loved. And at my time of life, I don't think it's really a possibility that it will happen again. I know what it's like to feel real love. My memory in that department is still working just fine. I'll always have that. I'm not looking for love any more.'

'But if it found you . . .' I trail off.

As the fairy lights on the market go out, I lie there, thinking about what it felt like to be loved. Was it when I was with Sam's father? Before we drifted apart and he finally left? Or maybe when I was a teenager on that school exchange trip. That's when I felt anything was possible, and really in love. I try to cling to that time when life was full of possibilities because I had someone who loved me before he broke my heart. I clasp that feeling as I try to drift off to sleep. It's a big day tomorrow, meeting Heinrich's family. I really need to be at my best.

# TWENTY-TWO

The clock on my phone slips round to 3.30 a.m. I haven't slept a wink. I slip out of bed very carefully so as not to wake Pearl.

I get dressed, putting on, well, practically all of my clothes. It's freezing. I worry my chattering teeth are going to wake her, but she's in a deep sleep, at last. I'm glad. I'm not sure she's been sleeping well, judging by her wakeful breathing at night. But last night she seemed to fall straight into a contented sleep. No doubt dreaming of Christmases gone by and *It's a Wonderful Life.* I mustn't wake her. I pick up my boots and creep towards the door. I turn the handle and slowly open it. It creaks loudly. I cringe and turn to look at Pearl in the soft landing light. She hasn't moved. Her hair is spread out across her pillow and, if I'm not mistaken, there's a hint of a smile on those lips.

I close the door. Let out a breath and tiptoe down

the dark wooden staircase to the hall, holding my boots to my chest. I slip them on, zip them up over the thick socks that I can now see don't match.

I let myself out of the front door and into the freezing misty morning. If you can call this morning. It's more like the middle of the night. The mist is rolling down the cobbled street, highlighted in the golden glow of the streetlamps, like a woollen scarf wrapping me up in a hug. I hurry into the deserted square, looking up at the big clock tower and the Christmas tree. I feel a frisson of excitement, like a child creeping downstairs to see if Father Christmas has been. I pull my coat around me. The smell of last night's waffles and woodsmoke hangs faintly in the cold night air, giving it a sweet, comforting tang. I make my way across the square, past the clock tower, the tree, and catch a whiff of the pine as I pass. The branches swing with big white fairy lights and homemade decorations from the local school, mixed with traditional wood ones from the market.

I want to savour every moment. I feel absolutely at peace. And a strange sense of something else . . . like a feeling of home, of belonging, like I'm falling in love with the place.

I walk through the square to the cobbled street on the other side. The only light is coming from the lantern over the alleyway I hid in. The shop's bay window and the sign above it, opposite, are barely visible in the early-morning mist. But the warmth from the shop draws me closer and, if I'm not mistaken, I can smell baking already. What's not to love about the smell of baking? It seems to say that everything is okay with the world. When Sam was growing up, I loved the smell of toast in the house. As long as we had tea and toast for breakfast, I felt he was set up for the day. Toast, amazing magic, caramelizing as it cooks.

I walk towards the shop, stop outside the window. I can see him, dark wavy hair held off his face with his usual bandana, standing in front of the ovens at the back, watching them as presumably they come up to temperature for his morning's work. I pull off a glove and place my hand on the cold brass door handle. I'm doing this for Pearl and the others, for Elsie and the Christmas memory list. It seems to have brought them all so much closer, and the problems they left behind seem to have stayed there. I need to help complete the list. Then we have to think about Maeve and her ice skating. Not easy for a woman who can't manage without her wheelchair.

I push the door open and am immediately wrapped up in the warmth of the place and the most enthusiastic greeting I've ever had. If only Fritz's owner was as keen!

'You made it then?' He cocks his head with a half-smile, wiping his hands on a cloth as he walks from the back of the room. I stand up from greeting Fritz, knowing Heinrich would be horrified to see him here, and imagine him sneezing at the sight of the dog.

He may be a rescue dog but he helps others too. He can sense when someone needs support.

'I can't believe I'm here and doing this!' I say, and he smiles. It's a nice smile . . . He's almost attractive, I think, then tell myself off. I laugh, a bubble of hysteria rising in me. It's early-morning madness.

'Come on, we're doing it for Pearl and the others,' he says firmly.

'Yes,' I say, thinking of Heinrich. I'm not doing anything wrong, I remind myself. I'm doing this for Pearl.

'Well, take your coat off and let's get started,' he says. 'I suggest we make some soft gingerbread for gingerbread hearts and some harder dough to make a small house for the window.'

'That sounds perfect. I loved making gingerbread houses with my grandmother.'

'Hopefully, I don't resemble her,' he says, and I realize he has a sense of humour.

'The ingredients have to be right and also at the right temperature for the magic to happen. If they're cold or too hot, it won't work. We need the room warm when we're cooking and cooler when we're decorating, which is why all my decorating work goes on in the workshop out the back. Much cooler. You can have all the right ingredients, but if the conditions aren't right, the alchemy won't work. It will be a disaster. Like the sticky sugar paste!'

I nod, watching him work.

'Like this,' he says, taking the rolling pin from me and showing me, so close I can feel his body heat, his breath. Goosebumps appear on my arms, and I think I should move away, but I don't. He smells of cinnamon and baking bread. Now possibly one of my favourite Christmas fragrances to join that of the early-morning mist and the Christmas tree.

Outside soft flakes of snow are falling.

'Now you.' He hands me the rolling pin and I begin to roll out the dough.

'Good.' He begins to work on his own piece of dough.

'So,' he says, 'you and Heinrich, have you known each other long? How did you actually meet?'

I give a little cough. 'We, er . . . we've been talking for a few months now,' I say, hoping to leave the conversation there.

'Really? So how does a girl from the UK end up talking to Heinrich in Germany?'

I suddenly feel quite warm. Very warm, in fact. I stand up and run the back of my hand across my forehead. I don't know why I'm feeling flustered. Everybody meets online, these days. 'We met online,' I say quickly, and go back to rolling my dough, ready to be shaped, baked and decorated.

'Online? This is the first time you've actually met?'

I bite my bottom lip. 'Uh-huh,' I confirm, not looking up.

'But how can you get to know each other from the other side of a computer screen?' He stands away from the counter, holding his rolling pin.

'You find out if you like the same things and want the same things in life.'

'And do you?'

'I think so.' I carry on rolling.

'Like what?'

'Well, obviously, you start with looks. As you said, I'd be the last person you'd be looking at.'

'I didn't actually say that.' He comes over, leans around me and adjusts the pressure on my rolling pin. Butterflies dance in my stomach. 'And after looks?'

'He has to be trustworthy,' I say. I bite my lip again.

'How do you know what you're looking for? Doesn't it come down to how you feel?'

'Well, I keep a list of all the things I'm looking for. Most people do.'

'A list!' He laughs.

'Yes, a list. To see if you have all the right . . . qualities. Ingredients, if you like.'

'And what's on this list?'

'Well, like I said, definitely trustworthy. And single. Always ensure they're single. Financially secure . . .'

'That counts me out,' says William, and I stop mid-flow.

'Oh, sorry, I didn't mean . . .'

'No, no, it's fine. I'm well aware that I wouldn't make anyone's tick list. I'm unreliable, not entirely divorced and practically broke. So you're saying it's like following a recipe, as simple as that.'

'Somehow it feels safer that way.'

'Safer than trusting your instinct? So, if the recipe said bake for fourteen minutes but you thought it was burning, would you follow the recipe or go with gut instinct?'

'I wouldn't say it was that simple. You can get caught out. That's why you have to stick to the list.'

'And have you been caught out?'

I breathe in, then out. 'Yes.' I increase the pressure on my gingerbread dough. 'Yes. I was very stupid once.'

'Stupid?'

I nod. 'I didn't follow the list. I didn't follow the rules of meeting and dating. I thought I'd met someone who really liked me. We got on and we made plans, but we never actually met.'

'So,' he frowns, 'how does that make you stupid?'

'Phffff.' I have no idea whether to say any more or not. But it's not like I'm going to be seeing William again. And there's something so warm and safe about being here in the early morning, making the day's gingerbread, that I just talk.

'He needed money,' I say, finding myself opening the lid of the box I try to keep this painful memory tucked away in.

'And you sent him some?'

'Said he needed it for his business, and once he had that sorted, we'd meet and start planning our life together. I didn't send the money at first. We talked about it. I mean, I'm not totally stupid. But somehow I felt I was in a relationship with this man and believed him when he said he could pay me back.'

'And he didn't.'

A single tear escapes from my eye. 'I never heard from him again.' Another tear falls and I step back from the work bench. 'He had every penny.'

William puts down his rolling pin.

'After my husband left me, and I really didn't see that coming, I thought I was doing the sensible thing, talking online first, building the relationship and trust. But I didn't keep to the list. I got carried away. Phffff!' I let out a long sigh.

'And he took everything?'

'All my savings. I was so stupid. And now my boss is selling his business and offered me first refusal, but I've had to turn it down because . . .'

'. . . all your money is gone,' he finishes.

'Like I say, stupid.'

'Not stupid,' he says, and puts his hand over mine, leaning into me ever so slightly. I don't move, smelling the cinnamon and baking. I feel I could stay there for ever. Only I can't. I really, really can't.

'We all do things that, at the time, we think are for the right reasons. It doesn't make us stupid. It makes us kind and considerate. Just because it didn't have the right outcome doesn't make it the wrong choice at the time. That's a chance we take to find happiness.'

I step away from him, reluctantly, and look at him.

He takes a deep breath. 'I went to Cologne to work, to better myself and make my family proud. My mother died a year after I left. Since then, we have never won the baking competition.'

'The Cologne curse,' I say quietly.

He nods. 'Like I say, you can have all the right ingredients, but if the alchemy isn't right, it's a disaster.'

He looks at me and I look at him, and a frisson passes between us. Maybe it's the setting, the sharing of stories, the fact that I'm off-limits . . .

His eyes are the colour of hot chocolate, dark, warm and spicy. I feel alive, on fire.

'I'm here with Heinrich,' I say, for some reason.

'I know. He's a lucky man.' He looks away, and I feel ridiculously disappointed. 'I hope he realizes it.'

My heart is pitter-pattering like the snow falling outside. 'He doesn't know I'm here,' I say.

'I know,' he says again. 'And I give you my word, I will do nothing to come between you two. I may not like him, but I won't do anything that will come between you. Unless you want me to, of course.' He laughs and I do too. A soft laugh, with the occasional sniff of a lasting tear. 'We all deserve a chance at happiness, however we find it. And, Connie?'

'Yes?'

'I'm sorry if I came across as rude when you first arrived. I—'

'It's okay.' I wave a floury hand.

'I was having a bad day. I think I'd just realized how financially unstable I'd become. Heinrich's made the right steps in life. Maybe I'm a bit jealous of him,' he jokes. Then, more seriously, he says, 'No wonder my wife left . . . I wonder if she had a list.'

There's a moment's silence and I don't know what to say. Then he claps his hands together. 'Come on, let's get these hearts made. We'll bake them and decorate them. What would you like to write on yours? These gifts mean a lot to people.'

I'd like to take some back for Pearl and the others, as Christmas presents.

'People can say how they really feel on them and give them from their heart. They're used a lot by people to tell the ones they love how they feel.'

I decide to do pictures on mine, an angel for Ron, a star for Maeve. I did think about doing a skater, but I decide not to in case it never happens. We work side by side as he prepares the morning's bakes and starts to hang out the gingerbread hearts on curly strings under the awning for passers-by to read and buy. And then he puts a small gingerbread house in the window, with a tealight candle inside it. It's getting lighter outside, slowly but surely.

I can't remember the last time I felt so relaxed and happy in a stranger's company, just being me.

'And now you have completed your Christmas memory,' he says, and I smile.

'I have. Thank you. If you had a Christmas memory, what would it be?' I ask.

He lets out a long, slow breath. 'To be back at the Christmas dinner table,' he says thoughtfully. 'I'd give anything to have Christmas with my mother again, just one last Christmas meal, to tell her how much she meant to me.'

'And who would be round your Christmas table?' I ask, warming to the theme.

'The ones I love, of course.' He looks down at my work and frowns. 'If that is meant to be a choirboy, it looks more like a seagull.' He chuckles. So do I, looking at my icing effort. I cannot wait for these to be a surprise for Pearl and the gang.

William looks up at the shop window and his face drops. A boy is staring in, a rucksack on his back, possibly on his way to school. Or perhaps he's glaring. He looks down at the little gingerbread house, lit with a candle, then up again. He and William stare at each other until the boy turns and runs.

# TWENTY-THREE

'Wait! Stop!' William runs around the counter and he launches himself towards the door. A cold chill sweeps in, making me shiver.

He throws himself out into the snowy cobbled street, the dog following. He looks down the road, then back towards the alley I hid in on that first morning. He puts his hands around his mouth and calls, as the snow falls around him, then throws them into the air in frustration.

His head covered with snowflakes, he comes back into the shop, guiding Fritz by his collar to his bed. The warm baking bubble has gone.

'Who was that?' I ask, wondering if it was a shoplifter.

He raises his head and looks at me with sad dark brown eyes. 'That,' he takes a deep breath, 'was my son.'

We finish making the gingerbread hearts and he

shows me how to finish my piping and wrap my gifts. But the happy, carefree atmosphere we enjoyed earlier is gone. There is sadness in the air.

'I have a son too,' I say, as we're clearing up.

He nods, as if he's slowly processing the information. 'He lives with you?'

'He did, until he went to university. Now he has a girlfriend and they're snowboarding together, for Christmas, with her family.'

'Ah,' he says, and I'm hoping that means he knows I understand something of how it feels to be separated from the boy he loves.

There's a silence and I think that's the end of the conversation. He pipes another gingerbread heart. My mouth is watering.

'My son lives with his mother. My wife.' He doesn't look up, his piping as steady as anything. There's just a twitch in his cheek.

'Your wife,' I repeat.

'My ex-wife,' he says slowly, 'soon to be. She left a year ago now. Just before Christmas. Just after we'd lost the baking competition for the ninth year in a row and she told me to choose between her and my work. I didn't expect my whole world to come crashing down around my ears, for her to take my son and for him to hate everything I stand for.'

And suddenly the date from the other night makes sense. It was his son who stood him up, not a woman. I feel my heart twist.

He straightens. 'Like I say, all the right ingredients, but . . . I came back after my mother died. Settled. Married a girl from the New Town and had my son. All the right decisions at the time, even if they haven't turned out well.'

'So, you're not together?' I ask dumbly, feeling daft, just filling in the silence.

'No,' he says flatly.

I can see the hurt and regret on his face, in his eyes, in the lines around them. 'She thought I chose baking over my family. That I was never there. Always baking.'

'And you?' I say quietly.

'She stole my dreams and my future when she left with my son.'

He stares at the window, and I turn to look at the little gingerbread house, its warm glow flickering as dawn and daylight finally arrive.

The door opens and the bell rings. Fritz jumps up happily to greet the new arrival.

'Ah! Good morning!' says the old man in German, pulling off his hat. 'What's this? A new member of staff?'

The moment of confidence between us is broken. The painful memories are pushed back to where they came from as we draw our eyes from the gingerbread house to the old man.

'Ah, Paps!' William reverts to his confident self. 'Yes, what do you think of my new apprentice and her work?' He indicates my handmade hearts.

'Apprentice?' the old man replies in English.

'Just for today.' I giggle.

'This is my father, Joseph,' says William.

'Pleased to meet you, Joseph.' Joseph's look of interest makes me explain: 'I'm just learning about gingerbread, to tell my baking group about it and create some Christmas memories.'

'She tried to learn how to make it when she visited Heinrich's factory.'

I catch my breath. That was supposed to be between us. My cheeks burn.

'Heinrich?' His father's bushy grey eyebrows shoot up. 'You can't learn to make anything there. It's all manufactured crap.'

I wonder how to respond.

'Connie is Heinrich's new girlfriend,' William says, with the teasing smile that infuriates me. We're back again to how he was when we first met. 'They met online,' he tells his father.

'Online!' His eyebrows rise even higher.

'Um, yes, we've been messaging for a few months. I've come to visit.'

'On a date.' William gives me the slightest of playful winks, letting me know he's only teasing, but still irritating me, just making me smile at the same time . . . I roll my eyes, letting him know his teasing doesn't touch me, even if it does. We both know we're keeping up appearances and distracting ourselves from the ones we're missing in our lives right now. Is that what

Christmas is about? Being with the ones we love, missing the ones we can't be with. Maybe finding new love.

'Yes,' I retort haughtily. 'On a date.' I feel we have the beginnings of a friendship that goes beyond his teasing and my irritation. 'And talking of dates, I really should be going. I have a lot to do before I meet Heinrich's family this evening.'

'Ah, his family. Yes, they'll be keen to meet you,' says Joseph. I want to ask what he means, but can't quite find the words. Maybe it's nothing, but something tells me there's more to it.

'Right, I must go.' I pick up my coat and bag.

'Don't forget these,' says William. I turn to him, not sure what he means. He's putting the gingerbread hearts in a paper bag with handles.

'Oh, of course! How much do I owe you?' I ask, rummaging for my purse.

He waves a hand. 'Call it a thank-you to Pearl and everyone for their help with the living Nativity and the film. I hear it was a great success.'

'It was.' We're transported back to that moment, me with Heinrich, William waiting for his son, and I want to say something, but there's nothing I can say. Hopefully today has built some bridges. 'Thank you,' I say. 'Oh, before I go, could you take a photograph of us with the gingerbread?' I ask Joseph.

'Of course, my dear. Just show me and I'll try.'

I set it up on my phone for him and pass it to him. 'Just press here,' I say, and go to stand beside William.

He puts one arm around my shoulders and holds up a heart in front of us. 'My heart,' he says, and we laugh as we wait . . . and wait.

Finally, 'I think I've done it!' I let myself breathe again, as does William when he drops his hand from my shoulder.

His father hands me my phone back.

I head for the door, telling William how much I've enjoyed today. I hope he realizes how much it's meant to me and I hope he gets his Christmas wish too. 'I wish things were how they were,' I remember him saying. I pull back the door, glimpsing the little gingerbread house that seems so warm and inviting in the window, a house full of hopes and dreams, pull my scarf tight and hold my hearts, with their Christmas memories iced on them, as I head for the guesthouse in the snow, with a glow inside, keeping me warm.

'Heinrich's girlfriend?' William's father said, as the door shut and the woman in the red coat disappeared down the lane towards the market square.

'That's right.' William didn't catch his father's eye as he rolled out more gingerbread dough to make hearts for the oven and the morning visitors to the town.

'Be careful, my boy. Be careful. There is enough bad feeling between our families. The last thing we want is for anything to spoil our chance at the weekend.'

'I know, Paps! It was just a favour. Nothing more. I won't be seeing her again.'

'Do you think Heinrich knows she was here?'

'No.' William shook his head. 'And he won't like it if he does find out. I've given my word I won't cause any problems there.' He gives his father a warning look.

Joseph shrugs. 'Now, show me the masterpiece. How's it coming on? All ready for Sunday?'

'Nearly finished. Come and see.' William and his father walk to the back room and William pushes open the door. His father smiles.

# TWENTY-FOUR

At 6.53 p.m. sharp, Heinrich meets me at the end of the cobbled street where I've parked the minibus. He jumps out of the car, kisses my lips and opens the passenger door for me. I slide into the warm car – with heated seats!

'I switched it on for you Hope it's the right temperature.'

'It's lovely. That's so thoughtful.' I snuggle into the warmth. It's bliss.

Heinrich gets in beside me. 'Okay?'

'Yes, lovely.' My body feels as if it's just got into a warm bath and my eyelids are heavy.

'Sit back and relax. We'll be at my parents' in no time. Six minutes, in fact.'

'Lovely,' I say again, feeling suddenly very tired. If only I'd been able to have that afternoon nap. But instead I've been back in the market, taking over from

Norman with the donkey, dressed as a shepherd in the living Nativity scene, while he visited the Christmas-jumper-maker to find out more about her knitting techniques. John has been to the church to listen to the choir rehearse. Ron is still the Christmas angel and Di and Graham are in the guesthouse, reading. But six minutes sitting in the quiet should be reviving, I think.

'I enjoy spending time with my parents. So it's good you're going to meet them. Hopefully you will be spending time here with them too.'

'Hmm.'

'Connie?'

My eyes ping open. 'Oh, yes!' I sit bolt upright and look around.

'What do you think?'

Was he talking to me and I fell asleep? I shake myself awake and tell myself off. Has six minutes gone?

'Six minutes, on the dot!' he says proudly, pointing to the clock on the dashboard.

'Well, it hardly felt like it.' I must feel relaxed with Heinrich if I was comfortable enough to drop off in the car while he was talking. Like a proper couple, I think. Connie and Heinrich. Like they've been together for years! I imagine friends and family saying, 'Are Connie and Heinrich coming over today?'

I see a man outside a front door, looking at his watch. It has to be Heinrich's father.

'Come. We're just on time. They'll be happy to meet you.'

Or that we're on time, I hear a little voice say devilishly, in the back of my mind. Connie and Heinrich, always on time! And I smile to myself as I go to push open the car door and find Heinrich is already there, opening it for me.

Walking down the path, I'm suddenly very nervous, but Heinrich's parents greet me with outstretched hands to shake. After the formal introductions have been made I'm ushered into the house, removing my shoes where everyone else does. It reminds me of being at home with Sam. He would have friends round and I would know they were there when I got in from work by the line of huge trainers and shoes beside the front door, the milk left out of the fridge and the empty cake tin. Crumbs everywhere. There would be no crumbs in this tidy house, I think, looking around. There are clocks everywhere. Everything in its place and running on time.

'Would you like a drink?' his mother asks. She's a slight woman, smartly dressed in beige trousers and a cream turtleneck jumper. Clearly not someone who eats a lot of cake. It doesn't look as if any of them overindulge in anything.

'Heinrich, serve the drinks. Dinner will be in,' she looks at a clock, 'twenty-three minutes. We have time for a drink and to get to know each other.' She gestures for me to sit. And I do, on the edge of the settee, and she looks down at my feet . . . my mismatched socks! As does Heinrich and his father. I stare at them too.

'They come like that,' I bluff, my toes curling with embarrassment as I try to cover one foot with the other.

'Tell me about your son and his father,' she says, and I'm taken aback, although no one else seems to be. I realize we're on a schedule and she wants all the important information so she can assess whether I'm a suitable partner for her son. 'And why did you choose a German man? Don't you like the men in the UK?'

I'm tongue-tied. Heinrich looks at me, clearly hoping I'll give all the right answers.

'Well, my son is Sam. He's at university.'

'And he's not with you now? In the run-up to Christmas?'

'He's with his girlfriend and her family this year, snowboarding.'

'Being together as a family is very important to us,' says Heinrich's father. 'Very important indeed. We need to know that anyone marrying Heinrich will be a part of his family.'

'And what are your plans if you decide to stay together after this week? Where do you intend to live?' his mother asks.

'Well, I—'

'Oh, it's time to eat!' says Heinrich, as at least two clocks strike the half-hour. It's as if they're calling time out in a boxing ring, and I retire to my corner for a moment to gather my strength.

'Dinner. I hope you have a good appetite.' His mother

gets straight up and his father goes to the table and pulls out a chair for me.

'Okay?' says Heinrich, standing in front of me – my coach giving me pointers before the next round.

'It's a bit full-on,' I try to joke.

He doesn't smile. 'They just want to know you're right for me. Isn't this why we're both here? Looking for the right one?'

He's right. No point in messing around. We have only a few days left to decide if we're going to make a go of it. This is like extreme speed dating.

'Talking of which, why did you go for a British woman, Heinrich?' I ask. 'I mean, I fell in love with a man from Germany when I was seventeen. I always thought he and I were meant to be together and . . .'

'I'm like him?'

'I suppose. But that was a long time ago. I guess I just have a thing about tall, blond German men.' I laugh. He doesn't. In fact, although we've smiled a lot, I don't know that we've actually laughed together.

'I think a British partner would suit me,' says Heinrich, just before his mother comes in carrying two hot dishes.

'As we have always told Heinrich, there is no such thing as luck. There is just good planning. That's how you get what you want from life. Now tell me about your health.'

Talking and eating at the same time is an art form. Trying not to talk with your mouth full but answer all the questions being fired at you is not easy. The food is lovely, if simple, and the portions are surprisingly on the small side.

An hour and a half later, the clocks signal it's nine p.m. and we move to the settees for coffee. I sit down and am overwhelmed by tiredness. I feel a yawn coming on and try to stifle it as coffee is poured.

I take the coffee, my hand shaking, as another yawn overtakes me. I tell them about Sam and his girlfriend Amy and they seem to like the idea that there may be grandchildren. Not yet! I assure them. They reiterate the importance of planning in life, and I have the impression they feel that Heinrich has let them down by not being married and producing grandchildren already.

I listen to Heinrich's parents telling me about Heinrich's academic achievements. I want to ask about their old partnership with William's family, what their plans are for the bakery if they win on Sunday and if William decides to sell to them. It's such an amazing little shop. It deserves to be taken on by someone who will love it as William and his father obviously have.

Heinrich's mother puts down her coffee cup as I stifle another yawn. My eyes are red and sore. 'Perhaps it's time you took Connie home, Heinrich. She is clearly tired.'

I could hug her.

'Either that or we bore her,' says Heinrich's father, and I'm suddenly embarrassed.

'Oh, no, not at all!' I exclaim.

'Just joking.' He laughs. I look at his face, which is just like Heinrich's. This is it, I think. He is just like Heinrich and this could be me in twenty years' time. It's not a bad place to be in life, is it? A couple. Dinner on the table on the dot. Life organized, safe and happy. Everything I thought was ahead of me when I was in love with my German exchange student. Sam's father liked life to be organized and wasn't happy in the months after Sam was born: everything then was chaotic. But when someone you love more than life itself comes into your life, you'll put up with the chaos and go with the flow, won't you? He couldn't. He wanted everything to go on as normal, and when it didn't, and I became more and more tearful and anxious about being a good mother, he couldn't cope. After that we were never really close. I didn't think I'd find again the kind of happiness we'd had when we were first together. But maybe Heinrich, ordered, kind, obsessed with time, is the one to make me happy again.

'It was a lovely evening, thank you,' I say, putting down my cup and glancing at the clock. Ten past nine. Brilliant. I can be in bed by nine thirty.

'I hope we'll see you again,' says his mother. 'When you are less tired.'

'I hope so too. It was a long day and I had an early start.' I say nothing about my trip to William's bakery. Whatever has gone on between the two families, it's best to stay out of it.

I thank them again, and this time they both embrace me in a tight hug. I have no idea if that means I've passed their test or good riddance.

'I hope to meet you again,' I say politely.

'It is best to plan these things, though, rather than hope. Otherwise time can start to run out.' She looks at Heinrich. 'No one wants to be a single forty-year-old,' she says.

# TWENTY-FIVE

'That went well,' said Heinrich, sliding into the driver's seat and starting the engine with a purr.

In the warmth of the car I feel even more exhausted than I did when we arrived.

'They liked you.' He beams.

I'm pretty sure they weren't that taken with me or that I have a grown son and wasn't spending Christmas with him. Or that I lived in the UK. They were worried that Heinrich would be spending less time in Germany. 'We are a very close family,' his father had insisted. I'm pretty sure they had a list like mine, and I'm not sure I ticked many boxes for them.

'They did,' Heinrich insists.

I'd hate to see how they'd interrogate someone they didn't like.

'You should see them when they meet someone they don't like!' He laughs loudly and naturally.

We must be totally in sync, I think. He reads my mind.

'Have there been a lot of people they don't like?' I ask cautiously, but feeling I can, that the tension has gone between us.

'A few. You know how it is. Internet dating is a precise science. It's hard to find the one who is exactly right.'

'And was there anyone before you started internet dating?' I ask gently.

He pauses. 'There was, once,' he says. 'But I have always found internet dating to be the best way of meeting someone you know you'll get along with. Why leave these things to chance?'

I agree. I might be taking a chance on love, but not on who it's going to be with. A sense of relief washes over me that we're relaxing into each other's company.

'I . . . I had a brother,' Heinrich says, and I feel the atmosphere changing. 'An older brother. Maurice . . .' He looks straight ahead.

I nod, encouraging him to go on.

'He died,' he says matter-of-factly. This is obviously his way of being able to pass on emotional information. 'He had his life ahead of him, all mapped out. He went to college, met a girl. They planned to marry. He wanted to join the business and expand it, make it an international name. But then, out of nowhere, his girlfriend decided she wanted to go travelling before settling down. She wasn't ready to fit into the plans.

So, he said he had to take the chance and they went. He wanted an adventure. They were in Italy, exploring, a car crash.'

Neither of us says anything. I want to put my hand over his, but something tells me not to. 'I'm sorry,' I say, a lump in my throat.

'I think life is better if you don't leave things to chance. Knowing the facts, you can make a decision.'

'And so you followed him into the family business?'

He nods.

'Did you always want to? Would you have liked to do anything else?'

He gives a little laugh, as if doing anything else would be impossible. 'Maybe engineering,' he says. 'I like things that work as they should. I studied engineering, before joining the business. I like clocks. Maybe I would have been a clockmaker. Who knows? One day maybe I will, when we grow old together.'

I try to imagine him old. Him and me old together.

'And what about you? What would you do differently?' he asks.

'Phffff!' I let out a long sigh. 'Honestly?' I think about when I was seventeen. I had met my soulmate, or so I thought. We had it all planned out, college, spending the holidays together and then we, too, would travel. But I guess he had other ideas or maybe his parents did. I try to picture his face, but now, with Heinrich, I can't see him at all. Was it love? Or was it just excitement at a time in my life when anything was possible? Was it that I loved being me, and nothing to do with the young man who had got away? Maybe it was me who got away and now it's time to find myself again. To take a chance on discovering love and happiness. Only none of this is about chance. It's about the list.

'I probably wouldn't change that much,' I say honestly. 'I love my job. I'd like it all to stay the same. That's the problem.'

'How so?' he asks.

'It's my job.'

'Delivering ready meals to old people?' Heinrich asks, and his use of 'old people' rankles with me.

'I bake, as you know.'

'That was the first thing that brought us together.'

'Well, I put the cakes I make into the boxes I deliver. I love meeting my customers, and many have become friends.'

'Okay. So you want to stay in your job?'

'Well, more than that, really. I'm not sure I'll have a job for much longer.'

'How so?'

'My boss is retiring, selling the business.'

'But that's great, isn't it?'

I'm a bit taken aback.

'I had hoped to buy it. That was my plan,' I say.

'Ah, a good plan. With the right employees you can run it from anywhere.'

I shake my head. 'I had the money saved, but now . . . I don't.' Because of my foolishness. Then I remember William's words: 'Anyone can make a mistake.'

'You don't?' Heinrich says, surprised.

'It's complicated,' I say and, for some reason, I don't feel able to admit my mistake to him. How I was taken in by a conman. If it was a man. I was a complete fool. And I will never let myself take a risk like that again.

'So, my plan may have changed.' Maybe this will work out just right.

'Like my parents say, there is no such thing as good luck, just good planning. I can't help but think that if Maurice had stuck to the plan he'd still be with us.'

This is why Heinrich is as he is. He likes to know where life is going. Not leaving things to chance. And he's right. We would never have found each other if it hadn't been for the internet. I like the fact that he has chosen me and I have chosen him. He leans in and kisses me. It's nice. He has soft lips. He smells lovely. As he pulls away, he leans back and looks at me.

'So, would you like to stay with me tonight?'

# TWENTY-SIX

'That would be very nice,' I say, tasting his lips on mine. I mean, we need to know if we get on in the bedroom as well as outside it. This is where we'll know for sure. I feel a flutter of excitement.

'We can go to my apartment.' He pulls away from his parents' house. 'I live on the outskirts of the New Town, in an apartment block there. I think I told you.'

'Yes.' I remember our initial messages, getting all the basic information from each other. 'Um, perhaps we can pick up some things from the guesthouse on the way,' I ask, reminding myself to tick 'own apartment' on the list.

'Of course.' He speeds towards the old bridge and the castle, which is lit up, looking down on the town like a royal bride on her wedding day.

As we drive towards the guesthouse, I'm excited and nervous, like a teenager all over again. I can't believe

I'm doing this! I'm actually going to have . . . I can barely think the word, it's been so long. And Heinrich is so good-looking. Just my type. I'm thrilled he thinks the same about me.

Heinrich gets as close to the guesthouse as he can, on the opposite corner of the square to the bakery. I run into the lounge, where Pearl is sitting by the fire with Anja and some of the others, and quickly explain to her that I won't be back this evening. She looks as pleased as Punch and gives me a quick thumbs-up.

'We're just back from seeing the choir sing in the church. John was there,' she says. 'Going to have a drop of glühwein as a nightcap. Enjoy yours!' she says, with a wink.

This is it! I think, as we pull up in his designated parking space outside his apartment block. Finally, I've met a man I want to be with, after all that searching online, after all the let-downs and one in particular. I'm finally about to climb back into the saddle. Just a couple more ticks to collect. And this is a big one. How do we get on together in bed?

I'm feeling hot and excited and nervous. I really want this to be right. More than right, I want it to be perfect. And so does he, by the look of it. He pushes open the front door of the apartment and I step inside. It's immaculate, new and modern, and everything is in its place. There are flowers on the table by the window at the far end of the living room.

'I didn't want to presume, but I had hoped,' he says gently.

'It's fine. Me too,' I say quickly. 'Yellow roses! My favourite!' I gasp.

He smiles at me. 'I remembered from our conversations. For you.'

It has been years since anyone bought me flowers. Let alone yellow roses. Tom bought them for me when I found out I was pregnant with Sam. He said they weren't as expensive as red ones. But I've loved them ever since. They remind me of one of the happiest days of my life, when I thought I'd got everything I wanted in life.

A bottle stands in an ice bucket beside two glasses and the flowers.

He takes off his coat, holds out his hand for mine, slips off his shoes and puts them into a cupboard.

Then he turns off the main light. There are small twinkling bulbs up a tall bunch of twisted willow in a big vase on the floor and more along the shelves, giving a beautiful white glow to the large open space. Then he lights candles on the glass dining table and on the coffee table. Outside, looking out of the big glass window, it's snowing. Perfect.

'Can I pour you a glass?' He gestures to the bottle and pads across the clean tiled floor. I start to follow, my boots squeaking on the floor. Heinrich looks down.

'Oh, sorry.' I slip them off, not as elegantly as I would

have liked. This time I take my mismatched socks off too, to reveal my specially painted red toenails. Then I take a deep breath, compose myself and walk across the tiles to join him. Ooh, underfloor heating. I smile to myself as my toes warm up and the rest of me follows. 'Anyway, a drink would be lovely.'

'I have this,' he points to the bottle in the ice bucket, 'or this!' He holds up a bottle of German Asbach brandy.

'My favourite!' I'm so moved by his thoughtfulness. I want to remember every bit of tonight. I want to be able to tell Pearl and Sam about every little detail.

'You said it was your all-time favourite drink.'

I'm barely able to speak. I had my first sip of it when I was on the exchange trip. It had made me cough. But I persevered. Now it's the drink I treat myself to at Christmas. I feel as if I'm in a beautiful dream.

As he pours the deep amber liquid into a waiting glass, I take in the views over the river, back towards the Old Town, lit with the soft white lights of the Christmas market. The snow, the lights, the castle and the bridge. It's beautiful, like a movie set. I almost think he's arranged the snow, just the right floating consistency, lit by the lights along his little balcony. I stare across the river and wonder about the others. Perhaps they're in the square now, drinking glühwein. I want to photograph this and show them, but I won't.

At the front of Heinrich's building the market in the New Town square will be in full swing with bands, the bars full to bursting. I hear the pop of a cork and something fizzy being poured into a glass as I gaze out over the river. I think about my morning at the bakery in the early-morning glow of the streetlight.

'For you.' Heinrich interrupts my thoughts and hands me a heavy, balloon-shaped glass. I swirl the brandy and smell its aroma. He toasts me with a glass of sparkling German wine.

'Thank you, Heinrich. This is just perfect.'

Then he holds up a little glass bowl to me. It's a bowl of Haribo. He's picked out all the little fried eggs for me. And I can't help laughing with happiness, as does he on seeing my reaction.

I take a little fried egg, then sip my drink, lifting the heavy glass to my lips.

He holds out another bowl to me. This time heart-shaped chocolates. I take one and bite into it. The centre is soft and liquid. Asbach brandy chocolates. I'm in heaven.

'Do you need to be up early?' I ask, holding my glass in one hand, a half-eaten chocolate in the other. I'm thinking of William's 4 a.m. start.

'Our machines are set to come on and I have staff to do the early shift. I can arrive at eight thirty.'

'Eight thirty,' I repeat. We have all night!

'I could maybe move things to nine, if need be. It's just a couple of calls. I have very good staff.' He puts his phone on the table. I take another glorious sip of the brandy, admiring the beautifully lit apartment and the snowy scene outside. The butterflies ricochet around my stomach.

He comes to join me by the window, slides an arm around my waist and takes a sip of his drink. I look up at his attractive jawline and watch the bubbles in his glass fizz upwards as he lifts it to his lips. It's the first time I've seen him drink alcohol. He doesn't drink much, he told me, and it's true. Another to tick off the list. Not a heavy drinker. I've had my fair share of dates that have ended with the bloke having had one too many and me deciding it's time to leave. This is *sooo* different.

We're staring at each other now, slightly nervous yet clearly looking forward to what's to come. From the square on the other side of the building I can hear a band on stage and the bierkeller in full swing. I shall have to bring Pearl and the others here. Why am I thinking about them now? I chastise myself. I should be thinking about me, with Heinrich, the beautiful setting. I should be drinking in every bit of our first night together.

He looks down at me and I look up at him. Then I reach up on tiptoe, put my hand around his neck, pull him gently towards me and kiss him. I need him to know I want this, tasting the wine on his lips mixing with the brandy on mine.

Finally, we pull apart, smile and even blush. I feel quite brazen at having made the first move, but I want this to work. Outside the band is playing and I look out over the river at the Old Town. It makes me feel warm inside, like I'm in the right place with the right man. I banish all thoughts of his parents and the dinner, and focus on now. I'm happy, really happy. This evening, the apartment, the drinks, the view and the snow, it's all perfect.

'So,' he says, and my heart lurches. This is it. We're going to the bedroom! I want to kiss him again, just to get really in the mood. 'I like to shower first. Is that okay with you?' he asks.

I'm put on the back foot for just a moment, but I say, 'Oh, yes, of course. Perfect!' We have time, I tell myself.

'Would you like to go first?' he offers. 'There is a clean robe on the back of the bathroom door and towels there too.'

'Lovely!' I say, suddenly a bit put off my stride. A shower first. Very hygienic. I like clean. Perhaps there's clean sheets too. That sounds fabulous. And a shower will wake me up a bit. Get me well and truly in the mood. 'Would you like to join me?'

He smiles. 'No, you go ahead. Enjoy. It has a brilliant shower head.' He tops up our glasses.

'Okay, I'll be as quick as I can,' I say.

'Take your time. We have all night,' he says, and presses a button. Suddenly my favourite Ella Fitzgerald album is filling the room. Heaven! I pop another chocolate in my mouth and head for the bathroom. He's thought of everything, tick, tick, tick.

*

William stared at his computer screen. His eyes were sore but he couldn't sleep. Nothing unusual about that. He usually had things on his mind, the business mostly, but this time there was something else. He stared at his screen, propped up in bed, one arm behind his head. The fingers of his right hand hovered over the keyboard. A message popped into his inbox. He opened it, then sat up straight and read it again.

That certainly wasn't what he was expecting, not from Marta. And it was a suggestion he wasn't going to turn down. He was now wide awake, his mind whirring. He'd never get to sleep.

# TWENTY-SEVEN

I can hear the shower turning on next door. Tall, blond, athletic Heinrich is getting into it right now. I can almost picture him. And in just a few minutes I won't need my imagination.

I walk towards the brandy glass he has put beside the bed, on a coaster, next to the bedside light. There are yellow rose petals over the duvet cover, and a chocolate heart on the pillow. I pop it into my mouth and pull back the covers. Clean white ironed sheets. I give the bed a couple of presses with my hand. Comfy! I sip my drink and sit on the bed, staring out over the river and the Old Town. The shower next door is still running. I wonder how I should look when he comes in. Sitting here, sipping my brandy? Or perhaps lying in bed, waiting, so I don't have to take my dressing-gown off with the light on. That's a much better idea. I may be ready to go to bed with him, but I am not ready to be naked before the lights go out.

I turn off my bedside light, leaving his on. I sit back on the bed and swing my legs up onto it, then rearrange some of the petals I've squashed. I sip my drink again. There are no books or ornaments. Nothing to look at. I wonder if I should check my phone. I put down my drink, which is making me even sleepier – I want to be as lively as I can when Heinrich gets back from the shower. I pull my phone out of my bag. I wonder if I should text William and thank him for today. I put it down by the side of the bed. Should I? I lie on my side, trying to be sexy, but my boobs look massive like that: two huge jellyfish. I turn onto my back, but the dressing-gown falls open. It's not a good look. The dressing-gown isn't big enough.

I throw back the covers and stand up. Maybe I should just get into bed naked. Yes. Under the covers. With all the lights off. Much better.

I slide off the dressing-gown and look for somewhere to lay it. There's nowhere, not a chair or chest of drawers. Everything seems to be behind built-in cupboards. I open one and see neatly pressed shirts, in colour-coordinated rows. I shut the door. When Heinrich said he was neat, he wasn't joking. He's nothing if not honest. I look around for my bag and notebook to tick off all the amazing things about tonight. After 'owning his apartment', I add 'thoughtful, kind and neat' to the list. Now all I need to find out is how we are in bed. I see a small hook on the back of the door and make a dash to hang the dressing-gown there, make sure it's straight, and then, hearing the shower go off next door, run to the bed and throw myself in.

Oh, if there was a heaven, this is how it would feel. I shimmy under the crisp, fresh-smelling covers, my eyes heavy again. If this is a sign of things to come, I could be very, very happy. I must make sure I don't fall asleep. This is a night I want to remember. The first of many, I hope, with a significant other. I want to enjoy every minute of it.

As I lie there, with nothing to read, I pick up my phone again. I look at the pictures of today, with William and the gingerbread. The photographs his father took, slightly blurry and skew-whiff. I smile at them.

I decide to send them to William by way of thanking him for today. Then I put down the phone, turn off the other bedside light, snuggle down under the covers, and wait . . .

# TWENTY-EIGHT

'Connie?'

I hear my name and I'm not sure if I'm dreaming. 'Connie?' I hear again and it seems closer, in the room with me.

'Uh?' I catch my breath in the pitch-black, heart thundering, no idea where I am. 'Who's there?' I'm suddenly wide awake.

'It's me – Heinrich!'

I sit bolt upright in bed, clutching a clean white duvet to my chest, having woken from the best night's sleep I've had in a long time. 'Heinrich?' I'm momentarily confused before last night floods back to me.

An overhead light goes on and I squint. Something tickles the side of my face. I put my hand to it and peel off a yellow rose petal.

'Your phone just pinged a message.' I see the outline

of Heinrich standing in front of me, dressed and smelling fresh from the shower.

'Did it?' I'm in a daze, confused.

'What time is it?' I ask, picking up my phone and squinting at it, waiting for my eyes to focus.

'Eight twenty-five. I should get going.' Heinrich is in front of me, adjusting his shirt sleeves under his soft V-neck jumper.

How? How can it be morning? What . . . happened?

I look at the screen of my phone and confirm the time.

'Someone left you a message, I think,' he says, running his hands over his hair.

'Oh, it's just William,' I say carelessly, and put the phone down, pulling the covers up higher around my chest. The bed seems barely slept in – his half looks untouched.

'What . . . ?' I peel off another yellow petal from my elbow. I'm trying to recall what happened after the lights went out. He seems to understand my confusion.

'You fell asleep,' he says flatly. 'I took the settee.'

'Oh, God!' I put my hand to my forehead. 'I'm so sorry. It was such a long day, what with going to the bakery in the morning!' I shut my eyes. I feel like I've got a hangover, only I really didn't drink that much. I just slept really, really well.

'The bakery?' he says, and my eyes ping wide open.

Did I just say 'the bakery'? He's agitated now, looking at his watch and back at me.

'You said it was William.' He nods to my phone. 'As in William's bakery, in the Old Town?'

My heart is racing.

'I . . .' I lick my lips. They taste of brandy and chocolate.

I have no idea what to say. Do I lie? Say it's someone from back home? Then I think about the list . . . and his list. If honesty is as important to him as it is to me, I can't lie. Last night was almost perfect. He is kind, generous and very genuine. I have to be the same if this is going to work. I take a breath, wishing I wasn't having this conversation naked, with only a white duvet to cover me, and him fully clothed. But I have to explain it was just a visit. Nothing more, I tell myself. And it wasn't! It was just a visit, by an interested tourist. Me.

'Yes.' There's no point in this if I'm not truthful. Trust is what a relationship is all about and I have nothing to hide from Heinrich. Not that he'll ever want to see me again after this fiasco.

'What were you doing at William's bakery?' he says slowly, and frowns, looking a little hurt.

I take a deep breath and sigh, feeling I need coffee. My stomach rumbles. I had hoped Heinrich and I would be sharing breakfast together, in bed. Doesn't look as if I've left time for that, especially as we never actually made it to first base.

'He was just helping me out, a favour,' I say.

'Helping you out?'

'Doing me a favour,' I explain, and point to the dressing-gown on the door. 'Would you mind?'

He hands it to me, but I have no idea how to drop the duvet and put on the dressing-gown. Heinrich seems oblivious to my situation.

'I needed to see the gingerbread being made. He offered to show me.' I slide one arm into an armhole but am at a loss as to how to get into the other without dropping the duvet and revealing everything that Heinrich didn't get to see last night.

'But I showed you how gingerbread is made.' His frown deepens and there is definitely hurt now.

'I know, I know,' I say quickly. 'And it was great seeing the factory and meeting your colleague – Klara, was it?'

'Klara,' he confirms, with a nod, but clearly he doesn't mix that closely with his staff. 'Didn't you see everything? Do you want to come again?'

'I needed to see it handmade. That's all. It was for a memory album we're putting together.'

'A memory album? Is there something you haven't told me? Some family illness?' He's clearly concerned.

'It's an album of photographs from our time here. I told you about my friends.'

'The old people.'

That grates on me. 'My friends,' I repeat. 'We're doing like a wish list. It's a list of Christmas memories we're all recreating, while creating new ones here. I had to make gingerbread and photograph it, for the list, for my friends on the trip. And then I get a candy cane for the cup.' I smile.

'A wish list.' He looks confused.

'Yes, in tribute to our friend Elsie. She loved Christmas. We all said what reminded us of it and what reminds us of the people we love. Something we wanted to do and see again. I wanted to make gingerbread like my gran used to make.'

'And William helped you,' he says slowly. He's now sitting on the edge of the bed, so I have no hope of trying to squirm further under the covers and get my dressing-gown around me.

'Yes. Look, Heinrich, I'm sorry about last night, I really am.' I sit up, still clinging to the duvet.

'It's okay.' He pats the duvet. 'You can't plan for everything, can you?' he jokes – I know he's joking because I've learned that Heinrich believes you *can* plan for everything.

'I'd like to . . . try again, if you would,' I say boldly. I haven't got this far only to ruin it all now. Heinrich is everything I'm looking for and I'm not going to let the mention of William ruin this.

He nods. 'I would.'

I feel so relieved that I loosen my grip on the duvet a little. 'But,' he stands up, seeming even taller from my sitting position on the bed, 'not today. I have to get moving.' He looks at his watch and then his phone. 'We have a big surprise coming for Sunday's competition.

The judges will see that we have the best market and the best bakery.'

'Great!' I say. 'What is it?'

'You'll see later, but there is a lot of work to get it up and running.' He checks his phone again. 'Okay, help yourself to coffee and let yourself out. We will speak later and plan our night, yes? This time, a plan we both stick to.'

'Definitely!' He kisses me, and I like it, and I wish he could be impetuous and come back to bed. But Heinrich has other things on his mind as he heads for the door. I sigh, letting go of the duvet and sliding out of bed into the dressing-gown.

'Connie?' He puts his head round the bedroom door.

'Yes?' I jump back into bed, hugging everything to me. Still not ready for him to see me naked in daylight – or any kind of light. But excited that he's changed his mind and decided to come back to bed.

# TWENTY-NINE

'About William . . .' Heinrich says.

'William?' My stomach jolts and my smile drops. Why are we talking about him?

'I just thought . . .' He's disappointed I went there. I shouldn't have gone.

'I told you it was just . . .' I'm cross with myself: I could have blown this, and all because of William.

'Did he . . .' He's choosing his words carefully. I watch him, wondering what on earth he's going to ask. My visit to William to make gingerbread hearts could just have ruined it all. I'm furious with myself.

'Did he mention me, or our meeting the other day?' he asks eventually.

I look at him. 'You?' I think back to yesterday morning. 'Um . . . Well, obviously he wanted to know how we met so I told him.'

'So, no mention of my business proposal to him?'

'No. We just talked about recipes.' Which was true, whether it was cakes, or relationships and their ingredients. I find myself smiling.

'Is there a chance you might see him again?' He cocks his head.

'See him again? No. It was a one-off. In fact, I promise you I'll never see him again. Suits me fine.'

He bites his bottom lip as he thinks. I knew I shouldn't have gone to the bakery. I knew Heinrich wouldn't like it. Why on earth did I not listen to myself?

'Maybe . . .' He looks at me with what I think may be a twinkle of excitement and I wonder if he's about to call off whatever he has to do and come to bed.

'Yes?' I smile back.

'Maybe it would be good if you were to see him again,' says Heinrich. 'He's in trouble financially. It's not a secret. The whole town is struggling. As you know, I've offered to buy him out, expand my business, but at the same time I'd be doing him a favour.'

'Expand the business,' I repeat, wondering who really is the winner here.

'Like I say, I'd take over the shop, keep it as it is, but sell my cakes and bakes from the factory there.'

'So the shop would stay the same?'

'Exactly the same.' He nods. 'And he would be able to walk away without going bankrupt and start again.'

'It seems like a good solution. And the town would benefit from the bakery being there,' I say, as if I'm thinking aloud. 'So what's the problem?'

Heinrich sucks his teeth. 'William is a very proud man. He thinks that the reason the business and the town are in trouble is his fault. He won't accept any help from anyone. Especially not from me, or my family.'

'But why not? Like you say, if he's in trouble and you're offering a way out, why wouldn't he take it?'

'It's like a drowning man turning down an outstretched hand.' Heinrich tuts, then turns back to me. 'Look, maybe you could talk to him, get him to see sense.'

'Oh, I don't know. William's not the sort of man who'd listen to advice, especially not from someone like me.'

'Why not?'

'Well, we're not really friends. Like I say, he just helped me out.'

For a moment, we say nothing. I wish there was a way I could help both men, heal the rift between them and build some bridges.

'Sounds like you'd both get what you wanted if he'd accept.'

'Well, I know it would certainly help him get his wife and son back if he accepted my offer.' He chews the bottom corner of his lip and checks his watch. 'Maybe you could go back to find out a bit more about the gingerbread. Get good at it. Post it for your Facebook group.'

I frown. 'But I've already done that. I don't need to go back.'

'Maybe you could go again, look interested. If he won't listen to you, or anyone, maybe the only way to make this happen, so he saves face, because he can't bear to accept my help, is if he doesn't win on Sunday. Maybe you could get a glimpse of his installation for the competition this year,' he says. 'If he loses, he's got to sell. It would mean that he has no other choice. He's not accepting my help, he's having to take it.'

'You want me to spy on him?'

'Not spy, just take a picture. Just one. Then it would really secure things for the deal. If I know what he's doing, I can make sure we are in the winning position. It works for all of us. He gets a hand out of the hole he's in, a chance to get his wife back, and I take over the shop and spread our market into theirs for next year, bringing back the tourists.' He taps his watch face. 'If I can get him to agree to sell to me, we could expand, get our cakes into his shop and have a really good image for our product. Take the idea to the UK too! Once we get the shop back into my family's hands. It could be our future.' He kisses me. 'We could sell the cakes all over the UK, with the old shop as the face of the business.'

I stare at him.

'That would mean you and me spending a lot more time together. Base ourselves in the UK, maybe. But William needs to save face. He doesn't want to sell to me unless he has to. If we win on Sunday, he will have to sell. His wife, Marta, I know, would be very pleased to hear he'd agreed to sell. This could be his second chance at happiness with his family.'

I'm speechless. This is all going very quickly – but it's what I'd hoped for, isn't it?

'Look, I want us to work. I think my parents like you.' I don't. 'And I do too. I want us to be together, a team, working to develop the business together. It's one of the things we really have in common . . . I am planning something special for our last night together. And if you're as happy as I am, I have a particular question I want to ask you.' He smiles. 'I know we will make a dream team.'

My mouth hangs open. Is he saying what I think he's saying? I hadn't expected this.

'I want us to be together, Connie. I know we've only just met, but we've known each other for a few months now. We know everything about each other, practically!'

I nod, dumbstruck.

'I hope that it's what you want too. Like I say, we have all the right ingredients to be a great team. And if we get the shop, we can move into the UK market too. And William gets a chance at a new start. Hopefully on Sunday we will all be celebrating a new chapter in our lives.' He kisses me, then looks yet again at his watch. 'I have to leave. Just go and see him. See if you can help this along a bit. You're part of the family now . . . or I hope you will be very soon.' And with that, he's gone.

I sit, staring around the empty room, replaying the conversation.

I pick up my phone. I wish I could message Sam and tell him what's just happened.

I look at my screen and read the message William sent earlier this morning: *You're welcome. Any time.*

Should I ring Sam, ask his advice? Or should I wait? I don't want to get it wrong. But I've done what Sam told me to do. I hold my phone to my lips. I want to be sure that that was what Heinrich meant when he talked about asking me a particular question. Is he going to ask me to marry him? And, if so, am I going to say yes? I've finally done what Sam said I should do and found someone online whom I want to be with. I took the chance and found love. I think about last night and all the effort Heinrich went to. It is love, isn't it?

# THIRTY

After last night's email from Marta, asking him if he wanted to meet to talk about 'where we're at', he wasn't going to turn down the olive branch and a chance to get things back to how they used to be. Did she mean where they were at with the divorce papers, or seeing if they could go back to how things were, when he felt like a father and a husband, when he had dreams and a future? If she wanted to meet him this afternoon, he'd do it. He had to make this work for his son's sake. He had to make Noah understand that he hadn't abandoned him. He thought about the look in the boy's eyes when he'd gazed in through the shop window yesterday morning and his heart twisted.

He picked up his coffee cup from beside the bed and wandered downstairs. Fritz was there to greet him as usual. He bent down and patted him and went to turn on the ovens. And then he saw the message from

Connie, thanking him for showing her how to make gingerbread and attaching the photograph Paps had taken. It wasn't perfect but he liked it. It made him smile. He didn't do enough of that, these days.

He wondered whether to reply or not. He probably wouldn't. He'd enjoyed talking cakes and patisserie with her. She'd been a brilliant student for the day. She had great skills. But, no, he wouldn't message her again. He probably shouldn't. Maybe just a quick *You're welcome. Any time* would do it. He typed it quickly, sent it and put the phone down. That was it. He wouldn't message again. No need to. Especially because she was involved with Heinrich. He needed to keep his distance. There was no way he wanted to get in the middle of anything going on between them. There was enough trouble between the two families. Besides, he had his own family to think about, Marta and his son. That was where he needed to focus. But he'd liked spending time with her. He'd made her laugh and she him. He hadn't laughed in a long time.

He wondered if she might know Heinrich's plans for his cake installation on Sunday. Would she? If she did, would he want to know? He didn't. He'd pulled out all the stops this year and his piece was the best he'd ever done. He didn't need to resort to espionage to win. Besides, the ice rink was arriving today. That would really add to the feel of the place in time for the competition. He hoped his son would join him down there. Spend some time together as a family. Feel like a family, feel like a father and son again, like he felt with his dad. Whatever happened, he mustn't miss this meeting with Marta. He mustn't be late. This was his chance and he had to try to get them back together and to how they once were.

# THIRTY-ONE

I'm doing this for William and the town, I tell myself, not just Heinrich, as I walk back from the New Town, across the bridge, peering up at the castle as if I'm seeking confirmation that this is right. I'm doing this to help heal the rift and bring the two communities together. I'm trying to save next year's market. I think about the hot-chocolate-seller, the toy- and jumper-sellers. I think about Anja and her guesthouse, everyone who relies on the Christmas market.

'It's all your fault anyway,' I say to the castle's turrets. 'If it wasn't for your competition, this war wouldn't have set in. I'm doing this for Heinrich and for William. I'm sorting out your mess.'

I'm doing it for both of them and their families, I tell myself. Isn't that what I do? Try to help where I can? Or am I really trying to ignore my own dilemma about Heinrich's question? I turn my thoughts back to

William, who, by all accounts, needs to see that selling to Heinrich could be the best thing for him, but also needs to save face. He said he'd poured everything into the market this year, and Anja told us that he'd borrowed up to his max to get the skating rink. If William is too proud to accept Heinrich's offer of buying the shop, I can try to help. If Heinrich wins on Sunday, William will have no choice and everyone will get what they need. I just have to work out how to do it . . .

By nine o'clock, William was finishing his morning shift in the bakery. He checked his messages. There was one from Marta, telling him where to meet and not to be late. He wouldn't be. He couldn't be. He had to show he was there for them. He wasn't choosing baking over his family, not this time, if there was a chance to get things back to how they'd been. If it meant walking away from baking, maybe that was what he had to do.

As he was about to close his screen to take his dog for a walk before opening the shop, a message popped into his inbox. He read it, reread it and smiled. Well, why not? Where was the harm? It was fine. He wasn't getting involved, just helping out a group of tourists with their Christmas memories album. What was the worst that could happen? He liked the woman. It was hard to say no.

'Hi,' I say, as I enter the shop, the bell over the door tinkling. I'm as nervous as a kitten and nearly back out as soon as I see him standing there. I remind myself I'm doing this for all the right reasons. It will put an end to the rift and help William.

'Hi,' he says, and we look at each other, both waiting for the other to speak.

'They look fantastic,' I say, pointing to the stollen he's just made.

'Would you like to try a slice?' he asks, picking up a knife, putting the cake on a board and cutting into it, placing the piece on the paper he'd normally wrap it in and handing it to me.

'Thank you.' I take a bite. 'Wow!'

'This is our traditional Christmas cake in Germany. It's bread, with nuts, spices, candied fruit, and sprinkled with icing sugar.'

I take out my phone and photograph it for the baking group.

'It was originally made of flour, oats and water. No sugar, fruit or alcohol. Then it began to have flour, oil, water and yeast. But as it was baked in the weeks leading up to Christmas, in Advent, a time of fasting, they weren't allowed to use butter. Finally, it got the royal seal of approval when a stollen was allowed to be made for royalty with butter. This is why it is known as the food of kings. Dresden is the home of stollen. They once made a huge one and it was carried through the streets for Prince Augustus in 1730.'

I take another bite, getting icing sugar over my hands.

'You've got some . . .' He points to my nose and I rub it, adding more to what's already there. 'Here.' He holds out a clean cloth. 'Would you like some hot chocolate to go with that?' he asks, as I take the cloth from him.

'That would be lovely,' I say. It's not the coffee I had been expecting to have this morning, but I find myself perching on the stool beside the counter, feeling strangely at home in the warm shop. As he returns, I dust off my hands.

'I see the ice rink is nearly ready to go.' I point in the direction of the workmen installing it in front of the clock tower and behind the big tree.

'Yes. Will you be trying it out later?'

I laugh and shake my head. 'No, not me! I know how much it can hurt when you fall. Still got the scar to prove it.' I run my hand along my nose and remember the bang as I went down, face first, and the blood that followed, when I was seventeen and with my exchange student boyfriend.

He raises his eyebrows. 'Sometimes it's worth the risk,' he says mischievously and, just for a second, holds my gaze. Something in me lights up, and goes out again as he looks towards the hive of activity around the ice rink.

I clear my throat. 'Is that what you're doing on Sunday?' I can't look him in the eye. 'At the baking competition. Taking a risk?' I take a sip of the hot chocolate and burn my tongue, which makes me cough, and spill half of my drink into the saucer.

He laughs, his hair bouncing as he throws his head back, his Adam's apple bobbing up and down. 'Did Heinrich send you to work out my plans? To try to persuade me to sell to him?'

'No,' I blush. 'Well . . . yes.' I swallow. 'A bit . . .'

'You'd make a terrible spy.' He laughs some more.

'I know.' I dab my mouth with the cloth, then hold it in my lap, laughing too. 'It's just . . . he asked me to get an idea. Said it would help you and him if he knew he was going to win on Sunday. He said you needed an excuse to sell to him and this would make it easier, to save face.'

'Did he now?' The laughter has subsided. 'Look,' he leans over the counter towards me and suddenly my insides leap around. This time I look straight at him, and can't turn away. 'I'm going to do everything I can to make sure I don't have to sell to Heinrich. I owe it to, well, everyone. My father, my son. My father built this place up with my grandfather. Everyone came here for the Christmas markets. Every year they looked forward to the Christmas baking competition. And when my father and Heinrich's rowed and went their separate ways, well, for a while, no one could touch us. Until I went away to work with one of the biggest bakers in Europe. Learn new skills.'

He tops up our hot chocolate. It smells just like it did in the market the other day. Then he walks back into the little kitchen and returns with a bottle. Asbach brandy. He holds it up and raises an eyebrow, as if asking permission to add it. Well, why not? I've blown it here. I might as well relax and enjoy myself. He adds a splash to mine and then to his. It makes me smile. I can't imagine Heinrich adding a splash of brandy to his hot chocolate, but maybe that's why Heinrich's making a go of things and William is taking a less structured path.

'You like it?' He nods to the hot chocolate.

It fills me with a delicious warmth as it slides down my throat and into my stomach. 'Very much.'

'I make the hot chocolate here and take it over to be sold in the square. It's my father's recipe. Never changed. Reminds me of my childhood.'

'Gingerbread does that for me.'

We sip in silence.

'Why did your father and Heinrich's father fall out in the first place?'

He shrugs. 'I think it was a difficult time, for both families. Heinrich's family had just lost their son, Maurice, and I think the business took the brunt of their distress. Heinrich's father wanted to make things more competitive and cost-effective. My father wanted to keep the soul of the shop and the baking. They fought over it and then Heinrich's father moved to the New Town. But the competition between the two of them just got fiercer and fiercer every year. The markets got better and better. More and more people came. The old man in the big castle loved the markets so much he left a legacy for the best Christmas bake and the battle lines were drawn. His family have to choose a winner every year. And every year my father won. But then, when we thought nothing could touch us, I went to Cologne. It was the year before my mother died . . .' For a moment, we are both lost in worlds that belong to another lifetime. Me with my grandmother, him clearly with his mother. 'So, I came back,' he snaps out of it, 'married, had a child and threw myself into the business. Sadly, it wasn't a happy mix.'

I wonder whether I should ask any more, but he goes on: 'Somehow Heinrich and his family have won the competition every year since then, creating bigger and better installations. My father fell into a decline.' He takes a deep breath. I notice he's busying himself making another batch of lebkuchen and I'm pretty sure he doesn't even know he's doing it. It seems to be his safe place. A bit like mine, I think. He lets out a big sigh and rolls out the dough. 'And then Marta, my wife, gave me an ultimatum. I had to choose between her and this place.' He pounds the dough. 'And with that, she left. I shouldn't have hesitated. I should have just gone with her.' He stops pummelling the dough. 'Overworked,' he says, and I'm not sure if he's talking about the dough or himself. He scoops it up and puts it into the bin.

He leans against the counter. 'But you still have hope – you're here to be with Heinrich!' He's teasing me. He scrapes off his hands and starts again.

'I was married,' I blurt out. 'I do know what it's like

to lose hope . . . your dreams. Everything. Well, nearly everything. But I still had my son.'

There is a moment of understanding between us.

'But now you're looking for love on the internet and here with Heinrich. And have you found it? Are you and Heinrich in love?'

'I . . .' Suddenly tongue-tied. Love. Where does love come into all of this? Is it something that grows, with time?

'Well, he must mean something to you if you came here to find out about my installation for Sunday.' He laughs.

I shrug. 'He . . . ticks all the boxes on my list,' I say. 'We're a good match, right for each other.'

'Show me,' he says, half teasing again.

I sigh, knowing I'm humouring him, and pull out my notebook.

'See?' I open it to the page with Heinrich's name and the list.

William pulls his thin, gold-rimmed glasses from his top pocket and begins to read, his finger stopping at each tick, nodding and agreeing. 'Yes, I can see what you mean. He does tick all the right boxes. You will make the perfect pair by the look of it.' He pulls off his glasses. 'But?'

'But what?'

'Nothing.' The book stays open on the worn countertop. He takes a sip of his hot chocolate.

'Go on,' I persist.

'Well, it's just . . . like I say, lots of good ingredients, a great recipe, but what about the alchemy? Do you love him?'

'I . . . Well, not yet,' I stutter. 'But I'm sure . . . that will come,' I say, gathering confidence. 'It's about finding the right match and then the love will grow.'

'You hope,' he says, draining his cup. 'Sometimes what looks perfect can be hollow inside.'

I take a sip of my brandy-laced hot chocolate. 'He told me . . .' I say slowly.

'What? What did Heinrich tell you?'

'That he'd offered to buy the bakery from you. That you needed the money. That if you sold to him, well, it might give you another chance with your family.'

There's a moment's silence.

'He told you that?'

'Yes.'

There is silence again. He's looking at the fresh ingredients on the work bench. Is he thinking about his own marriage? Was that hollow inside?

'He said that was the only reason you'd finally agree to sell.'

Again he says nothing. Then: 'Do you know what this place means to me? This place is everything. Who I am. If I'm not baking I'm not sure who I am.'

'And would you do that? Give it up for a chance to be back with your family?'

He lets out a long breath. 'Was that what this was all about? When you first contacted me to talk about the gingerbread, was it just so you could help Heinrich win on Sunday?'

'No! It wasn't. That was a mistake. I mean, I meant to send a message to someone else.'

'But that is what you're doing here, right?' He raises both his eyebrows, one higher than the other.

A hot red rash races up my chest, around my neck, into my cheeks and burns the tips of my ears. 'Today, yes. But not before, not the gingerbread. That was for Pearl. And me. And today . . . I thought I was helping, I really did.'

'Well, if I want Heinrich's help, I'll ask for it. But no. I've told him I'm not selling to him. This isn't over until Sunday and I'm not intending to lose. It's time we got that cup back here in the Old Town.'

I nod. My ears and cheeks are still burning.

'I should go now,' I say, sliding off the stool. 'Sorry, I shouldn't have come.'

I turn to leave, just as a crowd of holidaymakers opens the door and starts filing in, taking photographs and picking up handfuls of gingerbread hearts to buy.

'A coach party. Good for the till,' he says resignedly. He smiles tiredly as they pile into the shop, gathering up gingerbread and stollen. William begins to serve them, with his usual lazy smile and thanks.

In the background the clock-tower bell chimes. I stand and watch the large party, some coming out and more going in. I can't move. I see what William means.

This place could be a gold mine with more visits like this one. He can't afford to let these sales pass him by.

Suddenly William freezes. 'The bell!' he says.

'Yes, it's lovely,' I agree.

'No, I mean, yes! Oh, God! I have to go! I have to be somewhere. I can't be late! I am late!' he says, as the shop fills again, until it's full to bursting. 'I'm late! I promised I wouldn't be – not this time. Sorry, you'll all have to leave,' he calls. But no one hears him. The shop is heaving with people picking up gingerbread hearts, taking photos of themselves, selfie sticks waving around.

'I really have to go.' He glances at me and at the door. 'My father is coming to mind the shop later. After band practice. I just need help getting everyone out.'

'I'll do it,' I say quickly.

'Okay, ask them to come back in an hour,' he says.

'I mean I'll mind the shop,' I say, over the buzz.

'You?'

'Yes!' I say firmly. 'I'll mind the shop. I'll look after the customers. I'll work out the till, don't worry.'

The clock has long since stopped chiming. He looks anxiously at the door, frozen to the spot, clearly in two minds.

He looks back at me, and I know exactly what that looks means.

'You can trust me,' I say, 'I promise. I won't look. I owe you, for the lebkuchen lesson.'

He gives me another long look. 'I'm late – I'm always late!'

'Then go!' I say. 'Now!'

With just a split second of hesitation, he nods. A nod that says 'Thank you' and 'I trust you. I'm relying on you.'

'I won't look. I promise. I'll stay until your father gets here.'

He dips into the back room, grabs his coat and pushes his arms into it as he struggles to get through the smiling crowd in the shop. Then he's gone and I'm ringing up sales as hands are thrust at me with gingerbread and notes to fill the till. It's the least I can do to apologize for turning up to spy on him. I have to show him I understand and I'm not going to let him down.

# THIRTY-TWO

Finally, the bell over the door tinkles again as the last of the Japanese tourists leave, smiling, thanking me, taking selfies of me with them and wishing me, '*Fröhliche Weihnachten*! Happy Christmas!'

I'm still smiling as they leave. I loved it, but I'm exhausted. There's still no sign of William's father. I decide to see if there is any hot chocolate left to revive me while I wait, without the brandy this time. If another coach party comes in, I want to be ready. The till is looking pretty healthy after that visit. A few more customers would really help things along. And then I check myself. This isn't my business, any of it, I remind myself. William has made that clear. I need to stay out of it. And that's what I intend to do. By Sunday I just have to decide if Heinrich and I have a future, not whether William's business or the Old Town's market will survive another year.

It's not my business, I repeat, going in search of the hot chocolate, and I'm not going to get involved any more.

Fritz barks in a friendly way and I bend down to pat him, reassuring him after the busy half-hour in the shop.

I see a small hotplate with a pan on it and cups hanging on hooks. I head towards it. Then I stop, still. The worn wooden door to his workshop is there on my right, ajar. He can't have closed it properly when he went to get his coat. I feel guilty even looking at the door. My heart is thumping. Whatever creation he has behind it is the difference between make or break for him. I know it. He deserves every bit of luck. Heinrich has his life planned out already, so he can leave this one to Fate. I put my hand out to the brass doorknob.

'Just one photo,' I hear Heinrich's voice. 'Just to get an idea of what he's doing.'

I look at my hand on the doorknob as the bell goes in the shop. I slam the door shut. It's not my business. Or my battle. Everyone deserves a fair chance on Sunday. I turn to the shop expecting to see William's father standing there. But it's not him.

But he does look very much like him. From beneath the long dark fringe and dark glare, I can see the long straight nose. The wide jaw, with a twitch in it. He's not tall, but dark and broad. Just like his dad.

'Hello? Um . . .'

'Who are you?' he demands. He has his father's manners – I'm remembering the first day I met William.

'I'm—'

'Are you my dad's girlfriend?'

'No, no!' I put up both hands.

'I'm . . .' What am I? His nemesis's girlfriend? Here to spy on him?

'I'm a friend,' I say hopefully. 'Just helping out.' I hold out a hand to the shop. Fritz moves to sit at his feet but the boy doesn't respond to him. The dog doesn't move, staying by his side.

'Looks like someone's missed you,' I say, but the boy doesn't respond, doesn't look down at the dog gazing up at him, wagging his tail. I think ignoring him is maybe taking quite a bit of effort.

'Where's my grandfather?' the boy asks abruptly.

'On his way,' I answer, as economically as he has questioned me. 'Your dad is out too,' I tell him.

'Yes. With my mother. Talking. If he remembered,' he says, with an angry sneer.

'Oh, he did. He was really keen not to be late,' I try to reassure him.

'But he probably was. He always is. It's always baking first with him.'

I don't respond. I daren't tell him William was late, but it was because he was distracted. I distracted him, being in the shop, because Heinrich sent me. There is a chill in the air and it's not coming from outside.

The boy is looking around, as if it's been a while since he was here.

'I was, um, just about to have some hot chocolate. Would you like some?'

At first, I think he's going to say no. But then he nods, just once.

I turn to the little stove and wonder if he's finally greeting Fritz.

I heat the chocolate, stirring it, then pour it into cups. When I turn he's sitting on the wooden stool by the counter. He's so like his father and grandfather. But he's agitated.

I hand him the chocolate and take a sip of my own. It's wonderful. I watch him sip his, and hope this does the job of calming him down.

'What's your name?' he asks abruptly.

'Connie. What's yours?'

'Noah.'

I blow on my hot chocolate and for a moment we say nothing.

'Your dad told me about you.' I wonder how long it will be before Joseph is here to help out.

'Did he? When? I thought you were just helping out? Where did you come from and why are you here?'

'I'm with some friends.' I decide not to mention Heinrich. 'I've come to scatter another friend's ashes.'

'Her what?'

'Her ashes. She grew up in Germany and wanted her ashes scattered here. We're here to celebrate her life.'

'Ewww!'

'She grew up with the Christmas markets and she loved them. Said Christmas was all about remembering the ones you love, whether you were spending it with them or missing them. It's a good time to remember we're lucky to have people who love us.'

He shakes his head, clearly thinking I'm talking sentimental codswallop. I try a different tack, hoping to keep him talking until Joseph gets here or William is back. He'll be sad if he misses his son. I know that.

'Your dad is working really hard to win on Sunday. He's spent hours on his final cake. He won't let anyone see it.'

'Not surprised. He always preferred spending time baking than being with us. Mum said so.'

It's like walking through a minefield: I'm causing a minor explosion with everything I say. I'd forgotten what hard work young people can be. Sam never really gave me too much trouble, but occasionally there was the usual teenage sullenness when he felt the world, including his dad and me, had let him down.

'Well, hopefully they're talking now. That's good, isn't it?' I try not to take his rudeness personally. I sip the hot chocolate.

'Mum says he chose baking over us. He loved baking more.'

'Oh, I'm sure that's not true. He just . . . well, we all have to make a living. And baking . . .' I remember his words '. . . it just gets under your skin.'

He puts down the cup. 'Excuse me, I need to use the bathroom,' he says, as he slides off the stool.

At that moment, the bell tinkles and in come some more tourists. It's obviously the day for coach trips to the town. A smaller group this time, but I'm determined to make sure everyone is served, leaves happy and the till is even fuller. The shop fills again and I'm serving and smiling.

'Hey!' I call, towards the back of the shop. 'You could give me a hand out here!' I smile, hoping that when William gets back it'll be a nice surprise for him to see his son behind the counter helping out. At least I'll have done some good here today.

I strain my neck a little to see if he's back there. The door to the workshop is ajar again. Didn't I shut it properly? Or has it opened again? I need to shut it. I'll just serve these few customers. Looks like the ice rink has done its job in bringing more visitors to the town.

'Noah!' I call, hoping to get to the door to shut it before William comes back and wonders if I've looked in. I need him to believe I haven't. I need him to believe I gave my word and I intend to stick to it and stay out of this business.

'Thank you. *Danke!*' My schoolgirl German comes in handy at last, taking me back to that exchange trip and how I felt then. Happy and with a future ahead of me.

I strain to catch sight of Noah. But I can't see him at all. I look around the shop. I even stand on a small wooden stepladder, clearly there for William or anyone else to reach the higher wooden shelves behind the counter. I climb it and look over the heads of the tourists. But I can't see him. Has he slipped off without saying anything? I'm very disappointed. I really hoped he'd wait to see his dad. It might have made up for my earlier mess. If he'd been here when William had got back, it would have been good for both of them. I climb down the wooden stepladder and breathe out a big sigh. The coach party seems to be filtering out now, wishing me a merry Christmas, clutching lebkuchen hearts. As the last leaves I take my moment to shut the workshop door. I reach for the handle and something or someone moves.

'Noah! No!' I shout, just as William's son leans back, lifts his foot high and kicks. I throw the door wide as the huge sugar-crafted, chocolate-carved, painted paste sculpture of a winter wonderland – with huge polar bear, mouth open, showing its sharp teeth as it roars, protecting its two cubs on a melting ice cap behind an icy sea of water, with groups of penguins on ice islands – collapses into a massive cloud of rising sugar. Just as the bell over the door rings, Noah glares at me once more, pushes past me and runs out through the white cloud, past the figure in the middle of the shop. I stand rooted to the spot, waiting, heart thundering, for the dust to settle.

# THIRTY-THREE

Joseph is standing in the middle of the shop, white powder over his hat, his beard, his glasses and shoulders, like Father Christmas straight from the North Pole. Only he isn't Father Christmas. I feel sick. A piece of work as amazing as that, highlighting climate change, is now a pile of dust. The irony isn't lost on me. William had everything riding on his sculpture and now everything is ruined. Not just Christmas, but his business, the future of the market and the other businesses in it. It's all my fault! What was I doing, inviting the boy in, hoping I could fix things for William? What am I going to tell him? What am I going to tell anyone about anything?

I look around the shop, white dust covering every surface. Joseph still hasn't moved. I think he's in shock.

And then the bell over the door tinkles, letting in a freezing chill from outside.

*

William felt happier than he had in a long time. Marta had wanted to talk, to know his plans. He'd told her that if he won on Sunday, if they won the cup back for the town, he'd rethink. Maybe look at taking on staff, especially in the run-up to the Christmas markets next year. He'd enjoyed having Connie in the shop. It had made him remember how much he loved being there, doing what he did. He didn't want to sell up if he could help it. He wanted to compromise, make it work for all of them. He wondered if Connie would like to work with him, but of course he couldn't ask her: she was Heinrich's girlfriend. Heinrich and his family would never allow that. And if he didn't win on Sunday, well, everything would change anyway and he would have no shop to worry about.

He couldn't help but notice that Marta hadn't seen that idea as terrible. They could move away, start again, she'd suggested. But to where? To do what? It was a lot to think about. He would be back with his son and his wife. A family again. Back to how they were. But would it be how they were if he no longer had the shop, if he no longer baked? Or would it feel like failure?

He pulled his scarf tighter as the day grew colder. He passed small groups of people taking to the ice and stopped to watch them, then to talk with the foreman and workmen who were packing up and leaving instructions. He listened, took his receipt and care details and smiled at the skaters. He'd have liked it to be busier, but word would get around . . .

He hoped his son would want to come with his friends. He'd make sure they had a good time. He wanted to let Noah know how much he loved and missed him. If he won on Sunday, he'd take time out to show him how he felt, just the two of them. Maybe a trip to Cologne, to the market there. He just needed this win. This year he had a feeling things were going to be different and he hurried to the shop. He thought of Connie. He trusted her. He knew she hadn't let him down.

# THIRTY-FOUR

The three of us are standing in the shop. No one speaks.

I clear my throat and open my mouth, but no words come out.

I feel my blood freezing in my veins.

He stares at me with a darkness that goes right to his soul and mine.

There are no words, no words at all. How can I tell him it was his son who did this to him, ruined everything he and the town have worked for?

I grab my coat and bag and run out of the shop. The bell over the door jangles madly as I leave. A sob catches in my throat, and I cry all the way back to the guesthouse.

# THIRTY-FIVE

'Breathe, dear. Tell me what's happened,' says Pearl, beside the living Nativity's manger. 'Is it Heinrich? Has something happened?'

They all shuffle around in the straw and find a seat for me next to the donkey, which snuffles at me with warm whiskers against the cold air.

I stop crying for a moment. I take a deep breath and look up at Pearl. I shake my head. 'I think Heinrich's going to ask me to marry him,' I say between gulps.

Everyone stops fussing around and stands stock-still, like the perfect tableau, gathering around a bent-headed Mary.

Then they're all asking questions.

'Is there a ring?'

'Where's the list? Did we write "a proposal for Christmas" on it?'

'Will it be a winter wedding?'

'Will it be soon?'

'I've always dreamed of a Christmas proposal,' says Alice.

'Just a minute,' says Pearl. 'If you think Heinrich is going to ask you to marry him, why are you crying?'

They fall silent again.

'Oh, Pearl, I did something dreadful.'

I take a deep breath and tell them about Heinrich, the ring, William and the fallen cake. They are silent, as if they're staring at the debris of the town's hopes and dreams. 'It's all my fault,' I say, my face screwed up in mortification.

'Yes,' says Maeve.

'But you were just trying to help,' says Norman, kindly.

'And if I'm understanding things right, it was William's son who did this, not you,' Pearl says slowly.

'But I let him in. Told him to make himself at home. I was trying to get him to wait for his dad.'

'But not to sabotage his dad's year-long work,' Di adds, and Graham nods in agreement.

I take a deep breath as someone hands me a mug of glühwein. 'But I didn't look at the cake. I really didn't. I should probably explain to him,' I say.

They all agree.

'But I have no idea how to convince him I'm telling

the truth without hurting him even more by telling him it was his son. The son he's missed so much.'

'So does that mean the competition is off? The other town will win?' says Maeve.

They all mutter in agreement.

'Looks like Heinrich gets his Christmas wish,' I say.

'Which is what? You or buying the shop?'

'Both, I think, Maeve. It's all part of the life plan. Heinrich likes a plan and he likes it to happen on time.'

'What about William?' asks Pearl.

'He'll be . . . devastated. And it's all my fault. Why, oh why do I always think I can help? Why can't I leave things alone, leave people to get on with their own lives?'

'Because if you did that, dear, none of us would see anyone from one day to the next,' says Maeve, surprising me.

'And we'd be living off toast and marmalade,' adds Pearl, with a smile.

Back in the guesthouse, I pull out my phone and hunch over it, while perched on the edge of my bed, and try to write something but the right words won't come. I can't imagine how he must be feeling. But I must find the words. I owe him that much at least.

In the shop the little bubbles of writing appeared on William's screen and disappeared again. No words or explanation arrived. He closed the screen and held his head in his hands.

In my room at the guesthouse, I slam the phone shut. For once I can't do this. I may have spent the last few years carrying out all my conversations online, looking for a life partner, the biggest decision you can make in life. But I can't do this from behind the screen of my computer. This is something I have to do face to face.

# THIRTY-SIX

I pull on my hat and walk down the wooden stairs, decorated with swags of greenery and smelling of pine and beeswax. I look around. There's no one about, apart from Anja.

'Hello, dear. Looking for your friends?'

'I, er . . . Well, where are they exactly?'

'Down at the ice rink, watching the skaters. Sad that Maeve won't get to skate and the list will be unfinished.'

Pearl's Christmas memory list, unfinished. Our time here in the Old Town is definitely coming to an end. I have one more date with Heinrich. One more night to decide what I'm going to do, if I plan to make a life with him. I think of my list and the boxes I've ticked. Why am I feeling so hesitant? I said that if he ticked all the boxes, he'd be the one. And he does! I'm sure he does! But that's for later. There is something else I need to do first.

I head out of the heavy wooden door, the green wreath with ribbons framing the knocker. Outside flakes of snow are starting to fall, bigger than before.

Snow. Alice's Christmas wish. Tick.

I put my head down and hurry towards the market square. I stop as I reach the corner of the building. It's beautiful. The snow is swirling in the soft orange glow of the streetlamps and landing on the roofs of the little chalets, all lit up with white fairy lights that lead towards the covered terrace in the middle. Steam from the glühwein is rising to mingle with the snowflakes. The air smells of sausages, spicy and tantalizing, and roasting chestnuts. It smells like a place I've come to love. It couldn't be more perfect. Tears spring to my eyes again. And now, thanks to me, it will never happen again.

I head out into the square, where I can see the group all leaning on the side of the ice rink, watching, if I'm not mistaken, Pearl and Norman on the ice. I stop and stare. How fabulous is that? Neither of them is scared about falling: they're just doing it. I turn to the corner of the market and the street where the bakery is. I have to put this right. I have no idea how.

I put my head down against the snow and walk on, heart thumping. Why did I have to get involved? It was none of my business. Trust is what a relationship is all about. And trusting yourself. I'm cross with myself. And cross with Heinrich too, I realize. Am I cross? I ask myself. Is that what this feeling is? My insides are twisted and knotted, my heart is pounding, my mouth dry. Or is it something else? Is it that I feel something I haven't felt in a long time? If ever. Did I ever feel like this at seventeen when I thought I was in love? And when I was with Tom? I thought it was love. I thought I cared about him and him about me. But he couldn't have done, not when he'd left me for my 'own good'. That was what he said. He thought we made each other unhappy. Do you leave someone you really love? Or do you try to make it right?

I lift my head and stop in my tracks as a figure appears from the bottom of the cobbled lane. The snowflakes are tickling my nose and cheeks.

It's William.

He stands still and gazes at me. The snowflakes fall between us. I'm terrified. I'm not sure if it's because of what he's going to say to me, or how I'm going to explain what happened, or how just seeing him is making me feel right now and knowing I may never feel like this again.

Suddenly his dog shoots off at speed, legs and ears flying. We turn to look in the direction he's running.

'Fritz!' William calls, throws his hands into the air, turns back to me without a hint of anything I can read on his face, then races after his dog through the snow towards the ice rink and the group standing there.

I watch Fritz fly towards my friends, ears flapping, and to one person in particular. He skids to a halt and rests his head in her lap. Maeve rubs his ears, then holds his face in both hands and smiles.

William slows to a walk and allows Fritz to sit with Maeve, him staring up at her, her down at him. He glances over his shoulder at me and, again, my insides lurch and resettle, but this time in a whole new configuration. I take a few steps towards him, but stop. I can't say everything I need to say in front of everyone. He walks over to Maeve, bends and pats Fritz's head. I stand and watch as the group begin to chat. Pearl and Norman make their way off the ice and, smiling, begin to talk to William. He stands, listens, nodding, understanding. And then he holds up a hand and walks towards the skating kiosk. I watch from a distance, hugging my arms around myself as he reappears and sits down, takes off his boots and puts on skates. A small smile tugs at the corners of my mouth. Even at a time like this, he's making sure the visitors enjoy their time here. Having laced his skates, he gets up and walks over to Maeve. He bends to speak to her. Then, at a nod from her, he grasps the wheelchair handles firmly and pushes her to the rink, holding tightly as the wheels slide onto the ice.

Then, confirming everything I think about this caring, kind man, whose passion for baking runs through his veins, as deeply as it does for his family and his town, and who is far too engrossed in his passion to pay attention to timekeeping, he glides around the ice pushing Maeve in her wheelchair, her smile widening all the time. Finally, to Céline Dion's 'My Heart Will Go On', the *Titanic* theme, she holds out her arms in her plastic cape, as if she's as free as a bird, as she was before the wheelchair. Tears slide down my cheeks for Maeve, for the memories we've rediscovered and the ones we lost along the way.

I walk over to the group as William is wheeling her off the ice.

'Oh, that was wonderful!' Maeve's hands are clasped together, her cheeks pink, and she embraces Fritz, who is waiting for her. Everyone is gathered around her, all smiling and as pink-cheeked as she is. Anja is there, handing around glühwein.

'Thank you so much, William. You are a wonderful man. I hope things work out for you,' says Maeve.

He nods, sadly. 'I'm glad you enjoyed it.' But the market is half empty. 'I just wish we could have got more people here.'

'Don't know what they're missing!' says Maeve, still beaming and breathless.

'Oh,' says Norman. 'The New Town got a ski slope put in, on a big piece of land behind the theatre. I heard it from the knitters' circle I met with this morning for coffee at the jumpers stall.'

Pearl's surprise shows on her face. 'You've become

very friendly with the knitters,' she says. If I didn't know better, I'd say there was a tiny hint of jealousy there. But Pearl has always said she's never wanted another man. And if Norman has fallen for one of the knitters, good for him.

A ski slope! I look at William. He lifts his chin and breathes in deeply. So that was Heinrich's surprise. Always trying to go one better. Always wanting to outdo William and the Old Town.

I stare at William. Suddenly he looks straight at me. And in that moment, I realize it, like scales falling from my eyes. My exchange student when I was seventeen wasn't the one who got away. I just thought he was. When Sam's dad left me, I wanted there to have been more out there so I made myself believe I'd had a first love that got away. Made myself believe I was still looking for a version of him by coming here to meet Heinrich. I think about Tom leaving me, telling me it was better for me if he went. But if it had been love, real love, he'd have stayed and weathered the storm. You don't leave the ones you love when the going gets tough. He didn't love me. We just rubbed along. If it had been love, he'd have stayed with me. Is that what Heinrich would do for me or me for him? Would we stand by each other even when life was tough? Or would we just rub along?

'So have you found love?' William's words come back to me. Have I found love in Heinrich? Dare I admit I want more than just a tick list? Could I grow to love him? Suddenly there is a final box I need to tick: am I in love?

I back away from the group.

'Connie!' I hear William call.

'Sorry, there's somewhere I have to be,' I call back, and run towards the bridge, towards Heinrich's factory and shop, as fast as I can.

# THIRTY-SEVEN

'Connie? You're early.' Heinrich frowns.

'I know, but I really needed to see you,' I say, out of breath, standing in the brightly lit shop.

'That is very nice. Very nice indeed.' He attempts to smile but he's clearly a bit thrown: the sales assistant had had to explain that I was here and needed to see him.

'Is there somewhere we can go? To talk?' I ask.

'Well, I have a table booked for us at seven. I'm due to pick you up. I have a special taxi.'

'Special?'

He beams. 'It was supposed to be a surprise. I have a horse and carriage picking you up to bring you to the restaurant.'

'You did that? For me?'

He nods.

I wait for the butterflies to flutter in my stomach. But they don't come. Where are they?

He looks at me, clearly concerned. 'But I could cancel it . . . see if we could have drinks in the bar first.' He's still holding his watch, like a safety blanket. 'I'd have liked to organize this first, of course,' he says, as he dials. 'It is our last night after all, a special one.' He smiles, but somehow it doesn't reach me, although I really, really want it to, and I can't smile back. I need to talk to him. I need to work out exactly how I feel. 'Tomorrow is your last day here in the New Town,' he says, looking at his watch *again*!

If we got engaged, married even, would our life be one long schedule that we had to keep to? I clench my fists and release them anxiously. If he really is going to ask me to marry him, I have to know how I'm going to answer. Am I going to say yes and take this chance, a chance on us?

'Okay, we have a table for drinks at the bar. I'm just going to organize my desk, cancel the carriage ride . . .' he looks at my anxious face '. . . and check with my manager that everything is in hand. Do you need to change?'

'No, I'm fine,' I say, impatient to get off my chest what's on it.

He goes up to his glass-fronted office and takes his time organizing his desk. Then he speaks to his manager on the factory floor, checking his watch and going over the plan for the morning and tomorrow's early-evening baking competition.

Finally, we get to the restaurant and he leads me to the bar, overlooking the square and the ski slope.

'I pulled some strings,' he says, pleased with himself, still adjusting his jacket and hair. 'So, some champagne?' He reaches for the bottle in the ice bucket and pulls it out, dabbing off the moisture with a napkin before he opens it.

'Actually, could I have some water first, please?' I ask, my mouth dry.

Everything is picture perfect, even Heinrich, and yet, deep in my heart, there is someone I would much rather be with.

'Heinrich? Why me?' I ask, and it comes out blunter than I was expecting.

'Well, because we are the perfect match for each other. We like the same things. Want the same things.'

'Do we?' I blurt. 'I mean . . . I'm only just finding out what I want, who I am, and if I'm only just discovering that, how can you know?'

'Are you okay, Connie? You seem different this evening.' He frowns, and puts the bottle down.

'I'm fine. I'm good. I'm . . . actually, really good. Heinrich, if you could have one Christmas memory to stay with you, what would it be?'

'That's easy!' He looks at me with delight on his face, as if he has everything he wants right here in front of him. 'I will win tomorrow and make sure everyone knows who is the rightful winner of the competition, the best winter market.' He adds, 'And, of course, for you to agree to my proposal.'

I take a moment to let it all sink in, to work out why I'm disappointed by his reply.

'You can have all the right ingredients . . .' I hear William's words in my head and try and shake them. But I can't shake the urgent feeling of what I have to do now.

'Heinrich, if you could have anyone around your Christmas table, who would it be?' I'm thinking of William, wanting the ones he loves.

His face changes. 'My brother, Maurice,' he says evenly, and I nod.

'You miss him?'

He doesn't answer the question straight away.

'Things were different then. Maybe I would have taken a different direction in life, instead of working for the family business. He left a hole in the family. We never really got on,' he gives a small laugh, 'but, yes, I miss him. And how life might have been different,' he finishes quietly. The words hang in the air. This is the most I've seen of the 'real' Heinrich. All the rest of it is just . . . ticking boxes. For all those boxes, we don't really know each other at all. He's being the son his family want him to be. He's trying to take his brother's place. He's not living his life, he's living someone else's. And I'm not sure that's a great recipe for a relationship.

'Did you ever just take a chance on love?'

'Love'. The one word missing in all our lists.

'I did. Once.' He nods sharply. This is unknown territory for him, I can tell.

'What happened?' I ask, before he changes his mind and clams up.

'It didn't work out. We wanted different things. She went to America to work.' He's looking down at the empty champagne glass.

'Do you ever wish you'd followed her?'

He stares into the empty glass. 'It wouldn't have worked.' He shakes his head. 'I was needed here. And if it hadn't worked out . . .' He shrugs.

'But what if it had?' I say slowly, letting the words form in my head. 'What if it was worth taking the chance? If you'd just followed your instincts.'

'Instincts can get you into a lot of trouble,' he says, shutting down the conversation, and I know he's talking about his brother.

'Or maybe you find just what you're looking for,' I say, so quietly that I'm not sure I've even said it out loud. 'Heinrich, have you ever been engaged before?' I ask suddenly.

'Er, no. Not actually engaged.' He seems a little uncomfortable.

'Have you ever met anyone online and proposed before?' The thought suddenly appears in my head.

'Well, yes. A couple of times.'

'A couple?'

'Yes, we met, got on. But they . . . well, they haven't worked out.' Then, more brightly, 'But this time I'm sure you and I have everything that it takes.'

'All the boxes ticked,' I say sagely.

'Exactly.'

Except one.

'But actually, Connie, there's something I wanted to talk to you about.'

'Oh?' I focus on his face in the here and now, not ten years down the road.

'I've been doing a lot of thinking. Planning, really.' He looks up from the empty glass. 'You say your boss is selling your business?'

'Yes, but I can't—'

'And you don't have the money to buy it?'

I nod.

'Well, how about I move to the UK, buy the business and we run it together? I could tell my parents that we are pushing the cakes into the UK. Especially with Brexit, it might be a way to expand without all the complications that are going to go with it now. What do you say?'

He has it all worked out. This is everything I could have wanted. A man I know I can get along with, who is kind and thoughtful, and always on time. He is financially independent, successful even, and looks and smells lovely. He even knows which Haribo sweets are my favourite. And now he wants to move to the UK to be with me, and run a business with me that I really want to buy. If only I could forget the final question on the list.

'Heinrich, that's a really kind offer.' But this proposal isn't about love: it's about business and a plan coming together. It's also telling me he's trying to stretch the ties between him and his parents. He's looking for a way out.

'How would your parents feel about you moving to the UK?'

'Well, they would obviously take some time to get used to the idea, but I'm sure they'd come round when they saw the business sense in it.'

This is part of the reason Heinrich contacted me in the first place, looking for a UK girlfriend. It's part of a long-term plan. It's his escape route.

But he could be mine too, couldn't he?

'Heinrich, I could have bought the business. But I lost my money.'

'You said. Careless!' he tries to joke.

'Someone stole it from me. Someone I thought I trusted. I met a man online, and believed everything he told me because I wanted it to be true. I wanted him to be my perfect match. But I was fooling myself into thinking he was who he said he was. I lent him all my money because I wanted to believe I had found love. I hadn't. I never heard from him, or saw my money, again. The police said it happens all the time. That I shouldn't blame myself. I believed I was an intelligent woman, but I wanted to believe in something that wasn't there. I got it very wrong. But I think I've been fooling myself for a very long time.'

'It's okay.' He reaches over. 'We have both learned from the past and realize that this is the way forward.

We have been cautious and, that way, we can't lose. We won't get hurt. We are made for each other. It is science.'

Or is it because we can't get hurt if we don't love each other? That's the chance you take when you fall in love. It might really hurt. He is right. This is science. It's the right way. I want to say yes, but on the other hand, I need to be sure I'm doing the right thing. I need to listen to the voice in my heart, just to be sure that my head is taking me down the right path. Right now, my head and my heart are shouting so loudly I can hardly hear myself think. Everything I've been looking for is sitting in front of me, my future on a plate. But my heart keeps repeating, 'What about love? Will love grow?'

'Heinrich,' I say, looking down at the untouched water and champagne and take a deep breath, 'I'm really sorry, but there's somewhere I need to be right now.'

He frowns.

'Something I really need to do, to put right.' I stand up and grab my bag from beside me.

'But I have made plans. I thought we would eat, then go on the ski slope. I have a late slot booked. Then, I thought, back to mine. It is your last night.'

He has it all worked out, perfectly.

'And it sounds wonderful,' I say. It does. 'But I need to change the plans.'

'Change the plans?' He is aghast.

'Yes, Heinrich. Sometimes in life things happen and we need to change the plans.'

'But it's all booked.'

'Look, it's the competition tomorrow. You said yourself it's your Christmas wish to win. Ten years in a row.'

'And for you and me to become official,' he adds.

'Yes. You go and get ready for tomorrow. I need time to think.' If Heinrich wins tomorrow, because there is no other competitor, he wins by default, and the victory isn't worth anything, is it? It just turned up, ticked the box. For it to be a competition, for it to mean something, you have to put your heart on the table. The cake has to be made with love. I can hear William's words from our first email. Can a cake really make you happy if it's been made without love?

I have tonight to work out if I want to be with Heinrich. I can't mess him around. He's a good man, and is offering me everything I want in life right now, isn't he?

'I just need to think about . . . everything,' I say.

'Take your time. I understand. Making a list, checking it twice,' he jokes.

'Exactly.' I try to smile. 'I'll see you tomorrow,' I say and grab my coat, feeling bad about him sitting there with the unopened champagne, but I have to do this. I have to put this right for everybody.

'Tomorrow?' He stands and kisses me gently. It's nice. But no fireworks. I wish there were fireworks.

'Yes. Tomorrow.' I nod.

By tomorrow I need to decide whether I want to make my future with Heinrich, with a business I love, and a man I hope I could come to love. Tomorrow, we all have a chance to get what we want, but everyone has to have a fair chance. And I ruined William's. I can't leave feeling I did nothing. If Heinrich wins, it has to be because he won fair and square, not because I ruined someone else's chance of a Christmas memory.

# THIRTY-EIGHT

'William!' I'm standing in the snow outside the bakery under the orange glow of the streetlamp, snowflakes falling heavier, like feathers from the sky, tickling my face. The shop is dark and closed. So different from when I first saw it just a few days ago.

'William!' I push open the door, but everything is dark. There's no smell from the ovens. The shelves are bare. Not even Fritz is there to greet me. There is still a dusting of icing sugar over everything. I run my fingers along the wooden counter, making a line in the whiteness. My notebook is there, open at Heinrich's page. I brush off the icing sugar and see the ticks. I think about the effort he's put in to making this an amazing first few dates, an incredible Christmas memory. One I will never forget as I grow old.

I walk slowly into the back room where the fallen Christmas installation is, still in smashed pieces on the floor. I look around, for some kind of hope, I suppose. I pick up one of the penguins, still in one piece, but it cracks and crumbles in my hand. There must be a way of saving this, surely. I look down at the remnants.

'All the right ingredients,' I say sadly.

'But not the right timing,' a deep, gravelly voice says behind me.

I swing round to see William standing there. He looks like he hasn't slept in ages.

'Hi,' I say, waiting for him to be furious with me and tell me to leave.

'Hi,' he replies, stepping into the room, looking at the chaos that was clearly once a well-thought-out masterpiece. He paces around the room, passing the debris that was once his dreams and is now a crumbled mess on the floor.

'It was supposed to highlight how our actions and choices are destroying our world . . .' He trails off, with a half-hearted ironic laugh. His head drops and I can feel his despair. I reach out and hug him. I have no idea why, but I need to share the pain he's feeling. At first he doesn't move – he doesn't do anything. Then slowly he puts his arms around me, instinctively, and hugs me back, his face buried in my hair and mine in the crook of his neck, sharing his pain and mine for what I finally feel I've found and have been looking for all this time on a computer screen. Something that can't be found between the lines of a typed conversation or the pages of a recipe book, or a series of lists . . . a feeling of belonging. A feeling of freedom. And of loss, knowing I may never feel this again. Finally, we pull away from each other and I realize tears are rolling down our cheeks.

'I'm sorry,' I say, my throat tight with what feels like desire. 'I . . . I need to tell you—'

He cuts me off. 'It's okay. Maeve told me what happened, when I took her on the ice rink.'

'She did?' I say, surprised, and we finally break away from our impromptu embrace. 'What did she say?'

'She said that Noah had come here when I went to meet his mother. When I was late!' He runs his fingers through his dark hair, as if he's trying to get his thoughts under control too.

'That was my fault,' I say.

'No,' he says firmly. 'I should have kept an eye on the time. It's always been my problem. Baking, well, it just gets under your skin and everything else just comes after it. I get lost in my world. My wife, my ex, whatever,' he waves a hand around, clearly confused, 'she was right. I've always put baking first. And what have I got to show for it? A son who hates me, a wife who left me, and I barely noticed, just carried on as normal.'

'Baking is a good place to be when life leaves you feeling alone,' I say, my throat still tight with unspoken emotion, thinking about the times I'd baked after Tom, and then Sam, left home. It was the glue that held me together, connecting me to the past and who I used to be when I was younger, the dreams I'd had for life when I baked with my grandmother. Baking reminded me of who I was, connecting with me, even if I did end up delivering my cakes to the residents at the retirement flats. And it was Pearl and the others who brought me here. Pearl brought me to meet Heinrich. But right now it's not Heinrich I'm thinking about. It's me, who I am, how I'm feeling right now, and William, the town and the competition tomorrow, with a desire and a drive I haven't felt since I was a teenager. And whatever I might feel for Heinrich, however much I know he is a good man, and would do everything to make my life with him a good one, I know I have to make this competition fair.

'Look, about the competition . . .' I start.

He shakes his head. 'It's over. It's all over. I put everything I had into it this year. Borrowed against the business to get the ice rink in. I thought this year . . . I thought I'd done it. But it's time I admitted defeat. I can't win tomorrow now.' He walks back into the shop, behind the counter and rests his head in his hands, among the icing sugar. I follow him and stand beside him. I don't know what to say. I can't put how I'm feeling into words. He lifts his head. 'I will have to sell to Heinrich. It's time.'

I catch my breath. 'How is your father?' I ask suddenly.

'Upset.'

And I can't help but feel responsible still. If I hadn't tried to get his son to stay . . . But maybe I need to realize you only see what you want to see. I think about my first love. I was in love with the fantasy of being in love. I can barely remember what he looked like, other than his blond hair and that he was tall. Anyone who came afterwards, I tried to match up to this vision of my ideal man. But he didn't exist. I'd created an idea of a man I loved. But what if he'd loved me the way I wanted to be, and me him? No tick boxes. Just accepting each other for our differences, not our similarities. You can't choose who you fall in love with, I think. You can't invent a recipe for the perfect man and hope it will turn out right. He has to make you feel a certain way. He has to leave you thinking about him, wanting more . . .

Is that what I'm feeling now? Sometimes you have to follow your instincts. I step forward to William, take his face in my hands and lift it. He takes my face in his hands and looks at me with his deep, dark chocolate eyes, and I want to kiss him and keep kissing him, tasting this recipe: the one that doesn't have the right ingredients, that shouldn't work well together, but somehow you know is going to be amazing. And I suddenly feel a sense of freedom. To be me. Not tied to lists. Like I'm making the gingerbread my grandmother made, from memory, for the joy of it.

He drops his hands and turns away abruptly. My emotions are spinning and I'm desperate to be in his arms.

'Thank you for coming, but there's really nothing you can do now,' says William, standing with his back from me. 'Go to Heinrich. He'll be wanting to see you, I'm sure.'

He's right. There's nothing here that can be rebuilt. Heinrich is going to win tomorrow and buy the shop. I take a final look around. 'Are you sure I can't help clear up the mess?' I croak, as I finally realize that everything I've ever wanted and been looking for is right in front of me.

'Maybe I'll leave that for Heinrich when he buys the shop.' He gives another ironic laugh.

Heinrich buying the shop. Heinrich doesn't love the shop. It has all the right ingredients to sell his cakes but not the love that William puts into his. Real love. That's what our Christmas memories are about, remembering love, feeling loved. Not how big a present you can buy or receive. It's about remembering the ones we love, how we felt when we felt loved. Tom didn't love me. I let the words sit in my brain. My son, my grandmother, those Christmases cooking together: even when we didn't have money for big presents, that felt like love.

I walk towards the shop door. I grasp the brass handle and the bell tinkles. I look in the window, which is empty, except for the little gingerbread house. Its bright light has all but gone out, just a tiny flicker from the tealight, still trying to burn.

'I've got it!' I shout, and spin round to a surprised

William. Fritz barks as if he's heard me. And suddenly I'm beaming. 'Get your father! Meet me back here as soon as you can. And turn the ovens on.' I beam.

'What? What are you talking about?'

'Christmas! That's what I'm talking about. And your Christmas wish! Meet me back here!'

# THIRTY-NINE

I'm heading back to the shop, through the snowy square, barely half an hour later. There are a few families on the ice. Leaning on the barrier, watching them, is a small lone figure I recognize straight away. I stop and stare. All kinds of emotions fly around my head and my heart. Anger, sadness, empathy, loneliness . . . I take a deep breath and, instead of heading straight back to the shop, change direction and walk towards the lone figure, who looks as if life has forgotten him while everyone else enjoys the Christmas fun. Much like Pearl, Maeve, the others and myself before we got here, until we remembered the memories and the ones we loved and who loved us.

'Hey,' I say, leaning on the railing next to him.

He turns, startled, and glances around to see if I'm with anyone. He might be about to run.

'Don't worry, I'm on my own,' I say, looking at the

skaters, not at him. I remember that if I had to talk to Sam about something it was best done when I was in the car, driving, not making eye contact. 'Looks like you're feeling that too.'

I take another deep breath and wonder if anything I've got to say can make any difference. So far, all I seem to have done is create more trouble and mess for William. But one thing I am sure about is how much William loves his son, like I love Sam. No matter what happens in life, we never desert the ones we love. That's what love means: no matter where you are, how far apart, the memories are always there if you look carefully enough.

I'm at the front door of the bakery. The ovens are on. But nothing else is. I turn on the lights, pick up a cloth and start wiping down the surfaces.

William appears from the back room, holding two cups of hot chocolate and hands me one. I breathe it in, and detect a splash of Asbach. The scent of it will be imprinted on my memory for ever, like a photograph I can enjoy when I want to remind myself of being here.

'What's this all about?' He half smiles. He's clearly intrigued and possibly a little amused. 'I thought you'd be spending your last night here with Heinrich. I'm surprised he hasn't proposed yet.'

I raise my eyebrows, sipping the hot chocolate and wiping down the surfaces with my free hand.

'Ah!' William nods, as if maybe he's seen this happen before. 'Looks like everything's going his way.'

'He hasn't,' I say quickly.

'Yet,' he adds, looking at me with those dark eyes.

'Look, about the competition.' I change the subject quickly. 'We don't have much time.'

'There's nothing to be done. Really, I appreciate your concern, but—'

I cut him off. 'Remember? Your Christmas memory? Your wish?'

'Yes,' he says slowly.

'You said you'd want things back the way they were. And when I asked you who you'd have at your Christmas dinner table, you said the ones you love. You said, one last Christmas with your mum.'

'Yes,' he says.

'Then that's what we're going to do.'

He frowns.

'What?'

'Give you a Christmas with your mum.'

He frowns deeper and I can't help thinking how attractive he looks, as the half-smile widens. Something inside me flips over and back again.

'We're going to do Christmas here in the Old Town. The bakery. Your house upstairs. Your Christmas dinner table and the market in the square, outside, just like it was, with the ice rink for skating on Christmas Day with family and friends.'

He laughs. 'Really?'

'Yes, we're going to make a gingerbread town!'

'Just like that? You and me, in one night? It's a lovely idea but it will never happen.' He looks at me and my stomach flips. I feel tingles of excitement, like Christmas-tree lights going on, right down to my knees. 'We'd never get it done, I'm afraid.' He shakes his head and his dark curls bounce.

'We will,' I say, turning to the door, 'with all of us helping.'

The bell rings out brightly. There in the doorway are Pearl, Norman, Maeve, Ron, Alice, Graham with Di, Anja and, at the back, Joseph, looking less like Father Christmas now.

'Our way of saying thank you for all you've done this week to help make our stay so special,' says Pearl.

'Especially mine.' Maeve beams.

'What do you say?' I ask quietly.

He says nothing, staring at the group in front of him, standing in the sugar-dusted shop.

'We're all going to add our Christmas memories,' says Pearl.

'The merry-go-round!' says Ron.

'The ice rink!' joins in Maeve.

'The stall selling hot chocolate,' says Alice, dreamy-eyed.

'The Nativity,' adds Norman.

'The shop,' I say. Our eyes meet and lock as I think about the morning I came here to meet Heinrich.

'We'll make the gingerbread, you design and assemble

it,' I say quietly, thinking I've messed up again. Maybe it is a ridiculous idea. Maybe I've got it wrong again. 'I just thought, if we all want to remember Christmases gone by and our loved ones, if you recreated yours, before you left and your mum died, well, I can't think of anything more perfect for a Christmas baking competition. This place, the square, here, all of us with our memories.'

'It's worked for us!' says Norman, smiling.

William sighs. 'You're suggesting we make a gingerbread town – not just a house, a town, a Christmas market, with our Christmas memories in it. Overnight!'

'Connie can help us make the gingerbread. You tell us what to do and we'll have a go,' says Norman, cheerful as ever.

'I can help,' says Joseph, stepping forward. 'I'd love to be part of remembering your mum and our Christmases here when she was alive. I want to remember the love we felt.'

William has tears in his eyes.

'And me,' says a voice, and a smaller version of Joseph pushes himself forward through the small crowd standing there.

'Noah!'

'I'm sorry, Dad.' He flings himself into his father's arms. William hugs him, hard, his eyes screwed up tight. 'I just felt so angry. I thought you loved baking more than me.'

'Never,' says William. 'Never. I love baking because

of you. Because I thought it was a way to be a family, like it was for me as a child, growing up here. But your mum, well, she thought it was just a job. But baking isn't.'

'It's a passion, and once it's in your blood, there's no getting rid of it,' says Joseph, and Noah looks up at his grandfather.

'I'd like to help,' says the boy. 'To say sorry. Connie told me it was the right thing to do.'

'Connie?'

He nods. 'I was at the ice-skating rink. She saw me and told me she hadn't said it was me. But that I should. Being honest with yourself is the best way to be happy in life, she said.'

He looks straight at me and I blush. Am I being honest with myself? Do I want to commit to Heinrich? Do I believe that we have a future, based on our suitability on paper? Or should I trust the alchemy? Do I want a life that ticks all the boxes, or one that doesn't tick any but feels just right? Here and now, in this bakery, with him.

For a moment no one speaks.

'Then, yes, we should all put our Christmas memories into a gingerbread town. Not for the competition, but to remember the ones we love and why Christmas is the time to do that. It's not about being the biggest or the best. It's about how loved we feel and how much we love,' says William. Then he claps his hands together. 'Okay, let's get to work. Noah? You can sweep up the workshop. We're going to need all the space we can find!'

'On it!' Noah says, with a grin, grabs a broom and heads to the workshop.

'The rest of you, get your hands washed, aprons are by the door. Connie, you can start weighing the ingredients for the gingerbread, while I make a quick sketch.'

'Of course,' I say, as the bakery comes alive with chatter, ideas for what they want to make, everyone putting on aprons and sorting themselves into pairs. Once again William and I lock eyes, unable to drag ourselves away from each other's gaze as the shop busies into life.

'Would anyone like a Fox's Glacier Mint?' Ron asks.

'This watch hasn't kept time all week, I swear it's Aunt Lucy's!' Norman says.

'At least we have plenty of time in the morning. We wouldn't have done if we'd flown,' says Alice.

The shop, the back room and the kitchen come to life and begin to warm up as the ovens come up to temperature. Noah and Ron are clearing the ruined sculpture into big black bins. Pearl, Norman and Maeve are ready to make gingerbread.

'Di. You and Graham can make the icing to stick the buildings together.'

'We're the glue!' Graham smiles, resting on the stool.

'Start thinking what you want to make,' says William. 'Maeve, an ice rink in front of the town like this?' He makes a quick sketch, his glasses perched on the end of his nose, then shows her.

'Perfect!' she says, and gives an approving nod to Fritz, who is sitting happily in his bed, watching everyone, his pink tongue lolling out.

'And a merry-go-round.'

'And the bakery!' says Noah.

William sketches on his notepad as everyone calls out their ideas. He finishes and holds up the result. Everyone nods their approval.

'Okay, Norman, take the flour,' I say, as I climb the little ladder at the back of the shop, reaching for a big glass jar, remembering where all the ingredients are from my day baking with William. A day that will stay in my Christmas memories for ever.

In no time, the gingerbread is in the ovens and the temperature is rising. The whole place smells of cinnamon, ginger, and sweet golden syrup.

'Once the gingerbread is out of the ovens, we need to turn them off and bring the temperature in the room down,' William instructs, as he starts to cut out the templates for the buildings and Noah and Ron source the sweets for decorating.

'I'll cut the shapes and you can all start to assemble your buildings and memories,' he said. 'Who's on the living Nativity?'

'That's me!'

'Hope you've got room for one more,' says someone coming into the shop. 'Anja told me where I'd find you.'

'John!' we all say at once.

'Hope you're up for helping to build a church!' calls William.

'Indeed. With choir!' says John, rolling up his sleeves.

With that, Noah puts on some music on his phone, Christmas carols. His dad smiles at him and ruffles his hair, as Noah gets to work with Joseph creating a gingerbread bakery, with upstairs living room, dressed for Christmas with a tree and a laden Christmas table.

'My icing's gone hard,' says Norman.

'You have to keep it covered,' Pearl scolds. 'Like Connie showed us. Use mine.'

'Connie, can you do the icicles?' William asks, as he hovers over the busy work stations. Ron's attempt at icicles looks more like sausages but the gingerbread Old Town is starting to come to life. 'Like this.' He shows me how to use the piping bag to create the little icicles all around the gingerbread roofs.

'Leave it with me,' I say.

'Thank you,' he mouths, and I smile.

'This donkey looks more like a moose,' says Ron, standing back to scrutinize his modelling, and William steps in to tweak it.

'There's no way we'll get all this done by morning,' says Maeve. 'Not without a bit of magic.'

'Who's for hot chocolate?' Joseph asks, and they all smile. He winks at me.

Right now, I have no idea if we can do this. Right now it looks like organized chaos. All we can do is take the risk and go for it.

# FORTY

We work through the night, fuelled by brandy-laced hot chocolate and stollen. Flour and gingerbread off-cuts lie everywhere. Royal icing and food colouring streak our aprons, but as dawn creeps over the market square, the snow like a soft white blanket thrown over the huts, lamps, merry-go-round and Christmas tree, we open the front door to the bakery and the morning. The bell tinkles as we begin to carry the gingerbread town to the covered pavilion in the middle. Like the shepherds and Wise Men arriving, carrying their most precious gifts, to celebrate a new beginning.

William works to place each piece and set the scene. By the time the gingerbread houses and figures are all in place, everyone is tired but happy, really happy. William covers the whole construction in big sheets to hide it.

'Right, everyone. Let's get some sleep. Be back here

for Christmas-tree light-up and we'll light the candles in our little town.'

'And then it's the judging,' says Joseph, placing a hand on his son's shoulder.

'Whatever happens, we did the town proud here today, Paps.' He slings an arm around his father. His son comes to stand beside him and he puts the other arm around him.

Joseph pats the hand on his shoulder. 'We did, son. And I don't think you leaving for Cologne had anything to do with us losing our way in this competition.'

'You don't?'

'I think it had to do with Mutti dying and us missing her so much we forgot to celebrate the things we really loved, the people and the place, because we were just hurting too much.'

I can see William's eyes welling.

'She's here with us, son. Right here in this gingerbread town. I can feel her love.'

And they hug each other, tightly.

'I think so too, Paps,' says William, his voice cracking. Then he sniffs, pats his father's shoulder again and straightens. 'Now, come on, let's all get some sleep.'

'And . . .' I say slowly '. . . we need to pack. We'll be leaving soon.'

'Stay one more night,' Anja says quickly. 'As my guests. My friends. You can't drive on no sleep. Stay for the judging, the drinks and the band afterwards.'

'Besides, we still have to scatter Elsie's ashes,' says

Pearl, looking at me. 'I thought at the bridge would be nice.'

We all nod in agreement.

'We'll be home just in time for Christmas Eve,' says Alice. But no one seems happy about the prospect. In fact, everyone's spirits dip.

'But we still have tonight,' I say, trying to brighten them. 'We'll stay for the drinks and the band. Elsie's wake!'

'There'll be a bierkeller, a choir first, then a traditional band and entertainment,' says William.

'It sounds perfect. Elsie would have loved it!' says Pearl.

'Time to make some more new memories to take home,' I say, suddenly feeling as sad as the others. I have to see Heinrich and finally come to a decision about us. Are we going to come out as an official couple, plan our next few dates and a future together?

I lie on my bed but, even though I'm exhausted, I can't sleep. I roll onto my back, staring up at the ceiling, hoping for the answer to appear in front of my eyes, running through each of the qualities I was looking for in my perfect match, wishing I hadn't left my notebook at the bakery. Now is when I really need it. I try to visualize the page. Attractiveness, tick, timekeeping, double tick, financially secure, tick, thoughtful and kind. I think of our date at his apartment, triple tick. Tick, tick, tick. Heinrich's everything I've been looking for. This is my time to take the plunge, isn't it? They don't come more perfect than Heinrich.

But how will he feel when he knows I helped William? Will he still want me? Or will he think I've betrayed him? He may not even want to know me.

William's words keep coming back to haunt me. I keep trying to push them out. 'What about love?' This wasn't about love, it was about finding contentment with someone. But is it enough? Now I have a taste of what else there may be. Is it that I've fallen for someone else, someone totally unsuitable, who may not even want me? My head is saying, 'Pick Heinrich,' but my heart is saying something else. I can't hear either of them clearly. This is my chance to change my life, to start again and be content. To be a part of this place, which I've come to love. But is that enough for me now?

William lay on his bed, stroking Fritz's ear. No matter how exhausted he felt, he couldn't sleep. They'd done it. They'd made the gingerbread town. Connie had done it. She'd brought all their Christmas memories back for him and her friends. It was not just a work of art, it was a work of love. And, right now, that was how he was feeling about her too, that she was someone he'd come to love. But what about Marta and their son? He'd told her he was going to sell to Heinrich. She'd suggested they could try again. Would it work? Is that what they both really wanted? Could they be happy? Did he have a choice?

# FORTY-ONE

*Ping!*

My heart leaps into my mouth. I look at the sleeping Pearl. It's mid-morning and outside the market is starting to open up. I can't believe that tomorrow we'll have left before it opens and then I'll be back home, in my bed, waiting for Christmas to pass.

I open my phone slowly. My heart leaps again as I see the message is from William. *Can we meet?*

My hands shake and I wish I could put it down to tiredness. I go to reply but delete what I've written, no idea what to say. No idea what I would say if I met him.

The little dots bob across the screen. He's typing. *I want to thank you,* his message says.

I want to say yes, but I can't. I have to talk to Heinrich. I have to explain what I've done, helping William.

*Maybe later, after the judging and after we've given Elsie her send-off,* I type, and hope I've given myself enough time to talk to Heinrich and work out what I really want.

*Fine. By the Christmas tree. Six o'clock . . . ish!* he types, and I laugh.

*Ish! See you then.* I remember him being late for his meeting with Marta when I took over in the shop, wondering if his unreliability where time is concerned drives her mad and if he'll be able to change . . . if he goes back to her. Is that what he wants to tell me, that they're getting back together? I sit upright, then, sleep avoiding me, climb out of bed and pull out my case, ready to leave the following morning.

Just before four o'clock, as it's getting dark and all the lights start to shine in the market square, there's a buzz of anticipation. The judges, according to Anja, are gathered at the castle and are about to tour the two towns and inspect their creations.

Norman and the others are in place in the living Nativity and Ron, the Christmas angel, is walking the town. Norman has a plan to keep the donkey from running amok, which involves the gingerbread crumbs in his pocket from our earlier baking.

I'm on my way to see Heinrich, then to meet Pearl on the bridge with the others. Under the covered terrace, with snow gently falling all around, William is lighting the tealights inside the gingerbread village as I walk past. I'm drawn to it.

'It's beautiful,' I say, remembering a time when Christmas really was about feeling loved. I can practically feel the love in those windows, behind the doors and on the merry-go-round. The smell, too, of spicy cinnamon and golden syrup fills the air. And on a tiny track, a small train, put together by Ron and Norman, is running around the outside of the town, through the mountain, where the castle sits, and out the other side, just like it once had, according to Joseph, reliving his own happy memories of Christmases gone by.

William stares at the village as he lights each house, the church and the castle. The stained-glass window of the church, made with melted boiled sweets, shines beautifully, for John's choir memory. 'It is,' he says, then looks up at me as if he's going to say something.

'I have to see Heinrich,' I blurt, knowing he has promised to do nothing that would come between me and Heinrich. This is a decision I have to make for myself. To go with my head, and commit to being with Heinrich, or my heart, hoping something else is waiting for me.

William nods. 'Help me with these last few tealights,' he says, 'and the fairy lights around the market.' I take them from him as he turns them on and we string them around the gingerbread walls of the Old Town. And as we do, the wandering crowds turn to the gingerbread town, lit by candles and tiny fairy lights, and gasp. We look at each other and smile. All the right ingredients . . . and alchemy.

Suddenly everyone is standing around in groups, drinking glühwein. Shoppers, stallholders serving sausages and putting hot chestnuts into paper cones, stop and stare. There is a silence as everyone admires the gingerbread town.

The choir at the other end of the terrace begins to sing Christmas carols, bringing a tear to my eye. And I'm not alone.

'Look, it's John,' says Pearl, who's come to join me. There in the middle of the choir is John, singing his heart out, as if it's lifted and so full of joy it might burst out of him.

'So that's where he's been all week! Practising with the choir!' I manage, despite a tight throat.

'It's perfect,' says Pearl, sniffing into a hanky. 'It's Christmas. It's just everything we could have wanted to remember.'

'There's the Nativity.' I point to the gingerbread town.

'And the donkey!' Pearl laughs.

'And that reminds me of sitting with my mother as she knitted,' says Norman, pointing at a pair of figures at a fireside, knitting.

'And the church.' Pearl looks up again at John, singing.

'And the ice rink!' Maeve joins us. 'It's everything

we wanted to remember, bringing back the spirit of Christmas,' says Maeve.

'Do you know? When I get home I'm not going to my daughter for Boxing Day. I'm fed up of feeling like a nuisance,' says Alice. 'And I'm not going to buy my grandchildren all the big presents. They won't remember me for that. I'm going to send them gingerbread instead.'

'And I'm going to join a knitting group,' says Norman. 'Maybe start one up!'

'I'm going to spend Christmas with the ones I love,' says Pearl, and we all look at her. 'You lot!' she announces, with a wide smile. 'How about we all pitch in? Get out of our flats and make a Christmas dinner to remember! Who cares if we forget the bread sauce or overcook the sprouts? I want to spend the day with the people closest to me. And that includes you, Connie,' she says.

I look around for William. He is surrounded by people, excitedly asking about the gingerbread town. And then he looks round and sees me. We gaze at each other and the words we've been waiting for finally break us apart.

'The judges are coming!' someone says, from the back of the gathered group. Excitement and nerves fizzle in the snowy air.

A group of people in long dark coats, the castle owner's family, his son and wife at the front, is approaching the square, having visited the New Town.

It's my time to leave. I catch William's eye and mouth, 'Good luck.'

He nods anxiously. I wish I could stay, but Heinrich will be expecting me.

As I walk away from the covered terrace, through the huts, and past the merry-go-round, everyone is coming away from the New Town, towards the gingerbread town, and I feel as if I'm walking the wrong way, against the crowd, feeling the pull in both directions. Heinrich is a good man. He's the perfect match for me. And he lives here. I could be here more and more. But could I, if William was in the town living a new life with his wife? I don't think I could. Argh! My head hurts as the questions whirl in it, and the snow, whipping around me, falls heavily. I pull my coat around me, and my hat down further over my ears.

I lower my head and walk over the bridge. I hear it before I see it. The music is pumping out. Loud dramatic operatic music. I look up. Heinrich is exactly where he'd said he'd be. By the specially made outside pavilion with flashing lights, music playing across the square out of speakers. I stop and stand. The cake is amazing. The colours, the swinging pendulum, creating a moving arm, carrying a large chocolate egg on an immaculately timed journey from the top of the cake to the bottom, landing with a boom and a flash each time. The drama of it is outstanding. Just as I imagined it would be.

'Here!' he says, holding out a long arm to the cake,

under a big glass-like dome. Like a giant carriage clock. It is so much more than a cake. A landscape with swinging arms, carrying coloured eggs, and all in time to the lights and music. 'You're here!' he says triumphantly. He bends to kiss me. I go to kiss his cheek as he makes for my lips. We clash noses.

'Sorry,' we say, and laugh. I know he's embarrassed with everyone around him.

'Wow!' is all I can say, as I stare at the huge cake. 'It's amazing!' I say, and Heinrich beams.

'A piece of engineering genius!' he boasts.

But not really a Christmas cake, a voice says in my head, and for a moment I wonder if I've said it aloud. But if I did, Heinrich hasn't noticed. He is admiring the perfectly timed piece of engineering in front of him.

'Ah, my team!' he announces, as they come out from the factory, still wearing their white coats, hairnets and wellingtons, barely distinguishable from each other. Heinrich applauds them proudly, as do the bystanders around him. The ski slope is in full swing, as is the band on the other side of the square.

'Come, the judging will happen on the bridge,' says Heinrich, pulling me to him and kissing my forehead. 'Are you ready?'

The excitement here is just as palpable as it is in the Old Town. Heinrich's team, the stallholders and shopkeepers all start to walk in the direction of the bridge, where a crowd is gathering. He smiles down at me as we all move towards where the castle is lit up in all her pink and white brilliance, with a sparkling white tiara around the top.

We gather together on the bridge, watching the snow tumble and dance into the river below. It's beautiful. Perfect, in fact.

I look around for Pearl, Anja and William but can't see them.

'Actually, Heinrich, I need to talk to you about something,' I say, as the snow falls, tickling my face. 'About you and me, where we go from here.'

'And I you.' He draws me to stand to one side of the bridge, away from the castle.

I look around again and finally see Pearl and William, Joseph, Anja and the others arriving on their side of the bridge. My heart actually skips. I turn to Heinrich, but he's gone. I feel a tug on my hand and look down. He's kneeling.

'Are you okay?' I ask, concerned.

He's smiling up at me and suddenly the penny drops. Like one of the mechanical arms on his cake.

'Connie.' He looks at me, then at the magical setting, with the castle as its backdrop. 'I said I would ask you by the end of your trip here. When we'd both had time to consider our future.'

'Heinrich, please, do stand up.'

'I'm doing it properly, Connie,' he insists. 'Connie.' He pulls a small box out of his pocket and opens it. Everyone turns to us and sees Heinrich proposing. His parents included, taking pictures.

'Rubies, your birthstone, right?'

My birthstone. I'm not sure that many of the dates I've met would even remember my birthday, let alone know my birthstone. Again, Heinrich's thought of everything.

'So what's your answer. Will you marry me?'

It's everything I could have wanted . . . on paper. Heinrich is the perfect man, and he is the perfect match I've been looking for. I look down at the box and the ring he's placed in my hand. A ruby heart with diamonds surrounding it. Just stunning. So why isn't my heart racing and skipping, and why am I forcing myself not to turn and look for William?

Heinrich is still kneeling – on a small kneepad, I notice. Always prepared. Everything planned for.

'I . . .' I open my mouth but the words don't form.

Just then there is a crackle from the speakers at either end of the bridge. We all turn in the direction of the castle. The big, wide front door opens and the family of judges steps out onto the stone balcony there. Now everyone is watching them. Heinrich takes a moment to stand up, brushing off stray snowflakes and slipping his kneepad into his pocket. He straightens himself to his full height, and as he puts his arm around me, his smile spreads and his eyes sparkle as I look up at him. He's gazing at the gathered family on the castle steps. It's then I catch William's eye and this time my heart skips and flips.

'Thank you all for coming,' says the short, round

man. 'My father would have loved this.' Heinrich translates quietly into my ear, making it tickle and I feel a flutter of giggles, a combination of nerves and excitement as the crowd waits quietly. 'As you all know, my father loved Christmas time. He loved the markets and the way they brought people together.'

Not any more. They've driven two communities apart, I think.

'He left this fund to finance the market that showed the most initiative and flair with their markets and their Christmas celebration cake. The one that showed the spirit of Christmas, the town and its creators.'

Suddenly there's a crackle on the microphone and the sound dips out. Pearl looks at Norman, who shrugs. Joseph pulls Anja, wrapped in her poncho, to him and Maeve rolls her wheelchair closer to the speaker.

I gaze up at the castle as the snow continues to fall. I try to take in everything that has just happened. Heinrich has just proposed with a beautiful ring that is now tightly in my palm. I have to decide whether I want to put it on my finger. My eyes are instinctively drawn to William and his to mine. Have I actually found what I was searching for, without knowing I wanted it?

Just at that moment, the microphone crackles back into life.

'It's time,' Heinrich whispers, making me jump.

'I am pleased to announce, the winner of this year's Christmas Baking Competition, for its ingenuity and passion,' he says, 'without a shadow of a doubt, is . . .' We hold our breath collectively. 'And the recipient of the financial funding to go towards next year's market is . . .'

Heinrich is still translating, then tips his head from side to side, with a huge smile and says, 'The New Town!'

'The Old Town!' says the voice on the microphone, and Heinrich's face drops in disbelief. And, without thinking, I shout and punch the air. Then I freeze.

# FORTY-TWO

Heinrich is astonished, and I'm not sure if it's because he's lost the competition or that clearly I'm celebrating William and his town winning – a feeling that came straight from the heart and burst out of me.

I turn to Heinrich and take a deep breath. 'I'm sorry, Heinrich,' I start.

'About the fact that we didn't win with our cake or that you seem to be delighted for William and his team?'

I bite my lip. I sigh. 'They're my team too,' I say. 'I helped make and design the gingerbread town. It was my fault that William's cake was destroyed in the first place. I had to help.'

'You helped?'

'I had to put it right. It was my idea.'

He pulls himself up to his full height. 'I see.'

His parents are bustling towards us.

'I can't believe it! I have to see this cake!' his father is saying, and is heading over the bridge to the Old Town, somewhere I don't think he's ventured for a very long time.

'And so, I'm guessing . . .' He looks down at the space where he was kneeling just a few minutes earlier. The imprint of the kneepad is slowly being covered with snow, so there is barely a suggestion that it ever happened.

'I'm sorry, Heinrich, I can't marry you. I wanted to say yes. I really did. You are a lovely man. And there will be someone for you. The right person. But it isn't me. I think we'd make brilliant friends. We like all the same things. But, well, you need to listen to your heart. Like I'm learning to listen to mine. It's time we saw what was in front of us and stopped hiding behind our computer screens, too scared of getting it wrong. And your brother wouldn't want you to be trying to live his life. He'd want you to live yours.'

'I . . .' He swallows. 'I'm going to see my team.' He points over his shoulder.

I look down at the ring in my hand and decide to hand it back to him later, when he's on his own.

He turns to his team, who are disappointed, consoling each other. The tall woman, Klara, whom I've seen at the shop, pulls off her hat and hairnet, shakes out her blonde hair and unbuttons her white coat. Heinrich watches her, his eyes widening, as if he's suddenly seeing her for the first time. They smile at each other and I smile too. He'll be fine, I think. He turns and gives me a small wave, a wave of goodbye.

'Goodbye, Heinrich,' I say. 'Good luck,' I whisper, as the snow comes down over the river.

The crowds are heading towards the Old Town and Pearl is standing on the bridge with the others. It's time. It's time to say goodbye.

# FORTY-THREE

'Right,' says Pearl, producing Elsie from her handbag, as we gather around her on the middle of the bridge.

'Um, are we allowed to do this?' asks Norman.

'Bugger what we're allowed to do!' says Maeve. 'We'll be dead before they catch up with us!' And for a moment everyone is silent, then Graham laughs and nods in agreement, as does everyone else.

'Apart from Connie, of course, and she can just say she knew nothing about it. It was a bunch of loony pensioners she was driver for!' says Pearl.

Only this bunch of people are so much more than loony pensioners. They're my friends, as close as any family. Tears spring to my eyes again, and I have no idea why. Maybe I realize that William's right, that sometimes the most unusual ingredients work best together. Pearl, the others and I have practically nothing in common on paper, but we care about each other, and that's alchemy.

'Who's going to say a few words?' asks Norman, looking down at Elsie in Pearl's arms. Everyone turns to Pearl.

'You're the speaker, Pearl,' says Norman.

'I think you should do it, Norman,' says Pearl, stepping back and handing Elsie to him.

Norman clears his throat and takes a moment to think, looking down at Elsie. Then he says, 'Elsie, you have given us so much more than you could ever know, bringing us here and bringing us together.' Everyone mutters in agreement. 'You always said that Christmas made people smile, Elsie, and that was why you loved it. You have brought smiles to each and every one of us this week. Thank you. We only wish you were here with us. But I think you knew that you would be, and always will be when we think about our Christmas memories.'

He steps towards the wall of the bridge. We look out over the Old Town, lit with white fairy lights and the castle above us, smiling down from its rose-pink walls.

'Goodbye, Elsie, Elisabetta,' says Norman, and opens the urn over the edge of the bridge and shakes it. The little flakes of ash fly out and upwards, joining in the big fat snowflakes as they fall, like fairies from the sky, over the water, making us all smile.

We stand and stare as the last of the ashes flies up and away, mingling and dancing with the sparkling snow, then into the glistening river below.

'Goodbye, Elsie,' I say quietly. 'Thank you for making

me remember to listen to my heart.' I hold my fingers to my lips and send a kiss into the flurry of snowflakes.

'Now,' says Pearl, after a suitable pause, 'I think it's time we went and raised a glass of glühwein to Elsie and to William's bakery.'

'Yes, indeed,' says Norman, and everyone agrees, clearing their throats and blowing their noses.

'Just perfect,' I say. 'Just perfect . . .' and Pearl links her arm through mine.

'Think I've got something in my eye,' Ron says, bringing up the rear of the group as we walk away for our final night together.

# FORTY-FOUR

As we approach the Old Town and join the ever-increasing crowd heading that way, I look up at the clock tower. Nearly six o'clock. I can't wait to see William and congratulate him. William, I say to myself, and a big smile spreads across my face. As the bell in the clock tower chimes, I say, 'Pearl, there's somewhere I need to be. Someone I need to see.' I grin.

'Okay, love, you go.' She pats my hand and smiles. 'And good luck!' she calls after me, as I hurry through the crowds to the sound of the bell.

This time there are no tick lists or questions. It's just about listening to my heart. It's about William and needing to be with him. To tell him I'm not marrying Heinrich. I'm free, if he still wants to . . . To what? Kiss me? Take me to bed? Spend the rest of his life with me? All of the above, tick, tick, tick.

The snow falls, like glittery feathers, all around me

as I run to the square, squeezing past people on the narrow streets and emerging into it. I feel like I've run into a snow globe, right in the middle of my happy place.

The square is packed. Everyone is heading towards the gingerbread village, where the judges are congratulating Joseph.

I take a deep breath and turn to look at the big Christmas tree in front of the clock tower, just as the last bell rings. My heart leaps and swirls, as if someone's given the snow globe a gentle shake. He's there!

I take a deep breath, lift an arm and rise on tiptoe so he can see me. He's holding something in both hands. I can't see what it is. But I can't wait to find out. This is how Christmas should feel. Full of hope, happiness and new beginnings. Full of love, for those we're with, those we miss and those we've found. This is the best feeling, ever! I don't know what the future holds but, right now, it feels full of promise and excitement. That's what I fell in love with at seventeen, not the young man whose letters petered out. It was love of life, of promise and possibility.

I see him check the clock. He's on time. For once. For me! And so am I.

I call his name and wave. He spots me and waves back. And as I go to join him through the crowds, I hear his name being called, in a voice that isn't mine.

'William! Papa!'

William's head snaps round. He sees his son, waving

and trying to get to him through the crowds, who are sipping glühwein, meeting and greeting friends, families heading to the ice rink.

'We won!' Noah shouts and finally gets clear of the crowds and runs towards his dad. William opens his arms, still holding whatever it is in one hand, and lets his son run into them. They hug each other, their eyes closed, clinging to something they nearly lost and have found again. He spins his son round, holding him tightly. Suddenly I'm homesick, very homesick indeed. I'd give anything for one of those hugs from my boy right now. But that's not to be. I just have to remember them and think about them, like the memories in the gingerbread town.

I shut my eyes hard and remember the gingerbread house, and the feeling of being loved. It's there, in the gingerbread town, full of love. I slowly open my eyes and then I see her, standing at a distance from the Christmas tree. She steps forward, puts an arm around his neck and kisses his cheek. His son looks ecstatic. This must be Marta. William's wife. Then William looks at me, clearly torn. I try to smile, and wave.

'You go!' I say. 'Enjoy!' And I mean it. I want him to enjoy his time with his son. And Marta, if that's what he wants. I want him to be happy. I want what he wants for himself. His son tugs at his arm excitedly, and still he's looking back at me, apologizing. I wave again, and step back into the crowds, my heart racing and my tears falling. Much the same place as I started on this trip. Only I've found what I'm looking for: I just know I can't have it. It wasn't meant to be. My moment has gone. But I would have taken it, if I could. I would have followed my heart, wouldn't I? I guess I'll never know. I feel myself slipping back to the safety behind my computer screen and trusting to my tick list . . . because clearly my heart can't be trusted.

I watch William looking about for me, but I move quickly away. His son and wife are encouraging him towards the market, pulling him into the heart of the community where he is being embraced, engulfed and congratulated, people patting him on the back and hugging him, thanking him for bringing the cup home and the spirit of Christmas back to the Old Town.

My eyes sting as the snow meets the tears. It's time to pack and get ready to leave. First thing in the morning, at first light, we'll be gone from here and it will be just another memory.

# FORTY-FIVE

I walk back towards the guesthouse, in the shadows of the tall half-timbered buildings, watching the market as it comes to life. As I near the covered terrace with the gingerbread town, everyone is there, apart from William and Noah, who wants to go on every ride, even the ones he wouldn't have been seen dead on before his dad became his hero again. I watch as the two throw their heads back in laughter on the merry-go-round. Suddenly the scales have fallen from Noah's eyes and he can see the glamour and shine of the New Town for what they are, just like I realize I have spent my adult life looking for a man like the one I thought had left me behind, instead of grasping that I was seeing things wrongly. There's no shortcut to finding love. Love happens when and where it wants, whether it's right or wrong at the time. I see Marta watching her son, and his father, smiling, and my heart twists. Is this it? Has she understood what the shop and the bakery mean to William or is he still going to give it up for the sake of his family?

I walk through the market and stop at a distance from the gingerbread town. There is Joseph, and next to him is Heinrich's father. There is a gap between them. They say nothing, just stare as the little railway chugs its way from the village, through the mountain, over the bridge and back again. The choir are still singing and a band is setting up in the bar area next to them.

'Those were the days,' says Joseph, with a crack in his voice, 'when we were boys . . .'

'With a shared dream,' Heinrich's father joins in, with a matching crack.

'Before . . .'

'Yes. Before we lost Maurice. Before I took out my grief on you.'

'It all seems a very long time ago now,' says Joseph.

'And somewhere in all that time, this, the memories . . .' Heinrich's father waves a hand '. . . the spirit of Christmas . . .'

'. . . has been lost,' Joseph finishes.

They stare at the gingerbread town, letting the memories wash over them. Wave after wave.

'We were so busy fighting over who had the right vision for the business and the shop that we forgot what really mattered.'

They gaze at the two figures in the centre of the gingerbread scene.

'We forgot the magic of Christmas,' says Joseph, as his grandson and son come and stand by him.

Heinrich, too, has joined the group, with the beautiful Klara, who runs his factory floor like clockwork. She's smiling radiantly at him, as is he at her. Alchemy!

# FORTY-SIX

I join Pearl, and she knows from looking at me and at Heinrich. I shake my head and she hugs me to her.

'It wasn't right, Pearl,' I say.

'He asked you to marry him?'

I nod.

'And if it wasn't right, you did the right thing in turning him down,' she says, hugging me to her. Her eyes flick to William, as do mine, and his to me, but I quickly look down at the gingerbread town.

'Looks like everyone got what they wanted most for Christmas, their Christmas memory.' I sniff, lift my head and smile. 'Old memories and new ones.'

'Well, nearly . . .' says Pearl, as the choir comes to an end. Anja and the bar staff at the far end of the terrace hand around huge jugs of beer.

A group of schoolchildren come forward to the microphone where the choir have just been singing, and sing 'Silent Night' beautifully, then Pearl insists on trying to teach them 'The Twelve Days of Christmas' in English, getting muddled between her pipers piping and her lords a-leaping, and we all smile as our beer glasses are topped up, and laugh as, behind them, the band sets up.

Pearl rejoins the group around the table by the fire, laughing, wiping tears from the corners of her eyes and out of breath. She steps over the bench to sit at the wooden table and takes a swig of the beer that's been poured for her there. She looks totally happy and alive.

'Where's Norman?' she says suddenly, and we all shake our heads.

'No idea,' I say. 'I'm sure he'll be here soon. He won't want to miss this.'

Out comes a band, all dressed in Bavarian costume, with long shorts, white socks with tassels to hold them up, white shirts, braces and hats, many carrying their brass instruments. There's a tuba and a trumpet, someone sits at the keyboard and there's an accordion, played by Joseph.

'An oompah band!' Alice claps her hands in delight. Di beams as she picks up a glass of beer and helps Graham take a sip.

'Oh, where's Norman? He'd love this! He'll be gutted if he misses it,' says Pearl, her eyes darting around. I daren't look in case I spot William with Marta, and right now I can't bear to see that. In any case, the rest of the group and I are staring at the band in disbelief.

'Pearl.' I nudge her. She turns, and I point at the little stage.

'Norman!' she exclaims, putting her hand to her mouth. 'In lederhosen!' Norman takes centre stage with the band and looks at her, uncomfortable at first, but then, seeing her expression, he begins to enjoy himself as the band starts to play, the audience swaying. Norman plays the bells he's holding, and Pearl is transfixed, as if she's seeing him for the very first time, with different eyes, and I'm guessing that's alchemy too.

We all sway, drink and clap along to the oompah band and eventually everyone is dancing too. Di, encouraged by Graham, is on her feet, beaming, and I can tell Graham wishes he was up there too. Maeve is on the dance floor, wheeling back and forth like she has new dancing shoes on. And Norman leaves the band, grabs Pearl and swings her around. Then, much to my protests, he grabs me, too, and despite my wretchedness, I join in with them, my dear friends. When we're all exhausted, the band slows the music down and couples take to the dance floor. I can't look up. I don't want to see if William and Marta are dancing together. But despite my best efforts, I glance occasionally at the dancers, but I don't see them. Instead, Noah comes to dance with me and, once again, I can't say no.

Di returns to her seat by Graham, patting his knee and smiling. He looks at her and tries to struggle to his feet. Di stands to help him but he puts up his hand and tells her to stay where she is.

'Sorry, Noah, there's something I need to do,' I say, and he follows me towards Graham, who looks at me, no words needed. I put my arm under his. Noah helps, as does Ron.

Graham stands stiffly and says to Di slowly, 'Would you like to dance?', putting out a hand. Her eyes sparkle as she sees the Graham she fell in love with standing in front of her, not the friends supporting him to his feet. She takes his hand and lets him guide her to the floor, as we support his elbows until Di is in his arms, her body against his. She kisses him, then rests her head on his chest, holding one of his hands, her other arm around him, and they gently sway to the music as if it was their first and maybe their last dance together. Whatever it is, it's a special moment for them both. No thoughts of the illness that has worn them down, no Kindles to hide their worries, just the two of them in love, right now. That's love. That is real for-better-or-for-worse love. And if I can't have that, I'd rather spend my life remembering what it looked like than chasing something that isn't really there.

The snow has stopped and the sky is clearing. The moon shines, and a shooting star arcs across the inky blue. Di rests her head next to Graham's and takes the memory to her heart.

*

The band is still playing as Di and Graham finally leave the dance floor, her leading him, back to how life is today, but having for just a few minutes remembered how it used to be. More jugs of beer are being served but I decide it's time to slip away. Everyone else is dancing. Joseph has put down the accordion and is dancing with Anja, Pearl and Norman. William is with Noah and Marta, pulled onto the dance floor by their son. Every now and again William catches my eye but I just smile. It's time to leave them to it. It's time to get ready to leave for good.

William looked around. He still hadn't had the chance to see her and talk to her. What with Noah turning up, with Marta, she'd told him she'd see him later. But when? Was it that she didn't want to hear what he had to say, which he'd realized he'd wanted to say right from the start? That she was exactly the sort of person he would choose if he was searching for the right person online. That he couldn't think of anyone he'd rather be with, and she should think again before accepting Heinrich's offer, because if it didn't feel right . . . Well, she should listen to her instincts, just as she'd taught him to listen to his. And now he was listening, and despite the promise he'd made to himself, not to come between her and Heinrich, he needed to tell her, somehow. But had he left it too late? He needed to get Pearl to help him, but Pearl seemed blissfully preoccupied, drinking and dancing with Norman.

There was only one thing he could do, one last chance to tell her what he was feeling. He left the crowd and walked to the guesthouse, pushed open the door and looked at all the cases lined up there, ready for an early departure in the morning. Now all he needed to do was find the right one.

# FORTY-SEVEN

At barely first light, I'm up and keen to get going. I turn to Pearl to wake her, but her bed is empty. I smile. At least someone found their perfect date on this trip.

I get dressed and make my way downstairs to where the rest of the group is gathering. We hug and thank Anja for all she's done and make our way in the early-morning light towards the minibus. Norman helps with the cases and everyone helps everyone else onto the bus. John is still humming the carols he sang so beautifully yesterday, enjoying the memories they're bringing back for him. Maeve has stopped complaining about being helped onto the minibus as I load in her customized and decorated wheelchair, memories of her time here and her skating trip. She's sporting a new sparkly bobble hat and, by the look of it, feeling like Baby from *Dirty Dancing* still.

I turn on the engine and get the heaters going as I brush off the snow and de-ice the windscreen.

Norman and Pearl are cuddled up together, holding hands, as if to keep warm, but their smiles and the fact they can't stop looking at each other say something different, I think, as I climb into the driver's seat and adjust my rear-view mirror.

I turn the engine on. It stutters and cuts out. Is this it? Is the minibus going to break down and, by some twist of Fate, I'll have to stay here? I turn the key. It starts first time. No twist of Fate, then. I look around, one last time, towards the market square. Anja is still there, waving us off, and I know she and Joseph have a new start to look forward to . . . just like William, it would appear, with Marta. I can't stand in the way of that. I have to leave and let him try to get his life back to how it was. Just like he wanted.

I push the minibus into first gear, hoping against hope that William will appear and tell me not to leave, that it was me all along. But he doesn't. Even if he thought it, and Marta wasn't asking him back, he promised he wouldn't interfere between me and Heinrich. And I have a feeling he's going to keep his word. He said he wouldn't say anything to influence me about Heinrich. He kept his promise . . . but I wish he hadn't.

# FORTY-EIGHT

The following morning, I'm up early. There is no market outside setting up, no snow falling. It's Christmas Eve and it couldn't feel less like Christmas. The house is cold and empty, or maybe that's just how I'm feeling inside. But I can't lie here in bed. There is something I have to do, no matter how much I don't want to. I can't put it off any longer. I promised myself I would do this as soon as I got back, and I have to keep that promise to myself. I get up, pull on my Christmas jumper and head over to the retirement flats with my Christmas presents, the lebkuchen hearts I made, sharply reminding me of the morning I spent with William in the shop, one of my all-time favourite memories, along with making the gingerbread town. And when it's less painful, I will look back on it time and time again and smile.

As I approach the block, something looks different.

It's not just that the building work has stopped. Lights are coming from the unused day room. I push open the door and stop. It's different, nothing like it was a month ago when I turned up to see the ambulance doors closing and the door to Elsie's flat wide open with no one there. I was holding her order of vegetable soup and steak and kidney pudding. This feels very different, very different indeed. The first thing I hear is music. There is never music at the flats. Then I notice decorations, homemade paper chains and cut-out snowflakes, hanging everywhere, from the ceiling in Reception and along the corridors. Even po-faced Penny, the receptionist, is wearing a Christmas hat and a smile. A big sheet of brown paper, with potato-printed holly leaves on it, is covering the contents of the vending machine, and finally there's the smell. No longer cheap disinfectant, it's lovely, drawing me in and leading me down to the day room and the kitchen there.

'Wow!' is all I can say, as I stand and stare. 'This is beautiful!' Tears spring to my eyes, not for the first time over these last few days, and I'm surprised there are any left. Probably a combination of tiredness and sadness at what, or rather who, I found and had to leave behind in Germany.

'Ah, Connie, there you are!' says Pearl, poking her head out from the kitchen. 'Come and check our gingerbread, will you?'

I follow the smell into the kitchen, now warm and full of life. The oven there is humming away.

'Maeve used to be a school cook,' says Pearl, pointing to Maeve, in a sequinned top, tinsel covering her wheelchair. 'We've decided,' she says, 'that we're not going anywhere this Christmas.'

'Really?'

'Yes! Anyone who wants to see us can come and join us. We're having Christmas dinner here. Just as we like it.' She beams.

'Roast turkey, with bread sauce,' says Maeve.

'And decent red wine,' says John, then goes back to humming along to the carols as he cuts out more paper snowflakes. 'And carols,' he says, pointing to the radio. 'They're very good, this lot. It's a dementia choir, based in Scotland, and they're going on tour next year. Going to try and see them. Their album is called *Gin-gle Bells.*' He holds it up. 'Present to myself at the ferry port.'

'Talking of opening presents . . .' says Pearl, clapping her hands together.

'Er, Pearl.' I catch her elbow and pull her to one side.

'Yes, dear?'

'Talking of opening things.' I give her a firm look. She says nothing. I take a deep breath. I have to say something. I can't put this off. 'Isn't it time you opened the letter that's been in your coat pocket since we left home?'

'Letter?' She feigns innocence and I can tell she wants to distract me from the subject.

'The one from the hospital I gave you when we left for Germany,' I say quietly but firmly.

'Oh, I . . .' She waves a hand, trying to dismiss it.

'Pearl.' She looks at Norman, hanging paper chains from the windows, and Ron, decorating the artificial tree they found at the back of the cleaning cupboard with foil-covered chocolates. 'Do it for Norman. Now you've found each other, you can't ignore it any more,' I say. 'You have to know, whatever it is, so you can face it together.' A minute passes. Finally she nods and walks towards her coat. The letter hasn't moved from its pocket since she shoved it in there as we left.

She pulls it out and glances at Norman, who smiles and goes back to pinning up paper chains, the carols playing in the background, the smell of gingerbread and the warming aroma of turkey stock on the stove wafting to us. It feels a lot like home used to feel, filled with love. I think about Maeve and her family Christmas where she felt unwanted and unloved, and Alice only there to buy the expensive presents. Here, they're sharing the time because they want to be together. And I can't help but wonder what William's Christmas Eve is looking like. I try to push it out of my mind. I haven't opened my phone to check my messages and, right now, I don't intend to. I can't bear the thought of checking for messages. It's not the messages that count. I used to get hundreds from Heinrich and it filled my evenings, but that was all. They filled a void. A void that was left by Sam's departure and a space in my heart I'd ignored for a long time. A place for love. I thought I'd found love with Heinrich until I tasted the real thing, and now I have, I can't settle for anything less.

Pearl holds out the letter in front of her, hand shaking.

'Do you want me to?' I ask her.

She nods. I take it from her and squeeze her hand. 'Whatever it is, we're here for each other,' I tell her, and mean it. Because that's what love is. Being there through thick and thin.

I open the letter, my hand shaking too, and read it carefully, then reread it just to check. A smile spreads across my face as I pass the letter to Pearl and take her hand.

'It's all okay, Pearl. You're clear. No need to go back to the hospital. They didn't find anything wrong. Nothing unusual. The screening is clear.'

She looks at me in utter disbelief, and now I know why she was happy to share a room. I don't think Pearl has slept properly for weeks with worry.

'You should have told me!' I scold.

'Clear? Nothing wrong?' she repeats.

'Nothing wrong,' I confirm again. The letter is scrunched up as she grabs both my hands and tears of relief fall down her lined cheeks.

'Nothing wrong,' she says, a huge smile spreading across her face. 'I've been so worried. Thought Elsie's wake would take my mind off things.'

'And what you needed to do was share your worries.'

'Nothing wrong!' she calls to Norman, waving the crumpled letter. 'Got myself into a tizzy, waiting for my check-up results.'

He climbs down his ladder and comes over to hug her hard, then kisses her gently on the lips. 'Best Christmas present ever,' he says, looking at her wet face.

'Life is always better shared!' I say.

'Now, talking of presents,' says Pearl, wiping her eyes, then straightening from Norman's embrace.

'Let's open that prosecco,' announces Norman. 'It's Christmas Eve after all. And turn up the carols, John!'

John does so with a smile.

I grab some glasses and Norman fetches the prosecco from the fridge. He opens it with a pop and a cheer.

'Well I never!' says Penny, coming into the day room, with a couple of about my age just as another cork pops.

'Wow!' says the younger woman, admiring the decorated room, the gingerbread-house building and the prosecco pouring.

'Not what I was expecting!' says the young man.

'Thought we'd all be locked away in our flats, did you?' says Maeve, with a wink.

'Actually, we're planning lots of things for the new year,' says Norman.

'We could have cookery classes, get the kids from the school over to bake with us,' says Maeve.

'And have concerts. Maybe that Scottish choir could visit while they're touring,' says John.

'And a knitting group. I have lots of ideas for next year's Christmas jumpers,' confirms Norman.

'And wait until you see the gingerbread house we're making!' Alice joins in.

'What about adopting a donkey?' Norman puts it to the group.

'No!' we all answer and he laughs.

'We're having prosecco,' says Norman, handing each newcomer a glass.

'And presents,' says Pearl. 'In Germany you have presents on Christmas Eve and your big family dinner. And Christmas Day is for seeing more family and friends.'

'We bought the last turkey in the butcher's.'

'And you said I wouldn't want to go into a retirement flat!' says an older woman, about Pearl's age, pushing forward between the couple. 'You said I'd hate it here. It would be boring and dull. I'd be better off moving in with you, you said.'

'Well, we just thought—'

'More likely you wanted free babysitting.' She sniffs and the younger couple shrug to each other. 'Looks fabulous to me. Show me where to sign.'

'Come in, love. Leave your baggage by the door, we're all friends here,' says Pearl.

'Would you like a glass?' Norman offers.

'Love one! I'm Doris, by the way. Come to look at the empty flat.'

Elsie's, we all realize. But everything changes, I muse, and Elsie is very much here with us. Pearl, clearly thinking the same, winks at me.

Doris sits next to Ron with a puff.

'So you've come to see Elsie's flat,' says Ron. 'I don't suppose you like the purple Quality Street, do you?' he asks, offering her the box.

'As a matter of fact, they're my favourite.' She takes one and nudges up to him.

'Now then, presents,' says Pearl, with purpose, and walks towards the Christmas tree. I follow her and put the paper bag with my gingerbread hearts beside it, then step back and wrap my arms around myself. This is perfect. Almost. I try to push all thoughts of William out of my mind.

# FORTY-NINE

'I'll start,' says Norman. 'From all of us, Pearl, to say thank you for organizing the best wake ever.'

'Hear, hear!' They raise their prosecco glasses.

'And many more to come! Oh, no. Bugger. Not what I meant,' says Maeve. 'I meant many more years for us to come!' She raises her glass.

'And may I enjoy the ones I have with the people closest to me.' Pearl raises her glass and toasts them back. Her eyes rest on Norman. 'Thank you for being there for me.'

Once again I think of William, helping Maeve around the ice rink, bringing back my Christmas memories with the gingerbread-making. I hope he got his Christmas wish.

Norman hands her a large wrapped present. 'Go on, open it,' he says. 'It's a jumper, just like the ones we got in the market but with the date embroidered into it. The date our new life together started.'

'Oh, Norman! Thank you,' says Pearl. 'It's perfect!' She holds it up to herself. Then takes off her cardigan and pulls it over her head, kissing Norman as she does. 'Perfect!' she repeats.

'And this is for you, Maeve, from all of us,' says Norman.

Maeve looks at the snow globe as she unwraps it and beams with delight at the ice skater in the falling snow.

'Oh, and, Norman, I got you these,' says Pearl, cheekily.

'Lederhosen!' Everyone cheers.

'And I got you this CD of the choir singing in the church, John.'

'Thank you. Violet would have loved it. I'll play it every day,' he assures her.

'And I got one of these each for you,' I say, handing round the small gingerbread hearts, each with their Christmas memory.

'And, actually, this must be for you,' says Pearl. 'It was in my case. I think someone got them mixed up and hoped it would find its way to you. In fact, I made myself promise it would.'

She holds out the parcel tentatively.

I take it from her. It's just like the one William was holding under the tree at six o'clock so I know exactly who it's from.

# FIFTY

I unwrap the tissue paper carefully, my hands shaking. The smell takes me straight back, transporting me to the shop, to the moment when we looked at each other and I knew the alchemy was there. I feel like a string of fairy lights that's just been switched on and is shining brightly. I'm beaming.

I pull back the paper to reveal a large plain gingerbread heart, nothing on it, just the heart.

I feel ridiculously disappointed. I look at the heart again. It's just a heart. No note, no message.

I sigh deeply, resting the heart on the table in front of me.

I look up slowly.

'And this,' says Pearl, holding something out to me.

'My notebook.' I chuckle. 'I don't think I'll have much use for that any more.' I take it from her and flick through the pages. One last look at the hours I've spent on trying to find my perfect match before I toss it into the bin. I roll the edges of the pages under my thumb. All the thought and planning that went into finding my perfect match. I stop at Heinrich's page, and study the long line of ticks all the way down the edge. And then I look again. There's another question at the bottom of the page, not in my handwriting.

'Could you love him?'

There's more writing over the page. But my dating journey finishes with Heinrich, and I wrote the Christmas memory list in the back of the book. So what's this?

I turn the page and see a list, exactly the same as the one for Heinrich on the previous page.

'Appearance?' Beside it, there is a cross instead of a tick and a note: *A little shabby, to be honest, and always wearing a ridiculous bandana.*

'First impressions?' Another cross. *Rude and obnoxious.*

'Financially secure?' Cross. *Hardly!*

'Own accommodation?' *Shared with a loving but deaf dog.*

'Gets on well with his family?' *With the help of someone special, he does now!*

'Single?' Tick. *Yes.*

I read the words and reread the word 'single'.

Then: 'Could you love him?' followed by *There will always be a place at my Christmas table for you.*

I stare at the list with all its crosses, then at the final statement. Is it . . . is he . . . ?

I look at Pearl in disbelief. She raises an eyebrow. 'Well?'

'I think he may just be trying to tell me something!' I laugh. 'That he ticks none of my boxes, we have barely anything in common, apart from our love of baking but . . .'

She picks up the gingerbread heart off the table and hands it to me. 'He's giving you his heart,' Pearl says quietly. 'I knew you'd found your perfect match when you arrived out there. It just took you a while to realize it. But you had to do that for yourself.' Her eyes are twinkling mischievously.

# FIFTY-ONE

I've got a lump in my throat. I grab my bag and fumble for a tissue, putting my hand on something hard in there. I pull it out. Heinrich's ring. I hold it in one hand and look at the plain gingerbread heart in the other, then remember William's perfect Christmas dinner table: 'To be with the ones I love.'

Is he saying he loves me too? I look down at the heart and my own starts to soar. My hand tightens around the ring box.

'I have to go,' I say, quietly at first. 'I have to go,' I say louder, and back out of the room. I have to go! shouts the voice in my head.

'Connie?' Di asks.

'Go where?' asks Norman.

'Back! I have to go back!' I say.

And all their faces break into smiles.

'Go, go!' shouts Pearl, hugging me, then practically

pushing me towards the door. 'Go and get your man!' She's crying and I'm crying.

Suddenly my phone rings with a WhatsApp call. It's Sam. 'Hi, Sam,' I say quickly, brushing away the tears.

'Mum, are you okay? Do you need me to come home?'

'No, I'm fine. Don't come home. I won't be here.' I beam.

'Why? Where are you going?'

'Back to Germany!' There's another ripple of excitement in the room.

'Back to Germany? To be with Heinrich?' he asks.

'But I thought she'd decided Heinrich wasn't the one for her?' asks Norman.

'Not Heinrich,' Maeve, Pearl and Di say together. 'William!'

'I'll ring you tomorrow and explain,' I say to my son, over the noise.

'Okay, Mum. And you're happy, yes? You found him!'

'I think so.'

'Then go and get him!' shouts Sam. 'Happy Christmas!' He and Amy wave into the screen.

'Happy Christmas,' call my friends around me, waving.

And with that I need no other encouragement.

'I'll drive you to the airport. It'll be quicker,' says Norman. 'We'll take the minibus.' It's covered with tinsel and paper chains.

# FIFTY-TWO

I stand at the big front door and ring the bell. At first, there's no answer. I look up at the tall building. It's snowing hard. I ring the bell again. Then the door opens. Tall and in his socks, Heinrich looks surprised to see me.

'Connie? But I thought – I thought you'd gone. I thought you'd decided . . .'

I smile at him. 'I forgot something,' I say. He looks dumbfounded.

'Who is it?' I hear a voice from inside the apartment. A voice I recognize. I smile.

'Happy Christmas, Heinrich.' I reach up and kiss him, put the small black box into his hand and squeeze it shut. He looks down at it. 'Use it wisely, on someone you love,' I say, and turn to go.

'Connie?' I turn back. 'You too! Happy Christmas.' He smiles and waves, and I know I've done the right thing. I walk away from the New Town, towards the bridge, terrified and excited all at the same time.

Now I'm standing in the shadows, by the bins in the alleyway, looking at the shop, closed now for Christmas. The snow is falling heavily, like paper doilies, lit by the orange glow of the street lantern. The cobbles are covered. There are people skating on the ice rink and the market is buzzing. I'm dying for another look at the gingerbread town. But not now. I look at the door, from my safe distance, shaking with nerves. I take a deep breath, and feel the tickle of snowflakes on my face. This is me stepping out from behind my computer screen and living in the real world, in the now. Because I'm here and, right now, there is nothing else I can think about. I look at the door and step forward, when suddenly I hear voices. One in particular I recognize. It's William. I step back into the shadows. I hear him giving directions, then laughing, and shiver with excitement. That laugh! It makes me smile and want to laugh and cry at the same time. I hear a second laugh. His son! Then they come into view, carrying a Christmas tree between them. William reaches for his keys in his pocket, opens the door and they start to negotiate the tree through the door to the flat upstairs. I step forward to offer to help, hold the door or carry the tree, when I hear another laugh and an extra pair of hands is reaching out to help with the tree. I stop, and don't even dare to breathe.

It's Marta, dressed beautifully, in a baby-blue wrap-around coat and white hat highlighting her beautiful blonde hair. They get the tree through the door, where Marta stands smiling, dusting off her hands. My heart is crashing around inside my chest, throwing itself against its walls. Did I really think I could jump on a plane, fly out here and he'd be waiting for me? Did that gingerbread heart really come from him or was Pearl just trying to make me feel better? Or did he think I wasn't interested as I hadn't replied? Or was it all just a lie?

Suddenly he appears again, the tree inside the front door and his son shouting about getting it upstairs. Fritz is barking. William comes to stand in front of Marta, takes hold of her elbow and says something to her that I can't hear. I don't want to – I just want to get out of here. Then he kisses her cheek, and I feel as if my heart has been ripped into tiny pieces, smashed like the polar bear into thousands of pieces. I feel so foolish. My cheeks burn, as do my eyes, and I shut them tight, wishing I was anywhere but here.

I hear her laugh, then him. Noah calls for his dad to get a move on: he wants to decorate the tree. A cold wet nose is pushed into the palm of my hand. Oh, no! Not now! My eyes fly open. Fritz is wagging his tail.

'Hi there,' I say quietly, and rub his head. 'Now, go home,' I instruct, and point. 'Go on, go home.' But he just barks at me. 'Go on,' I encourage him and step further down the alleyway, backing once again into the bins. This time, I managed to steady myself and not fall. If only my heart had learned the same lesson. Next time I'll stick to a list. Next time? I laugh at myself. There won't be a next time. No. This is me done. Just like ice skating, it hurts too much when you fall. I'm not falling again.

Fritz nips my coat sleeve and tugs it, as if playing.

'No!' I try not to but a laugh comes out anyway. It's a mix of pleasure and nerves. 'Go home!' I try to be firm but the bubble of laughter rises up in me again.

And he pulls me a little further forward, under the lantern, as I try to pull away. And as he does so, William sees me. My stomach lurches and my body tingles. I'm wishing he hadn't noticed me, but he has. And in that moment, all I can see is him, with the snow falling around him, and it's a moment I will never forget. Just like the memories we brought to the gingerbread town, this one is etched into my heart. He cocks his head. His mouth is tugging into a smile. I stand rooted to the spot, despite Fritz's efforts to take me home.

William straightens himself, looks left and then right, no doubt checking to see if my friends are with me. Then his smile widens and he walks towards me.

'Oh, no,' I say, backing away. I don't want Marta to see me. My eyeballs sting even more. I take another step back and this time I feel myself lose balance as I hit the bins and start to fall. A hand catches me before I hit the ground and pulls me upright. He stares at me, and all I want to do is fall into his arms. Our eyes flicker from lips to eyes and back again and I want so much to kiss him. But I can't. He's not free. And I have to leave.

'You got my message! You came,' he says.

'I'm sorry, I shouldn't have.'

He frowns. 'Why not?'

He's still holding my arms and I don't want him to let go, because I will be letting go of everything I want. But he's not mine to have.

'I . . .'

Noah calls from the shop. 'Papa, come on! Let's get the tree up!'

William smiles. 'It's Christmas Eve, and we're putting up the tree. Come and join us!'

I shake my head, tears filling my eyes. He got his Christmas wish.

'I should go. Happy Christmas,' I say, and start to walk away.

'Wait!' He follows me and grabs my arm.

'You did get my gift?' He's confused.

'That's why I came,' I say, my voice hoarse.

'Then, why leave again? Didn't you come here . . . for me?'

Tears slide down my face, mingling with the snowflakes falling there. 'I came back, because I thought . . . I thought . . .'

'We have alchemy?' He smiles a lopsided smile.

I nod, and this time let out a little sob.

He puts his finger under my chin and lifts it. 'That is exactly what we have,' he says softly. 'And I always want to feel like this.'

'But Marta? She's here with you and Noah. You have your Christmas wish.'

He throws back his head and then nods, understanding. 'Everything changes, Connie. Nothing stays the same for ever. We can't go back, we can only remember the good times and go forward.'

I have no idea what he's talking about.

'Marta and I have talked. We are better as friends. We share a son and we want the best for him. She has dropped him off to spend Christmas Eve with me and my father.' He points down the lane to where Marta is getting into her car. 'She'll be back for him in the morning. We have agreed it's important he has us both in his life.'

He holds my hands. 'She knows I can never give up the baking. It gets under your skin.' He smiles. 'I can't sell the shop. Someone taught me that. It's in me.'

'And now maybe Noah has found it too.' I smile and sniff.

'I think so . . . because of you. Everything has changed because of you.'

He leans in and kisses me under the lantern light, as the snow falls on our faces. I feel I've come home.

'Now, come and join us.' He takes my hand. 'We are putting up the tree and lighting it. Paps is cooking the Christmas dinner. He'll be delighted to see you.'

I stop. 'Are you sure? I don't want to intrude on your time with your loved ones.'

He kisses me again.

'You, frustrating and eccentric and totally not my type,' he says, 'are my loved one. And I hope to be yours.'

I smile widely, then kiss him, and he leads me into the shop with Fritz at my side.

'Hey!' says Noah, and throws his arms around me in a hug that takes me by surprise, but then I hug him back. 'Come on, we're decorating the tree,' he says, as if me being here is the most natural thing in the world and he's been waiting for me to come.

'Happy Christmas,' says Joseph, as if he's been expecting me too. And I think maybe he has. 'Have a seat. We saved you a place. Dinner won't be long.' He hands me a drink with a smile.

That evening, we decorate the tree, place the presents, mostly for Noah, around it. The fire is lit and candles give out a soft light as we eat melt-in-the-mouth roast goose, with apple and sausage stuffing, scented red cabbage and soft potato dumplings, followed by glorious, brandy-soaked fruit stollen. Finally, when we finish, still holding glasses of red wine, William says, 'Okay, Noah, you can open a present. Maybe save some for the morning for when you go to your mum's,' but I think that's fallen on deaf ears.

'Yes!' he says, and dives in.

'This is from me and Grandpaps,' says William,

guiding him to the first gift. Noah rips it open and finds his own set of chef's whites . . . only they're black, like his dad's, with his name and 'Becker und Sohn' embroidered on them. He beams and pulls them straight on. I have a feeling he may sleep in them.

Then William hands me a gift, in a box.

'But I didn't have time to . . .'

'You have given me everything I wanted this Christmas by being here,' he says. 'Now open it.'

'But how did you know I'd be here?'

'I had a feeling.'

I open up the box to find a beautiful snow globe, with a house just like the bakery inside it. Home, I think, and hold it to my heart. I'm home.

# FIFTY-THREE

The next day, after a lazy breakfast cooked by Noah and Joseph, we're dressed in our best, and by lunchtime the town is alive. The clock-tower bell is ringing and everyone is spilling into the market square to meet friends, eat, drink and skate. Everyone is there.

I watch William and Noah skate, leaning on the barrier drinking warm glühwein. My phone rings. It's a WhatsApp call from Pearl.

'Merry Christmas!' I hear, as I answer. They're all there, waving, with paper hats on, holding glasses of beer and wine.

'Merry Christmas!' I say.

'We miss you,' says Pearl. 'We had the most wonderful lunch. Turkey, all the trimmings, cooked by Maeve.'

'And a lovely drop of sherry. I don't know why no one has sherry any more,' says Maeve, who is wearing Christmas sparkly glasses and a Santa hat.

'We've had it nice and early so we've got time for a snooze and then the Queen's Speech.'

'And then a proper game of charades!' says Norman.

In the background I can hear John's CD playing.

'So tell us . . . how's things?'

'Well, you may find you've got a new delivery driver for your ready meals soon.'

'What?' they shriek.

'William needs help in the shop and, well, I thought I might stay on and help out.' I beam. 'After a bit of a holiday . . .'

'Whoop!' I hear them cheer. 'And there's no need to worry about a new delivery driver, love, we've got it covered here.'

'Yes, we're reopening the café! We're all going to run it. Take it in turns and eat our meals together. There'll be no more TV dinners for one!'

'And we'll bake our own cakes, although we might need some pointers,' says Maeve.

'You can Skype or WhatsApp me anytime. I happen to know a master baker.'

William skates up beside me and waves to the screen.

'It'll all be happening here in the lounge. No more hiding away behind closed doors, or computer screens for that matter. Life's for living in the now,' Pearl says.

'Elsie would have loved that,' I say, and we all nod.

'To Elsie and Elsie's Diner!' says Pearl, and they all cheer.

'Merry Christmas,' William and I say. They chorus back and the line goes dead but I'm still beaming.

'Mum!' Noah shouts, waves in my direction and skates over, arms flailing.

'Um . . .' Suddenly I'm not sure what to say and my snow-globe bubble looks like it might burst.

'Connie.' Marta is beside me and smiles. She looks at her son and his father as William helps Noah to stay on his feet and nearly topples with him. 'You made this happen. I realize I've been wrong keeping William and Noah apart. Thank you. You brought them together and we all need this. We would never have made it as a couple again. But as parents, we need to be there and we can make this work.'

I'm taken aback by her directness but also totally ecstatic. There's no reading between the lines. We all know exactly where we stand. And I like that!

'Merry Christmas, Marta.'

'And you, Connie,' she says, as she goes to meet Noah from the ice and wraps an arm around him. They hug Joseph and say goodbye, and she guides Noah off to his second Christmas with her family, everyone wearing big smiles. We watch them go, and as I turn around, William is smiling at me, just like the smile I woke up to this morning and will wake up to, I hope, every morning for the rest of my life.

'Right, your turn!' he says.

'What?'

He holds up a pair of skates.

'No, no!' I shake my head.

'Connie!' I turn as I hear my name. It's Heinrich!

'Er, Heinrich! Hi!'

He takes me by surprise and hugs me, hard. Once he releases me from my face-plant in his anorak I see Klara standing beside him.

'Hi,' she says. 'Merry Christmas.' Her blonde hair is draped around her shoulders and she's wearing a cream beret.

'You remember Klara?' Heinrich asks.

'Of course! You work in the factory.'

'Runs it, more like!' Heinrich laughs. 'And she's going to keep running it, while I look for engineering jobs.'

'Oh, Heinrich, not in the UK?'

He shakes his head. 'No, I'm not going anywhere. I'm just going to do what I want to do. Maybe even start clockmaking.' He takes Klara's hand and leads her onto the ice where they skate in perfect unison hand in hand.

'Come on, your turn,' says William.

'I tried it once. Hurt like hell when I fell,' I plead.

'Well, it's a good thing I'll be by your side if you fall again. Falling hurts far less when you've got someone at your side. Someone taught me that you never walk away from the ones you love. Falling hurts far less if you do it together. And getting back up again takes far less time.'

And with that, he hands me the skates. I put them on, and he takes my hand and leads me onto the ice and doesn't leave my side . . . and as the bell in the clock tower chimes again, I finally have my own special Christmas memory. I have all the right ingredients, and alchemy. I have someone I love who loves me back. And as I turn to look at him, I catch the toe of his skate, making us both stumble, and flail, reaching out to steady each other as we start to fall. We manage to balance ourselves and then, once we're straight, he leans in to kiss me. I slip and this time I do fall, but he's there, smiling. I check my nose, and there's no blood. He pulls me to my feet and into a kiss, and I hope this is how life will always be from now on, maybe not perfect, but just perfect for me.

*Read on for recipes with all the festive flavour of the Christmas market*

## Lebkuchen (German gingerbread)

Gingerbread fresh from the oven smells just like Christmas! Try making your own, inspired by the recipe that William teaches Connie in *Finding Love at the Christmas Market.*

100g butter
250g honey
120g dark muscovado sugar
1 tsp cinnamon
1 tsp ginger paste or chopped ginger
½ tsp allspice
1 vanilla pod, seeds
2 whole eggs
2 tsp cocoa powder
440g plain flower
1 tsp baking powder

**Method**

1. In a small pot, over a low heat, melt the butter, sugar and honey. Stir regularly until the sugar has completely dissolved.
2. Meanwhile, mix together all the other ingredients in a big bowl.
3. Add the liquid honey/butter/sugar mix to the dry ingredients (you'll either need a spoon and strong arms, or an electric mixer with a kneading-hook attachment).
4. Leave the dough to rest and cool for an hour at room temperature. Pre-heat your oven to 180 degrees (160 if fan-assisted).
5. After the dough has cooled, roll it out to 1cm thickness and cut out your preferred shapes with a biscuit cutter. (If the dough is too sticky, place it in the fridge for a few minutes to firm up, or knead it with your hands and add a bit more flour.)

6. Place the biscuits on a tray lined with baking paper, and bake for approximately. 10 minutes (they will still be slightly soft to the touch; this is what you are aiming for!). Once cool, you can decorate with icing, or anything else you'd like!

## The ultimate hot chocolate

Simple but luxurious, a delicious treat in a mug!

200g plain chocolate, broken into pieces
600ml milk
150ml single or double cream
Sugar, to taste
Optional garnishes: marshmallows, peppermint candy canes, grated cinnamon

**Method**

1. Put the chocolate in a pan with the milk over a gentle heat. Stir until all the chocolate has melted, then continue to heat until steaming. Remove and stir in the cream.
2. Divide the hot chocolate between 6 mugs, and add sugar and garnish to taste!

## Smoked sausage casserole

A warming meal that's perfect for a cold day – or at any time of the year! Garlic bread or potatoes go well with this.

1 tbsp olive oil
1 red onion, finely chopped
3 garlic cloves, crushed
1 celery stick, finely chopped
2 red peppers, sliced
6 smoked pork sausages
1 tsp sweet smoked paprika
½ tsp ground cumin
½ tsp chilli flakes
2 x 400g tins chopped tomatoes
400g tin cannellini beans, drained
2 tbsp breadcrumbs
1 tbsp chopped parsley

### Method

1. Brown the sausages on a high heat under the grill, while you prepare the vegetable base for the casserole. Make sure the sausages are browned all over.
2. Put the oil in a large heatproof casserole dish over a medium heat and add the onion, cooking for 5 minutes until starting to soften. Add the garlic, celery and peppers, stirring to mix. Cook for a further 5 minutes.
3. Add the sausages to the casserole dish, sprinkle in the spices and season well. Then add the tomatoes and bring to a simmer. Cover and continue simmering gently for 40 minutes, stirring every now and then.
4. Heat the grill to high and uncover the casserole. Add the beans, spinach and most of the parsley, and stir to mix. Scatter over the breadcrumbs and grill for 2-3 minutes until golden and crisp.
5. When golden brown, sprinkle over the remaining parsley and serve.

# ACKNOWLEDGEMENTS

I loved writing this book. The research was fantastic. I had always wanted to visit a German Christmas market and on this research trip I got to visit not one, but three!

I firstly want to thank a lovely woman, Nicola Burgraff, whom I met some years ago at a writing retreat in Chez Castillon in France, for sowing this seed and sparking this idea off in my head.

And of course, my research companions Katie Fforde and Bernadine Kennedy. It wouldn't have been half the hoot it was without my writing buddies there with me to try the glühwein, the sausages and to walk the markets with. Then, of course, there was the river cruise itself, along the Rhine with Titan Travel River Cruises. A glorious way to travel and see the countryside, the villages and Christmas trees and lights.

I need to give a big thank you to my daughter Ffi for becoming a bakery and patisserie student and giving me the background to this story. Ffi has grown in confidence and skills since she began her course at Cardiff and Vale College and I can't thank her course leader, Linda Burns – otherwise referred to as Chef – enough. She is wonderfully encouraging and caring and I know her students thrive under her leadership . . . I know I would! Chef invited me into the kitchens for the day to watch and help out making gingerbread. I loved that day. I felt like I'd been wrapped up in a great big hug. Thank you for allowing me in, Chef, and for letting me get hands-on with gingerbread and make the gingerbread village. And to all the students on the Bakery and Patisserie course there who welcomed me in too and let me be part of that world for the day. I loved it! I wish all of you luck and success in this wonderful profession you have chosen. I'm so excited to see where you all go on to!

A huge thank you to Sally Williamson for guiding this book through the process and helping make it the best it could be. I have loved working with you. And the rest of the team at Transworld, Julia Teece and Hayley Barnes. And as always the fantastic VP, Vicky Palmer, for cheering loudly from the sidelines, and my wonderful agent David Headley for his support, guidance and friendship.

I hope you all enjoy your trip to the German Christmas markets and make your own Christmas memories while you're there.

**A place to heal broken hearts and find new beginnings . . .**

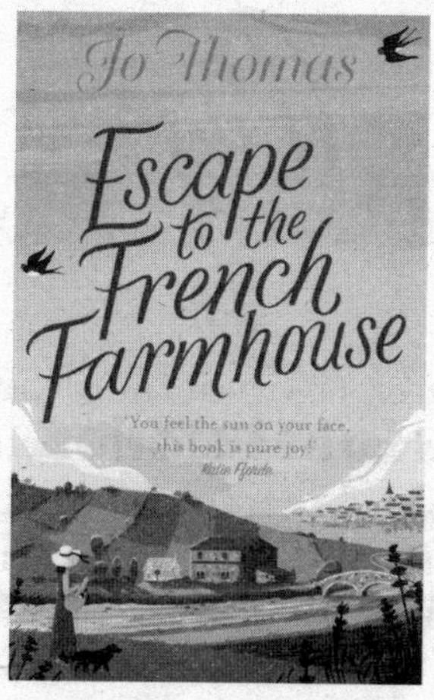


Del and her husband Ollie moved to a beautiful village in Provence for a fresh start after years of infertility struggles. But six weeks after they arrive, they're packing the removal van once more. As Del watches the van leave for England, she suddenly realizes exactly what will make her happier . . . a new life in France – without Ollie.

Now alone, all Del has is a crumbling farmhouse, a mortgage to pay and a few lavender plants. What on earth is she going to do? Discovering an old recipe book at the market run by the rather attractive Fabian, Del starts to bake. But can her new-found passion really help her let go of the past and lead to true happiness?

**'This book is pure joy' Katie Fforde**

**'A proper treat!' Milly Johnson**